# Secrets in Retribution Bay

Aussie Heroes: Retribution Bay

## Claire Boston

BANTILLY
PUBLISHING

First published by Bantilly Publishing in 2022



Secrets in Retribution Bay: Aussie Heroes: Retribution Bay

EPUB format: 978-1-925696-94-3
Print: 978-1-925696-95-0
Large Print: 978-1-925696-96-7

Cover design by Mayhem Cover Creation
Edited by Ann Harth
Proofread by Teena Raffa-Mulligan

I would like to acknowledge the Bayungu people, Traditional Custodians of the land on which this story is based, and pay my respects to their Elders past and present.

# Dedication

*This book is dedicated to Bayungu Elder, Hazel Walgar and Yinggarda woman, Toni Roe. Thank you for your help, ladies.*

<h1 style="text-align:center">Chapter 1</h1>

Georgiana Stokes drove towards Retribution Ridge, driven by the need for comfort and home. She raised her hand to her mouth, stopping just short of biting her nail, and shook her head, tucking her hand under her thigh. There was nothing to be nervous about. The interview with Parks and Wildlife Services had gone well, which meant she might have a big decision to make.

She *liked* her job as a crew member on the whale shark tour boats in Retribution Bay, and she loved spending her days swimming alongside the biggest fish in the ocean. But it did little to challenge her, and conservation was more her passion.

The only problem was, two jobs were going with Parks and Wildlife Services; one land based, dealing with Cape Range National Park, and one ocean-based, caring for Ningaloo Reef and the outlying islands. Her contact at PAWS had said one of the other interviewees had all the skills needed for the ocean-based job. Georgie sighed. Either role would be a good step towards putting her marine biology degree to work.

Jimmy would be pissed off if she left him in the lurch with still a few months left of the tourist season. The boat was almost fully booked and she couldn't leave him one crew member down.

Georgie would have to find someone to replace her — if she got the job.

Her breathing deepened and slowed with each kilometre on the one-hour drive home. Red dirt flashed by her window and she kept her eyes peeled for kangaroos and wild goats blending in with the dull green bushes on the side of the road. The sun was low, making long shadows across the road. Her stomach rumbled.

Maybe she should have called Amy to tell her she was coming home.

Her shoulders slumped. Could she still call the Ridge home?

The homestead now belonged to her oldest brother, Brandon since her parents had died two months ago, and he'd married Amy last week. It wouldn't be long before they built their own family.

Georgie's mum had always welcomed her home, even if she turned up out of the blue. There was always shortbread and a cup of tea, so they could have a chat, and always enough food for one more at the table.

Georgie blinked rapidly to clear her vision.

She turned onto the road which led to the Ridge and slowed when she reached Hangman's Bend. Only a few broken branches were left to show her parents had died there when they'd been forced off the road and the car had rolled. Her stomach clenched and her throat closed over, forcing her to pull over to the side to breathe.

They didn't deserve to die. Not so young, not at all. Her parents were the best of the best, welcoming everyone, always with a kind word and a huge hug. She'd been so excited they were finally taking a day off to come out on the tour boat with her, to see what she did for a living, to share her excitement about swimming with the whale sharks. She'd told everyone who would listen, not realising she had to be careful who heard her.

Georgie leaned her head against the steering wheel as the tears ran down her face. She'd been so happy, so unaware of what was to come, with no idea a Singapore consortium by the name of Stonefish Enterprises wanted something from the Ridge land and would go to great lengths to get it.

If only she'd stayed silent, Stonefish wouldn't have known her parents would be heading out early to catch the tour boat, they wouldn't have told someone to cut the brake line in the four-wheel drive, wouldn't have had anyone in place to force them off the road.

She tried not to blame herself, but the niggling thought wouldn't go away, spitting its hissing tongue whenever she was down. It had been the same with her brother, Charlie's death as well. Maybe she was cursed.

Georgie sucked in a breath as a car roared past her and she sat up, brushing the tears from her face. Enough. If she turned up to the Ridge with red eyes and blotchy skin, everyone would want to know what was wrong. Her brothers were annoyingly observant like that and so overprotective.

Taking another deep breath to calm herself, she put the car into gear and continued driving.

The same couldn't be said of Matt. He still had no clue she was in love with him and had been for years. He was as dense as a block of wood.

She huffed out a breath. That wasn't fair. Matt was highly observant when it came to the land and usually to people as well. He must know about her feelings but pretended he didn't because he didn't feel the same way.

And that was a kick in the teeth.

Last time she'd been out to the Ridge, she'd slept in the shearers' quarters, right next to Matt's room, because Ed and Tess were in the spare bedroom. She'd fantasised about sneaking into his room in the middle of the night to tell him how she felt, but smart Georgie knew how stupid an idea it was.

She scowled. It really was time she got over him. He would never view her as more than his best friend's little sister and it was time for her to woman up and move on.

She drove through the gates of the Ridge, the angry-looking sheep on the sign reminding her of Charlie. Guilt stabbed her again and she slowed to breathe through it.

Swallowing hard, she continued on to the homestead. She had to stop this pity party for one before she saw anyone. Charlie had probably met up with their parents in heaven and was entertaining them as he always did.

She smiled at the thought and some of her guilt dissolved.

The newly cleared campground was full of caravans and tents, and kids crowded near Maggie, the kangaroo, watching her as she lazed by the camp fire.

Georgie's smile grew as she pulled up next to the house. Only Reg and Wesley were in the horse corral. As she walked to the verandah, she scanned the surroundings for her niece, Lara, Lara's soon to be step-mother, Faith, and whoever was riding with them.

No one, but maybe they'd just left. If Georgie was quick, she could radio to find out where they were and join them. A ride always made her feel better.

She pushed the kitchen door, but it didn't budge.

Locked.

Frowning, she pulled her keys from her pocket. It was Stonefish's fault they had to lock the house now. Bastards.

The anger helped to push away her remaining sorrow.

But a locked door meant no one was home.

She unlocked the door and breathed in the slightly dusty, old house scent. The kitchen was empty and the building was silent. Georgie rubbed her arms. Her mother always had music playing, usually some eighties mix.

She flicked on the stereo and smiled as sound filled the room.

Her brothers and Matt would still be working on the station, but Ed, Tess or Amy should be around somewhere.

She didn't want to be alone. That's why she'd come here. "Ed!"

The last thing she wanted to do was interrupt her brother and his new girlfriend when they thought they had the house to themselves. Though she hadn't seen his hire car outside, so maybe they'd gone into town, or down to the gulf for a swim.

"Ed!"

She wandered down the photo lined corridor, checking the lounge room first and then the bedrooms. No one.

In the room with twin beds she'd normally shared with Ed, his backpack was on the floor and a few clothes Tess had bought since she'd fled the scene of a murder were folded neatly on the chest of drawers. Despite the horrific circumstances, the event had led Tess to Ed, and the two were very much in love.

The love bug had bitten all her brothers. Brandon had married Amy a week ago, and Darcy was engaged to Faith. Georgie had no one, not even her parents anymore.

Was she destined for heartache all of her life?

She couldn't even be happy the man behind the issues plaguing the Ridge was now dead. He would have someone mourning for him, and others would take his place.

Georgie scowled and tried to shake off the mood.

She headed back to the kitchen and filled the kettle, flicking it on through habit more than any genuine desire for a cuppa. She reached into the cupboard for the jar of shortbread and stopped short. Empty.

No reason it should be there anymore. Her mother had died months ago.

She shook her head to shake away the pain. Focus on something else.

They still hadn't figured out why Stonefish Enterprises wanted to buy the Ridge. The police had discovered evidence they were searching for something on Retribution Island which lay just off the shore of the gulf near Ridge land, and Darcy and Matt had explored the new tracks they'd discovered, but they led nowhere of note.

Still no concrete answers.

Georgie's steps took her into the laundry, and she opened the recently uncovered hatch to the cellar. There had to be answers in there.

She moved down the stairs and breathed in the musty scent of the room, which had been hidden for decades. One wall of shelves had been dusted since Georgie had last been out, probably by Amy. The old glass jars of preserves still lined them as the family hadn't decided what to do about it all. Why the cellar had been hidden was a mystery.

She ran a hand over the surface of the wooden desk. Everyone had looked for secret compartments, but they'd found nothing.

Lara had reminded Georgie so much of Charlie with her excitement and theories.

Georgie hugged herself and sank onto the bottom step, rocking back and forth as her despair overpowered her. Charlie would have loved this place.

The grief and guilt she'd forced away earlier swept in with a rush.

It wasn't fair Charlie had died at only twelve.

She squeezed her eyes closed. "I'm sorry, Charlie. I didn't mean it."

What nine-year-old wouldn't curse her brother who

scared her with a fake spider? The curse had been in a book she'd just read and she still remembered the words. *May your actions rebound on you triple-fold and may you rue the day you crossed me.*

The fake spider had scared her half to death. And Charlie had died only days after she'd cursed him. She swallowed hard and wiped the tears from her eyes. She didn't believe in curses, not really, but at times like this, it was hard not to let the guilt overwhelm her.

Charlie would have loved the idea of a cellar hidden away for decades. Ever the prankster, he would have lured his siblings in here, then locked them in and turned off the light. Georgie smiled. The dark didn't scare her, and she'd already checked for spiders lurking in the corners.

They'd found Great Grandma Charlotte's journals, full of her discontent and unhappiness, which referenced locking her own children in the cellar for misbehaving. But the cellar pre-dated her. Brandon thought it might be part of the original house, built in the 1870s by their ancestors who had settled this land.

Georgie stood and moved over to the shelves again. She and Tess had taken every single bottle from the shelf to check for hidden boxes, or more journals, and had found nothing. Each stone in the wall had been carefully laid, each one finding the perfect place next to the others.

They would have carted the stone from the nearby ridge, or the dry riverbed, working in the searing sun. Her fingers brushed the stones, the cool hard surface centring her.

A stone under her fingers wobbled.

She frowned and examined it closer. It was a larger stone, long and thin. She traced around it with her fingers and it wobbled more. Curiosity mixed with excitement as she pried her fingers behind it. Not very thick. It couldn't be part of the actual wall holding it up. She lifted the rock away and gasped.

Hidden behind it was a small metal box, less than a ruler's length long.

Georgie glanced at the ceiling. No point waiting for the others to get home. They could be ages. Besides, like the chest they'd found down here, it might contain nothing of value and she didn't want to get their hopes up.

The guilt prickled her skin as she tugged on the metal box. No, her family hadn't waited for her to explore the cellar, so she didn't have to wait for them now.

She scraped at the dirt surrounding it, wincing as it stuck under her fingernails. Looking around, she found an old screwdriver and stabbed at the sand, loosening it enough so she could drag the box out. It was an old biscuit tin, a little bigger than an A5 ream of paper.

Georgie carried it to the table and used the screwdriver to lever the lid open. She paused before opening it. Something closed this tightly wouldn't have spiders inside. Still, she stood to the side, reaching over to flick the lid away. Inside was something wrapped in oiled cloth.

Heart pounding, she wiped her hands on her pants, lifted out the parcel and slowly unwrapped it.

Two books—one was brown leather-bound and the other a red hardback. Both had yellowed pages, and the red book had signs of water damage. Its cover creaked in protest as it revealed the first page.

*This journal belongs to Lilian Stokes.*

Georgie's mouth dropped open as she wiped the dirt from her fingers onto her shorts and then brushed the small, neat handwriting. Her ancestor, the one who had settled the land with her husband, Reginald back in the 1870s. Georgie had always fantasised about what her great-great-great-grandmother's life had been like and now she'd find out. But why had it been hidden away?

She opened the first warped, brittle page to discover neat and flowing handwriting.

*26 September 1870*

*It is done. One short ceremony at the registration office and my identity has been erased. I am now Mrs Reginald William Stokes. Mother is of course thrilled I am no longer a spinster, and Father is pleased I am no longer a financial burden.*

*Perhaps I should not be so dour. Reginald may become the great love of my life like I read about in novels.*

*I should not blame him for his lack of interest in me during the lead up to the ceremony. I imagine a lot of planning is required when moving across the other side of the world. We will have plenty of time to get to know one another during the three-month voyage to Western Australia. For yes, that is my destination. Not only did I have no say in who I was to marry, but I am also to be sent to the new colony in the antipodes. My heart is torn. The thought of leaving everyone and everything I know behind grieves me, but I will not deny the glimmer of excitement at the adventure my husband and I are about to undertake.*

Upstairs, the floorboards creaked. Someone was in the kitchen. Georgie tensed, glancing up. Perhaps she should have locked the kitchen door behind her.

"Georgie! You here?"

Ed. She breathed a sigh of relief. "Down here," she yelled. She opened the other book, another journal, but this one dated a hundred years earlier than Lilian's journal. She didn't recognise the Dutch name on the title page.

Ed trotted down the steps, wearing hiking boots with shorts and an astronomy T-shirt, his light brown hair mussed like he'd been swimming. "What have you got there?"

"Lilian's journal."

Ed did a double-take. "What?"

She grinned. "Found it in the wall." Georgie pointed at the hole she'd left behind.

"Let me see." Reverently, he took the journal from her and read. "This is amazing. Tess will flip." Without another word, he ran up the steps with the journal in his hand.

Georgie's heart squeezed. Only a few weeks ago, they would have pored over the journal together. Now he had someone better to share it with. Ed hadn't even asked her permission to take it.

She rubbed her eyes. Stupid to be upset. She was happy Ed had found someone to love. If only it didn't make her feel so alone.

She spread out the cloth to make sure she hadn't missed anything, and then double-checked the tin. Upstairs, she heard Ed's and Tess's excited voices.

No use moping down here. She gathered up the brown journal with the tin and cloth and carried them upstairs.

***

Matt Roe placed the last of his fencing tools in the back of the ute and lifted his Akubra to wipe the sweat from his brow. The sting from the sun was harsh this afternoon. He grabbed a bottle of water from his esky and radioed Darcy. "All done here."

"See you back at the house."

Matt hesitated, taking a swig of water. "I might visit my folks first."

"Roger that. Say hi to them for me."

Matt cradled the radio and stared off to the red ranges of the Cape Range National Park in the distance. He'd promised Darcy he wouldn't go off alone to explore the tracks they'd found, but what he hadn't told his best friend was some of those tracks led toward places that were sacred to his people, the Bayungu.

Though he knew the words to appease his ancestors and to allow Darcy to come with him, the discomfort still sat on his shoulders. Darcy wouldn't judge him for following his traditions, but Matt always felt weird discussing anything spiritual. He'd heard the dismissive tones of people discussing indigenous 'superstitions' before, and he hated the judgement, hated being torn between the two worlds.

Easier to avoid the topic and go by himself.

He climbed into the old ute, twisting the key a half turn back before turning it the correct way to start the car. After double-pumping the clutch, he put the ute into gear, and slowly headed towards the ranges. He could ask his father to come along, but the tracks had been made by someone at Stonefish, and he didn't want to put his father in danger.

As Senior Constable at the Retribution Bay police station, his sister, Nhiari would be pissed off at him for going alone. Though in his defence, she hadn't explicitly told him he couldn't explore the tracks when Matt had first told her about them. Back then, he and Darcy had found nothing out of the ordinary, but Matt wanted to take a closer look to ensure Stonefish wasn't desecrating sacred land.

The ute bumped over the rough red dirt. Matt kept his speed low and an eye on the temperature because the old beast had to be babied. They didn't have the funds to buy a new one and though Brandon had brought a new ute when he'd returned to the Ridge, Matt was the only one who could get this old thing to run reliably.

The sun low in the sky made it hard to see more than a few metres ahead and he slapped down the sun visor, squinting against the glare.

He was wasting his time. There wouldn't be anything out here. He could be at the homestead having a cold beer rather than roasting in the ute.

Matt flicked on the air-conditioning and the engine groaned. Damn it. He switched it off and wound down the window instead. The warm breeze helped a little.

It took almost an hour to reach the ranges, and he slowed, scanning the ground for the tyre tracks. There.

He followed them and reached the base of the ranges where he turned off the engine and sat for a moment, listening.

A few bird calls, and in the distance the hush of the ocean, but it was mostly silent. The slam of the car door echoed as he got out.

He greeted his ancestors and moved towards the caves in the rock face. To his left he heard a faint thump like something hitting plastic. Not normal.

Frowning, he moved into the bush, walking carefully, scanning the area for more footprints. Only a few metres in, he discovered a plastic container buried in the ground, about the diameter of an old dustbin lid and a foot deep. Inside was a thorny devil lizard trying to clamber up the smooth sides.

Had to be a smuggler's trap.

Matt scowled. So that's what the bastards were doing out this way. Always stealing from the land. He lifted the trapped thorny devil from the hole and placed it on the hard dirt. The animal lumbered off into the bush as Matt checked his phone for reception. Nothing. He'd have to wait before he called the police. This was men's land, and Nhiari wouldn't be pleased when he insisted they send Constable Colin Lipscombe to investigate.

Matt explored the surrounding area and found another four traps, so took photos of each one. He wasn't on Ridge land anymore, so there was no need to involve Darcy. This was Bayungu land.

He drove to his parents' place, a collection of house and buildings not too far away. His mother came to the door before he'd got out.

"Matt! What are you doing here?"

"I was in the area, *Bibi*." He hugged his mother and followed her inside. His father sat at the kitchen table peeling potatoes. "Hi, *Babu*."

"Good to see you."

Matt took the glass of cold water his mother handed him and took a long sip. "Do either of you know about the animal traps over by the ranges?"

They both looked up at him, surprised. "No. Where?" his father asked.

"Near the men's caves. I found a *nganaraji* in one."

"You should call Nhiari," Bibi said.

"Get Colin to check it out," Babu added.

Matt nodded. "Can I borrow the phone?" His mother handed him the landline, and Nhiari answered on the first ring. "Hey, *gunyjan*."

Nhiari sighed. "Little brother, what's happened now?"

He chuckled. "Can't a brother call his sister for a chat?"

"Not at work, and usually not at all."

Fair enough. "I found some smugglers' traps out by the range near the men's caves."

"What were you doing out there?"

"Men's business," he lied. "I can show Colin tomorrow."

"You telling me I can't do my job?"

"It's a sacred men's area." Nhiari would know if she'd paid more attention to her heritage, but Matt understood why she didn't.

Her sigh was long and suffering. "You think anyone would know if I went?"

"I'm calling from Mum and Dad's."

She swore. "Fine. I'll call you in the morning to arrange a time. Give Mum and Dad my love." She hung up.

Matt handed the phone back to his mother. "I'll take Colin out tomorrow," he said. "Probably best to stay clear until the police can catch them."

"It's our land," his father said.

"And they likely have guns," Matt pointed out.

His mother patted her husband's hand, and asked Matt, "Will you stay for dinner?"

He hesitated. The Ridge homestead would be full of couples now Tess and Ed had hooked up. Over the past couple of months he'd felt more and more like a third wheel. A night's reprieve from that would be welcome. "Yeah, that would be great. What can I do to help?"

His father passed over the remaining potatoes with a grin. "Peel."

# Chapter 2


As Georgie reached the kitchen, Faith, Amy and Lara trooped in from their horse ride, all dressed in jeans and loose long-sleeved tops. Ed and Tess pored over the journal at the table and Lara plonked down in the seat next to them.

"Whatcha reading?"

Ed grinned at his young niece. "Lilian Stokes's journal."

"What?"

Faith rushed over.

"Georgie found a hidden pocket in the cellar wall," Ed said.

"That's incredible." Amy placed the backpack she carried on the bench. "Should we wait until the others get here before you read the whole thing?"

Georgie grinned at the looks of utter outrage on Lara's, Faith's and Ed's faces, but she'd felt left out when they'd gone through the cellar without her. "Good idea. They won't be long."

"They'll take forever," Lara complained.

"Why don't you have a shower?" Faith suggested. "We'll get dinner ready."

Lara pouted, but did as her future step-mother suggested.

"Where did you find it?" Amy asked.

"There was a loose rock in the wall," Georgie said.

Tess shook her head. "I felt a loose rock the day we discovered the cellar," she said. "But then the lights went out, and I forgot about it."

Amy took the lamb out of the fridge. "Do you think she wrote the journal after they'd set up here?"

"She started it the day she married Reginald," Georgie said. "That's all I read before Ed stole it from me."

Ed closed the journal and smirked. "It records her journey out here from England," he said. "Did you know they came on a convict ship?"

Georgie gaped at him. "They were convicts?"

Ed shook his head. "No, but they came on the same ship as a bunch of convicts. There weren't many paying passengers."

At that moment Bennett, their blue heeler, trotted up to the back door and Amy let him in. "They're back."

Georgie's heart clenched, and she braced herself to see Matt. The first glance was always the hardest. Her two oldest brothers clumped up the stairs to the verandah and toed off their boots. Brandon, and then Darcy, hung their Akubras on the hook by the door, just like their father had always done. Georgie wrapped her arms around herself as sorrow filled her. She'd never see her father do that again, or greet his wife with a smile and a kiss. Her brothers' chocolate brown hair was flattened with sweat, but the same colour as their mother's, Brandon's hair shorter than Darcy's, still growing after years in the military.

"You gotta see what we discovered," Ed said.

"Hey, Georgie. You got tomorrow off?" Darcy asked.

Georgie forced a smile. "Thought I'd come out and check how everyone is."

"Good to see you." Brandon swept Amy up in a hug and kissed her. Moments later, Darcy did the same with Faith. Georgie almost wished she hadn't come. She felt like the third wheel with everybody loved up and happy. Though if she hadn't come, she wouldn't have found the journal. Georgie glanced towards the door. "Where's Matt?"

"He's gone to visit his parents," Darcy answered.

She relaxed. At least she wouldn't have to deal with him as well.

"What did you find?" Brandon asked, coming to stand next to Ed and Tess at the table.

"Lilian's journal," Georgie answered. "Found it in the cellar's wall."

Both her brothers jolted and stared at her. "Seriously?" Darcy said.

"Yeah."

"What's in there?" Brandon asked.

"We haven't read it yet," Amy said. "We were waiting until you got home."

"Bet Lara wasn't happy," Darcy said. "Where is she?"

"Having a shower," Faith answered.

Lara rushed back into the room, showered and dressed in her Wonder Woman pyjamas. "Dad, you're home finally." She hugged Darcy and then turned around. "Can we read the journal now?"

Faith laughed. "How about somebody reads it aloud while we make dinner?"

"Georgie should," Tess said. "She found it."

"Good idea." Darcy passed around drinks, and they settled at the kitchen table, Amy and Brandon chopping vegetables to go in a stir-fry.

Georgie gingerly turned the brittle pages of the journal, scanning the contents.

"Start from the beginning," Lara said. "I want to hear it all."

Georgie read about Lilian's unhappiness with the wedding and her shock at discovering she was going to Australia on the convict ship, Retribution. Only a week into the voyage, things got interesting.

*4 October 1870*

*I awoke early this morning. Not only does Reginald snore most disagreeably, but the bed is uncomfortable, and a bell tolls every half hour to mark the passage on watch. Over time I am sure to become used to it, but at the moment everything is still new and different. With the sun up, I decided to go for a walk about the deck. The aft has been set apart for those of us on board who haven't committed a crime, however when I emerged from my cabin, many of the sailors seemed shocked to see me. Perhaps it was the early hour. When I reached the aft, I looked down upon the deck to see a group of men taking a turn in the early morning air. The wardens were with them, but the men weren't chained and did not look like the type of convict I had imagined. In fact, aside from their matching clothing, one would not have been able to distinguish them from people one might meet at a luncheon.*

*The first mate approached and bid me to return to my cabin. On my query, he told me the men were Fenian prisoners, Irish political prisoners sentenced for treason.*

*I pretended more shock than I felt, for I had regularly read my father's newspapers and knew of how the Fenians strive for an Ireland independent from England. I will admit some sympathy for their cause, for I have longed to be an independent woman, but society will not allow me to be.*

*Then something miraculous happened. One of the sailors cried, 'There she blows!' and in the water not far from us was a huge whale, leaping and slapping its fins. I must have shrieked in delight, as a voice with an Irish brogue called, 'Magnificent aren't they?'*

*One of the Fenians was speaking to me! He was perhaps a*

*few years older than me, with the same colour black hair as Reginald's, and a cheeky grin. I will admit my heartbeat increased at his smile and familiarity, but before I could answer, one of the wardens chastised him and dragged him away.*

*He glanced once over his shoulder at me, and the first mate insisted I return to my cabin.*

*My thoughts return to the man more often than I would like. He, like myself, had no choice over the voyage we both find ourselves on and his smile brightened my day. It is the first affection I have received since starting this journey. Reginald is busy with his papers and rarely smiles. I hope in time he will share his worries with me and I will be able to share whatever burdens him.*

The kitchen was silent. Georgie glanced up. "Lilian doesn't seem thrilled with her marriage."

"She had no say in the matter," Amy pointed out. "It can't have been easy."

"I like the sound of the Fenian prisoner," Faith said. "It's nice she received some affection."

Georgie continued reading the details of Lilian's three-month journey to Australia—her frustration and boredom with the other passengers, her despair at the lack of attention from Reginald. It was not a marriage to be envied.

Disappointment filled Georgie. She had always fantasised their ancestors had had a strong and loving relationship, although there'd been no evidence to support such an idea.

The only joy for Lilian had been her limited interactions with the Fenian convict, John.

"It sounds as if she admires John more than her husband," Amy said.

Georgie nodded. "He sounds like a nicer person." Reginald was secretive, spending hours locked in their cabin going over paperwork or talking with the other men on board. He refused Lilian's attempts to engage in conversation and her offers to help him with whatever he was working on. Only occasionally he'd play cards with Lilian and a couple on board who Lilian despised.

By the time dinner was ready, the journal noted that the ship had reached Fremantle, and Lilian and Reginald were staying in a hostel with no permanent housing arranged.

"Let's stop while we eat," Darcy suggested.

"Da-ad," Lara protested.

"We don't want to get food on the journal," Darcy responded.

Lara's pout caused Georgie to smile as she put the journal on the counter behind her.

Everyone dished up faster than normal, keen to get back to Lilian's story. Darcy tried for conversation. "How was school, pumpkin?" he asked Lara.

She grimaced. "All right, I guess. I've got homework."

"Need any help with it?" Ed asked.

So sweet and just like Ed to offer. He'd always been the most academic of them.

"Maybe," Lara said.

"What did you two get up to today?" Brandon asked Tess and Ed.

Ed had another week before he was due back in Perth for work.

"I took Tess to the ranges," Ed said. "And then we went snorkelling around in Turquoise Bay."

Georgie straightened. "See anything interesting?"

Tess grinned. "Some turtles and so many fish." Tess was learning to swim and snorkel, but she'd taken to it enthusiastically. It was nice to see her happy, especially after the ordeal she'd been through, and the issues with her family. Ed squeezed Tess's hand. "She's a natural."

They smiled at each other, their affection clear.

Georgie turned away hating the jealousy shooting through her.

What she needed was time with the girls, where she didn't have to see them with their partners. Maybe it was time for a girls' night. There were plenty of tourists in town and she could find someone to keep her distracted for a while.

She finished her stir-fry and carried her bowl to the sink.

"Leave the dishes," Amy declared. "Let's get back to the journal."

No one protested. They reconvened in the lounge room to finish reading Lilian's journal. Her stay in Fremantle was short, only a few days. Reginald had bought the Retribution and was setting up a shipping business transporting goods between the northern ports and Fremantle. The delay was for him to find a new crew because most on board didn't want to stay in the colonies.

"I never heard anything about a shipping business," Ed said.

"If the cyclone story is true, that might explain it," Darcy said.

Good point. The legend was that a cyclone had hit the Retribution and it had run aground in the gulf. Lilian and Reginald had set up the station where they landed. Georgie smiled as she read the next bit. "Guess who else was on the ship north?"

"More convicts?" Lara asked.

Georgie nodded. "But which ones?"

Tess ventured, "John?"

Georgie nodded. "He was contracted to work for a pastoralist, Mr Clarke, who had leased land up north."

*I can barely believe it. I went to watch us set sail, and I stumbled as the boat shifted and who should catch me? John.*

*It seems Mrs Clarke took my suggestion and John, Patrick*

*and Tom have been contracted to work with Mr Clarke. I am not sure whether this work will be more difficult than that which the chain gangs do, and I said as much. John told me he was pleased with the opportunity to see me again. Oh, how I blushed.*

Georgie smiled as she scanned ahead and noted the three pearl divers on board. She glanced at Tess. "What was your pearl diver ancestor's name?"

"Da Lim."

She continued reading. "There are three pearl divers on board heading to Tien Tsin and one of them is Da."

Tess gaped at her. "We know she was on board when the cyclone hit. Her name is on the commemoration plaque at the beach."

Which would mean the maiden voyage of their shipping business ended in disaster.

Georgie tensed as she read aloud the details of Lilian's voyage north. After several days becalmed in the gulf, the cyclone hit.

*Reginald has ordered all passengers below deck. I had time to grab my journal and ink, and a pack of cards only. The wind bellows outside, a noise so loud it hurts my ears. The sailors have curled the sails and let out the anchors, hoping we will stay in place in the middle of the bay. The waves are not monstrous, but we are being tossed about nonetheless. Everyone is silent, waiting, listening, as the storm picks up outside. Reginald is too busy yelling at the sailors to notice my fear, and John only risked squeezing my hand once.*

Georgie could feel her fear. Next to her Lara clutched Darcy's arm, her eyes wide as she listened to the tale.

By daylight it was all over and the ship was stuck on a reef on the northern side of what would become known as Retribution Island.

"Poor Lilian," Faith said. "Being the only woman on board and with an uncaring husband."

"Reginald sounds like a real douche," Ed agreed. "It's disappointing. I always pictured him as more heroic."

"Me too," Georgie said. It was John, the Fenian prisoner who had found Lilian somewhere safe to sit while they salvaged as much as they could from the wreckage. Even the pastoralist, Mr Clarke showed more concern to Lilian.

The next few pages described the salvage, the search for fresh water and deciding who to send in one of the salvaged life boats to get help. Reginald offered to stay behind on the island. Georgie had been sure he'd be the first to leave.

"Reginald is definitely hiding something," Brandon commented after listening to Lilian describe his behaviour.

Georgie agreed. It wasn't until she turned the page that she discovered what it was. Sunken treasure. Reginald had made the pearl divers dive off the shore to the east, and one diver had found a cup. Another ship had crashed offshore a century earlier and Reginald had found the Dutch captain's journal, leading him right to it.

Georgie stiffened. "Where's the other book?" At the blank stares she got to her feet. "The one which was with Lilian's journal." She hurried back to the kitchen where she'd left it on the bench. On opening the book, excitement filled her, and she returned to the lounge room. "This is it," she said. "The captain's journal." The Ridge desperately needed extra funds. After their parents had died, they'd all been stunned at how bad the finances were. If any treasure was still there, it would save the station.

Ed took it from her. "Could that be what Stonefish is after?"

"Possibly." Darcy tilted his head to the side. "But if the Retribution found the treasure, there'd be none left today."

"Where did Reginald get the captain's journal from?" Brandon asked.

"Lilian doesn't say," Georgie said. She frowned. "Surely there'd be some record of another shipwreck in the gulf."

Tess nudged Ed. "The coin."

His eyes widened. "You're right." He raced out of the room and came back a minute later holding a large metal coin. "The other week when I was going through my stuff in the shed, I found this. I discovered it years ago, when Charlie was still alive. I never told anyone about it. Tess took one look and realised it was a seventeenth century Dutch coin."

Georgie gaped at him. "Where did you find it?"

Ed shook his head. "That's the thing. I can't remember. It might have been one day when we were exploring the island, or it might have been out horse-riding. Charlie was with me and I hid it from him, because he would have pinched it from me."

"Can I see it?" Lara asked.

He passed it to her and she squinted at it.

"I can't believe you didn't tell anyone," Darcy said.

"I didn't know what it was. I figured an old prospector had dropped it, and I couldn't have been more than Lara's age."

"Charlie would have gone nuts," Darcy said, with a smile. "He would have dug up the entire area."

Ed frowned. "Yeah," he said slowly. "Maybe that's why I said nothing." He pursed his lips.

"Keep reading," Lara urged. "The answer is probably in the journal."

Georgie smiled and continued. Mr Clarke was saving as many sheep as he could and investigating how he could transport his salvage to the mainland, so he didn't have to cart it all back when they were eventually rescued.

John, as part of his Fenian convict allocation, helped him. Elsewhere on the island, the sailors discovered what Reginald was up to and wanted their share of the bounty.

"Things are sounding quite nasty," Darcy commented. "Perhaps that mutiny isn't a rumour."

Lara clasped her hands together and leaned forward. "Keep going."

Georgie broke off mid sentence as she read Lilian's words. Her eyes darted across the page reading and Lara shoved her. "Aloud Georgie, we all want to hear too."

*Something tragic happened today and I am bereft with grief. Mr Clarke was bitten by a snake. Though Tom and Patrick did what they could for him, he died within hours. I weep for him and for Mrs Clarke and her daughters waiting back in Fremantle.*

"What will happen to John?" Faith asked. "Will he have to go back to prison?"

Georgie hoped not. It was clear Lilian liked him more than Reginald. John and the pearl diver, Da had been her only comfort on the island.

"Keep reading, Georgie," Darcy urged.

Her eyes scanned the page. "There was a mutiny," she exclaimed.

The divers had discovered a small treasure chest and when the sailors wanted their share Reginald refused.

*I raced onto the far beach. It was a massacre with bodies lying all over the ground and Tom was bent over John. I shrieked as I dropped to my knees beside him. He had a deep cut in his side and Tom was wrapping a torn piece of his shirt around it to stem the bleeding.*

*Oh, I cannot describe the fear in my heart. I thought he might die and begged him not to leave me. I realised how much I loved him.*

*The sailors who had arrived behind me swore and one ordered his men to help 'Mr Stokes'.*

*It was not until they bent to help John that I realised they'd mistaken him for Reginald. I was too distraught to correct him, but it made me look for Reginald who was lying dead not far from us. Both he and John had the same bushy beard, so it was easy to see how the mistake had been made.*

"How can Reginald be dead?" Faith asked.

"Lilian must already be pregnant," Amy answered.

"But she couldn't have set up the station on her own," Brandon argued.

*It was then the reality of the events hit me. I was a widow. With Reginald dead, I had the freedom I longed for, but what I really wanted was John. The irony was not lost on me and when a sailor arrived to ask 'Mr Stokes' what to do with the bodies, a most shockingly bold idea came to me. I sent the sailor away with instructions to bury the dead and then told John my idea.*

*The sailors already believe him to be Reginald, and with none of the mutineers left alive, it would not be difficult to continue the deception.*

Georgie gaped at her siblings. "John took on Reginald's identity."

"We're descendants of convicts not lords." Ed grinned.

The ruse was pulled off because those sailors who'd spent any time with both men were now dead.

Help arrived three days after the mutiny. The men they had sent to Tien Tsin Harbour returned with a ship to rescue them and the first mate didn't realise John was not Reginald.

With John taking Reginald's identity they needed to avoid anyone else who might have spoken with him in the short time he'd been in Western Australia. The constabulary at the harbour sent letters to Fremantle requesting permission for them to buy the lease and keep the convicts and it was a long month before a response was received.

During that time the captain's journal which had led Reginald to the sunken treasure ship had been stolen, though they still had the English translation. The original was never recovered and Lilian suspected it was the other pearl divers who had taken it as they were the only others who knew of its existence.

"Could one of Stonefish's employees be a descendant of those pearl divers?" Darcy asked.

"Could be," Brandon answered. "Dot mentioned people had been digging there, and Lilian said some of the treasure from the ship had been buried on the island."

"What happened next?" Lara asked.

Georgie continued as Lilian and John received permission to buy the pastoralist's lease and to take responsibility of Tom and Patrick. They set out on the long journey over land taking the supplies and being led by an Aboriginal tracker named Jimmy. Along the way Lilian wrote of encounters with the indigenous tribes of the area. Likely Matt's ancestors. Georgie would have to show him the journal later.

By the time they returned to the gulf, Lilian had figured out the location of the buried treasure, and the four of them had dug it up and shared it between them. Tom and Patrick agreed to stay to help them build the house and set up the station, but afterwards they planned to return to Ireland without serving the rest of their sentence.

"So the treasure's gone?" Lara slumped back against the couch.

Georgie read the final page and shook her head.

*Reginald and I have no need for such riches yet, so we have buried ours and I have included clues in this journal and elsewhere. Where shelter, food and water collide, you will find the treasure hide. The money will help us, and our family, during times of need. For that is my other news. I am with child.*

"Where?" Lara demanded. "Where did they bury it?"

"She says she'll tell her children when they're old enough."

"Then it could be gone," Darcy said. "Any of our ancestors could have discovered it."

"It said, 'Where shelter, food and water collide, you will find the treasure hide,'" Faith said.

Ed frowned. "That's not a great clue."

"Is there anything else?" Tess asked.

Georgie shook her head.

"Read it again," Amy suggested.

*I have decided to put this journal and the English translations of the Dutch captain's journal together, and bury them in the walls of the cellar. I shall inform my children of the truth when they are old enough, and one day maybe our ancestors will find the journals. If they do, I wish them luck on this land and they will know the truth of who their great grandfather really was.*

*Know my children and my children's children that I loved my husband with all my soul. I ask them not to judge too harshly the decisions we made for the good of our family.*

Georgie's chest tightened. Lilian had found her happiness. She deserved it after her ordeal.

"So is the treasure still there?" Lara asked.

"Only one way to find out." Brandon grinned. "Looks like we're going treasure hunting tomorrow."

# Chapter 3

The house was dark by the time Matt arrived home and even at the camp sites few lights were on. His headlights illuminated a small blue car parked out behind the homestead. Georgie was here.

Disappointment filled him. Maybe he should have come home for dinner. It was always fun when Georgie was home. She had such an optimistic way of looking at the world, though she could be quick tempered when something set her off. He enjoyed seeing her riled, maybe because it was so easy to do it. He parked outside the shearers' quarters and got out, trying to be quiet now he knew Georgie was sleeping in one room. His body tightened and he shook off the feeling, annoyed by the reaction. This was Georgie, his best friend's little sister.

He ducked inside his room to get a change of clothes and then showered off the dust and dirt of the day's work before he returned to his bed. He should be more tired than he was. As much as he loved his parents, sometimes it was hard work visiting them. They wanted him to be more involved in their culture, making sure it stayed alive, but it was difficult. So few people knew the old ways and fewer cared to. His people were a dying tribe and he struggled between fighting for it and letting it go. But he didn't want to let his parents down either. They'd been disappointed enough when he'd dropped out of high school in Year Ten.

They were talking about setting up a business running cultural tours and he'd brainstormed ideas with them. To be honest, it was a great idea as there was nothing like it in the area, yet so many tourists came to explore Ningaloo Reef or fish. He'd also agreed to help Parks and Wildlife redo their signs so they contained more cultural information. His mother would call him with the meeting details.

Darcy shouldn't have a problem with him taking a day off. It wasn't as if the station was thriving.

That was another concern. Money was tight, and it might not be long before Darcy had to let Matt go. He'd worked at the Ridge since he was fifteen, he had no other skills, no place of his own. He couldn't imagine working anywhere else, and the idea of having to apply for work made him cringe. Who'd want to employ someone who hadn't even graduated from high school?

Matt lay on the single bed, staring at the ceiling. Outside, the occasional bird called, and Lara's pet sheep, Flotsam and Jetsam bleated. The sounds of home.

He exhaled, trying to calm his mind, but how was he supposed to sleep? On top of family expectations, and the threat of losing his job, he had to deal with the whole animal smuggler thing. Someone, probably Stonefish, was stealing native animals and selling them for profit. Matt had seen photos of how creatures were treated, squashed into tubes and plastic containers. Hadn't people stolen enough from his family and his people?

Darcy would be furious when he found out. He was very protective of the station's land and Stonefish had already taken so much from him.

Then there was Nhiari. Matt would have to deal with

her unhappiness at being left out of the investigation.

The verandah creaked and he stiffened. Sure, it always made noises in the night, but the first creak was followed by a second and then a third. Someone was outside.

There'd been too much sabotage over the past couple of months for Matt to ignore it. Quietly he threw on a T-shirt and moved over to the door. He opened it and peered out. The figure stood on the steps just down from his room, leaning against the verandah post, staring across the yard. Small and lean, with short hair sticking up in different directions. Though it was dark, he had no trouble recognising Georgie.

Delight filled him. He grinned and crept quietly over to her. "Not tired?" he asked.

She shrieked and whirled, almost tumbling over in shock. Matt grabbed her before she fell, pulling her against him to steady her. Her warm body pressed against him in a way it never had. Feminine, curvy, soft. It felt right.

Shocked by the thought, he let her go and she swore.

"Matt! You scared the shit out of me." She ran a hand through her hair and sat on the step.

The edge of fear in her voice made him contrite. "Sorry, I couldn't resist." He sat next to her. "What's up?"

She shrugged. "Couldn't sleep."

It had been a long time since they'd sat side-by-side with Georgie confiding in him. Not since before she'd gone to university. With a jolt, he realised he'd missed it. They'd always been able to make each other feel better. He bumped her shoulder with his. "Come on, spill, Freckles."

She was silent a long moment and then sighed. "Where to start?"

The next silence was longer than the first, so unlike Georgie. His concern spiked. "What happened?"

"I went for a job interview today, and then when I got here, I found Lilian's journal hidden in the cellar wall."

Matt blinked. "What?" He thought she was happy on the tour boat. Was the new job somewhere else? Was she moving?

"There was a loose brick in the cellar and I found a cavity behind it. Lilian's journal was wrapped inside a tin along with the journal from a Dutch East Indies captain from the sixteen hundreds. Lilian mentions run ins with your ancestors."

Matt's head spun with questions, but before he could ask any, Georgie continued.

"Lara insisted we read the whole journal before she went to bed."

He smiled. "Of course." But damned if he was disappointed he hadn't been there for it. "Did Lilian say anything interesting?"

"A lot. Turns out we're not descendants of an English lord after all. He was killed in the mutiny and a Fenian prisoner stole his identity. So I have Irish convict ancestry." She chuckled softly. "Maybe Charlie was a throwback."

Matt stared at her, but in the dark he couldn't see her face and whether she was kidding. "Seriously?"

"Yeah. But there's more." She lowered her voice. "The treasure rumours are true too."

Matt leaned back. "What do you mean?"

"Just what I said," Georgie answered. "The Dutch East Indies ship was wrecked a century earlier in the gulf and it carried treasure, but only the captain was aware of it. Reginald got hold of the journal somehow and discovered the wreck after the Retribution had come to grief on the island. He found a small chest of treasure, but Lilian realised most of it had been buried and when she returned to the island, she found it and split it between herself and the three Fenian prisoners."

Georgie twisted her finger in her hair. "She and John didn't need the money so buried it for later. We don't know if it's still there, or whether they used it during their time setting up the station."

It was quite a tale, but Georgie was too agitated for it to be a lie. "So, where is it buried?" The funds would be a lifesaver for the Ridge.

"We can't figure it out," Georgie answered. "We're going to study the clues tomorrow."

Matt could imagine Lara's excitement. She was probably lying awake, staring at the ceiling, imagining finding the treasure. Darcy would have had his hands full getting her to bed at all. He smiled. "Are you too excited to sleep too?"

She shrugged. "Not really. It would be a miracle if it was still there."

She sounded glum, and Georgie was rarely glum. He could always count on her to be optimistic or to snap back at him if he felt like poking her. Rarely was she defeated. "Then what's wrong?"

Georgie sighed and looked at him. "Can you imagine how excited Charlie would have been?"

Matt grimaced. His best friend in primary school was never far from his mind. They'd spent their childhood roaming the Ridge and whenever Matt worked, he thought of Charlie. "He'd be out there now with a torch and a shovel," he said. "There'd be no waiting for morning for him."

Georgie nodded. "It's times like this when it hits me hard how much he's missed."

Such a tragic accident. Charlie had died at twelve in a cattle stampede when the Stokes were trialling cattle instead of sheep. Needless to say, they'd stuck with sheep.

Matt slid his arm around Georgie's shoulders and she leaned into him. So simple, yet her trust and the fact he could comfort her made him feel so good about himself. He stroked her arm. After Charlie's death, he'd grown closer to her. She'd been all of nine and he'd been thirteen, but they'd come together in their grief. He'd felt lost and his steps had kept carrying him back to the homestead and the Ridge as if Charlie would magically appear. Charlie had made school bearable.

The Stokes had always been the most warm and welcoming family but after Charlie's death his parents were lost in their own grief. Matt and Georgie had comforted each other over those first few months.

He'd told her about the bullies at school who wouldn't leave him alone now Charlie wasn't there to stick up for him. Jerry, in particular, had made his life hell. He took every opportunity to make a snide comment, to put him down, tell him he was stupid. One day he'd even locked Matt in a storeroom and told the teachers he was wagging school. Matt had spent the last period in the small dark space, banging on the door for someone to let him out, but outside no one went past. He'd thought he would be stuck in there the entire weekend.

It was lucky the football team had had training after school, and the sports teacher had let him out. Matt had run all the way to the front of the school so he didn't miss the bus home.

Come Monday, no one had asked him how he'd got stuck in the storeroom in the first place, so Jerry had got away with it.

Matt had counted the days until he was old enough to leave and then asked Bill Stokes to give him a job as a station hand. Bill had agreed and he'd moved out here permanently and become part of the family. By then Brandon had been long gone and he and Darcy had become best friends as they'd worked side by side.

Georgie trembled and he shook off the tension of the

memory, his focus on her.

"It's not fair, Matt." Her voice was full of tears. "First Charlie, then Mum and Dad." The next words came out as a whisper. "I cursed him."

"What?"

"I cursed Charlie after he scared me with a fake spider. Not long afterwards, he was dead."

Matt stared at her. Why was the normally sensible Georgie talking nonsense?

"And it was my bragging about Mum and Dad coming out on the boat that told Stonefish their movements. If I hadn't opened my big mouth, maybe they'd still be alive."

"You're talking shit." Annoyance made him less patient. "You don't really believe you're responsible for anyone's death. Charlie's death was a tragic accident and Stonefish would have got to your parents eventually."

"It feels like my fault."

"It's not. But that doesn't mean the situation doesn't suck."

She leaned her head against his shoulder. "I know."

He wasn't sure he'd convinced her, but they sat like that, side-by-side, Matt's arm around her until the night grew cold. Georgie shifted, sitting more upright, and rubbed her arms. "It's getting late. We'd better get some sleep if we're going treasure hunting tomorrow."

Matt missed her warmth against his side, but stood and offered her a hand up. "Yeah. You OK now?"

She nodded and moved back to her room. "Night, Matt. Thanks."

He didn't want her to leave, but couldn't think of an excuse to make her stay. "Any time." He waited until her door clicked shut behind her and then entered his own room.

His words seemed to resonate in his mind. He would do anything for Georgie, be there whenever she needed him. They had a bond he had with no one else, not even Darcy or Charlie. If only he could take away her pain and sorrow.

Tomorrow, after he met with Colin, he could go into town and get her a box of those little cakes she liked from the Saturday evening markets.

They always made her happy.

It wasn't until he lay down that he realised he hadn't asked her about the job she'd applied for.

***

"Georgie! Georgie! Are you awake?" Lara's shouts from outside woke Georgie and she groaned.

"If she's not, she will be now," Matt called from the room next to hers.

Lara giggled. "Sorry!" Rapid knocking followed her words.

Georgie grimaced. It was light outside, but it was the pastel glow of early morning. This was the one downside of staying over at the Ridge. She threw the rugs back. "Gimme a minute." She stretched and checked the time. Six o'clock. Far too early on her day off. Opening the door, she asked, "What's up?"

"We're going treasure hunting, but Dad said I had to wait until everyone was awake." Lara grinned, her brown ponytail swinging behind her as she jigged on the spot.

Georgie's breath caught as she remembered last night. "Make me a coffee and I'll be there soon."

Lara squeezed her. "You're the best." She skipped to Matt's room and called, "Do you want coffee too, Uncle Matt?"

"Sure, La La. Thanks."

Georgie's body warmed. For years she'd tried to become immune to Matt's voice, but it was impossible. Even when he was teasing her, it made her feel secure. Georgie shook her head, more resigned than upset. She had no sense when it came to him. She was like a bug attracted to a bug zapper, always drawing close even though she knew she would be hurt.

But how could she resist, especially in moments like last night when she'd needed his comfort?

Quickly she dressed and brushed her blue hair back as well as she could. Going short was easier most of the time, except in the morning when it stuck up in every direction. Only water tamed it.

She ducked out of her room, hoping to get to the shared bathroom before Matt, but she crashed into him as he stepped out.

"Oof," Georgie grunted. Pressed against his hard chest, she clenched her hands to stop herself from running them all over him to feel how firm and muscular he was.

"In a rush?" Matt grinned as he steadied her and her heartbeat ratcheted up to a hundred. His grin widened as his dark brown eyes swept to her hair. "You know you shouldn't stick your finger into an electrical socket."

She grimaced. "Yeah, very funny." He looked totally put together, even though he wore work jeans and a blue-checked shirt, his Akubra already hiding his dark hair. As he stepped into his boots, she darted around him. "I'll see you in the house."

Inside the small bathroom, she took a moment to calm her pounding heart. It wasn't fair his touch affected her like this. He didn't get short of breath or all tingly when he saw her.

She wet her hands and used the water to dampen the more significant clumps of hair sticking out, and used her fingers to comb through it. The blue had seemed like a good idea, but it faded quickly, particularly because she spent most of her days in the ocean. Perhaps next time she went to the hairdresser she should go back to her natural light brown tones.

With her hair as tamed as it was going to get, she left the bathroom and trekked across the red dirt to the homestead. Maggie was begging for breakfast at a camp site with younger kids who were already awake, and Flotsam and Jetsam were resting under a tree.

Voices floated out of the house through the fly screen door. Bennett ate his breakfast on the verandah. He wagged his tail as he saw Georgie and she patted him before slipping inside to find the kitchen full. Her family was always up at this time. Work started at first light to get as much done as they could before the heat of the day hit, and it was an hour's drive into town where Lara went to school. Even Ed and Tess were awake and dressed, but Georgie put it down to Tess's excitement at the treasure hunt because Ed was not a morning person.

Lara handed Matt a mug of coffee and then spotted Georgie and held up the other mug she'd made. "Here you go, Georgie."

"Thanks, La La." Georgie sniffed the strong aroma before taking her first sip and wandering to the table. Brandon, Darcy and Amy were hunched over a photocopy of the journal they'd made last night while Ed read the copy of the Dutch captain's journal.

They hadn't finished when Darcy had ordered Lara to bed. "Find anything interesting?" Georgie asked.

"Yeah. After he was rescued, he lied about the exact location of the shipwreck. In those days, the people in charge only dealt with the captains. He was planning to return at a later date to take the treasure for himself."

That was interesting.

"But what about the other sailors on board?" Matt placed bread into the toaster. "They would have known about it.

Ed smiled. "The captain salvaged and buried the treasure at night when the others were asleep. Only he knew he was carrying such precious cargo."

Darcy frowned. "But the company would have known he was lying when they got there and found no treasure."

"When they returned to the wreck, they probably thought someone else had beaten them to it," Tess said.

"The journal ends the day before he leaves on the salvage mission," Ed said. "He says if he doesn't return, he's left clues in his journal for his family."

"What are the clues?" Lara said.

Ed shook his head. "If they're in there, I missed them. Maybe they're lost in translation."

"They must be there if Lilian found them." Matt took the toast that popped up, and added two more slices to the toaster. He handed Georgie one piece of toast and sat at the table to spread his slice with butter.

Her heart clenched as she passed him Vegemite and got jam for herself. She'd bet her car he didn't realise how much the subconscious action meant to her.

"Can we go yet?" Lara asked.

"We need to decide where to search," Faith said. "We can't dig up the whole Ridge."

"Does it say how deep they buried it?" Georgie asked.

"No," Tess answered.

This was like looking for a needle in a quarter of a million acre piece of land.

"It might be over by the windmill," Darcy said. "There's an old well which probably dates to Lilian's era and some bush tomatoes grow there."

"What about the shelter aspect?" Faith asked.

"It's close enough to the house."

"Not that close," Georgie said.

"There has to be something marking the spot, otherwise they'd never have found it again," Amy pointed out.

She was right. It was a long shot, but they had to start somewhere—and Lara was dancing around the kitchen, too excited to sit. If nothing else, it would burn some of her energy.

"Let's go!" Lara shouted.

"Has Dad still got his old metal detector in the shed?" Brandon asked.

"It was there the last time I looked," Darcy said.

Georgie raised her eyebrows as she spread jam on her toast. "You think it will detect a chest?"

"Depends on how deep it is, and what it's made of, but it's worth a try."

Amy finished adding food and drinks to an esky, and they trooped out to the two utes. Somehow Georgie ended up in the front seat with Matt, with Tess and Ed riding in the tray. She finished her toast as Matt followed Brandon to the well.

A spark of excitement stirred.

They were hunting treasure.

# Chapter 4

Matt's faint aftershave drifted over Georgie's nose, dampening her excitement. It wasn't fair he should smell this good. She wound down the window and looked out at the camp site as they drove past, trying to ignore her body's longing.

"What do you think our chances are?" Matt asked.

"Somewhere between slim and none," she admitted. "But it will be fun to look." The words came automatically, years of practised nonchalance making it seem as if she wasn't yearning for him to touch her.

She squeezed away the thought and focused on the treasure. If the treasure actually existed and they could find it, it would be a lifeline for her family. Darcy and Brandon had been babying the station along since her parents died, and it would be nice for her brothers to catch a break.

"What are the ownership laws on buried treasure?" Matt asked.

Georgie glanced at him. "I hadn't considered it. It's on our land."

He shot her a look, which spoke volumes.

"Right, it's on Bayungu land first, but you know what

I mean. If we found anything, we'd split it with your family."

"But isn't it stolen property? The ownership can be traced back to the Dutch East Indies Company."

"Does that even exist anymore?" She sighed. "We can worry about that if we find it."

"Good point. You feeling any better today?"

She didn't want to talk about last night. He wouldn't tease her about it, but he was also too clueless to realise how much it had meant to her. Besides, he hadn't even asked her about her job interview, which meant he didn't care if she stayed in town. "I'm fine." She so needed to get over him. All this moping was pathetic. Definitely time for a girls' night. She grabbed her phone from her pocket and sent a text to Gretchen, Dot and Nhiari while she still had reception.

"Who are you texting?"

It was on the tip of her tongue to say a random man's name, but she didn't. "The girls."

He grunted as if satisfied which needled her. "Did you hear Sam's moving here permanently?" she asked sweetly. "He bought Faith's dad's boat, and he's asked me to check out a few houses for him."

"Why you?"

"I live in town and he probably trusts a woman's eye more than Brandon's."

Matt's mouth set in a line.

"Why don't you like Sam? Everyone else does."

"I like Sam," he said. "I just think he's too old for you."

Georgie laughed. "You have no clue." Sure, she'd had fun flirting with Brandon's best friend, but he did nothing for her. Not like the man sitting less than a metre away.

They arrived at the windmill and she got out. "Tess, you want to go out tonight?" Georgie glanced at Ed.

"Girls' night."

Tess smiled. "Yes, that sounds like fun."

Georgie called to Faith and Amy. "Girls' night tonight?"

Amy gave her the thumbs up and Faith nodded.

"Can I come?" Lara asked.

The hopeful expression on her face made Georgie cringe. "Not tonight, La La, but I'll organise a day you can come to soon."

Darcy placed a hand on Lara's shoulder. "Besides, you might be too busy sorting through treasure."

Lara brightened and nodded. "OK."

Georgie remembered all too well feeling left out because she was too young, and watching her brothers go off and have all the fun. Perhaps she could arrange a pamper day for them, and there was still Faith's hens' night to organise. She'd have to ensure Lara could attend an aspect of it.

"So where do we dig?" Ed asked.

Brandon was setting up the metal detector. "Why don't I do a sweep with this first, and you can search for clues around the old well?"

The old well was about two and a half metres wide and had a stone wall about waist height. Long ago, someone had placed a metal grid over the top so no one fell in and hurt themselves. It rarely contained water these days.

Brandon swept the area, starting closest to the well and moving out in circles.

"This is so exciting." Lara clutched her hands together. "I can't wait to tell Mischa about it."

"No, pumpkin," Darcy said. "You can't tell anyone about this. The last thing we need is word getting back to Stonefish."

Lara bit her lip, her eyes wide. "Please! She'd think it's epic."

"No." He gave Lara a stern look so like their father's that Georgie's heart twinged.

"Not even Dot and Nhiari?"

Darcy glanced at Matt and then Brandon. Brandon shook his head. "Not even them."

The police didn't need to get involved.

While Brandon swept the area, Georgie examined the stones, searching for a similar structure to the one that had hidden the journal in the wall. The others spread out, looking for clues. Every time the metal detector shrieked, Lara rushed over, but inevitably it was an old piece of wire, or scrap metal.

Georgie traced her fingers over the rough rocks, looking for a loose one. She didn't notice the bush tomato shrub right next to her, not until she'd walked into the sticky web which stretched between it and the well.

Fear gripped her and she shrieked, leaping back and slapping away the webs, her heart pounding, her breath coming in pants.

Was a spider on her? She moaned as she imagined it poised to bite.

She shuddered and continued swiping at her skin. Darcy grabbed her and she pushed him away, not wanting him to get bitten as well.

"Hey, Freckles, it's all right." Matt stood in front of her, his mouth moving, but his words wouldn't process.

"Sp-spider," she managed to gasp as she stepped away from him.

"You're OK." He clasped her hands, stopping her from brushing off the web. "It's just a Golden Orb web and the *garrawarla* is still there. Look." He turned her so she faced the web, and sure enough, the spider still sat in what remained of it.

Georgie sucked in a breath.

"Let me check you." Matt brushed a few stray strands

from her arms as he scanned her for spiders. Georgie trembled. "It's OK," he murmured, his hands gently caressing her skin.

As the fear receded it was replaced by a warmth at Matt's touch. She wanted to lean into him, wanted him to touch her everywhere.

With a jolt, she stepped back. Their eyes met and she couldn't read his expression. He cleared his throat. "Better?"

She nodded. "Thanks." One day she would have to do something about her phobia. She glanced around. Lara appeared worried and formed a heart on her chest with her hands. Georgie forced a smile. Ed called, "OK, Mermaid?"

"Fine," she called back, though her voice was shaky. How she hated this fear. "Damn you, Charlie," she murmured. He'd triggered her phobia by making a plastic spider drop onto her head when she'd entered her bedroom. She'd taken to carrying an umbrella whenever she went room to room for weeks afterwards.

"He always regretted the prank," Matt said.

Georgie stared at Matt. "He said that?"

Matt nodded. "Yeah, it was just before he died. You were giving him the cold shoulder, and he felt so guilty about it. He told me he'd never thought it would scare you so much, and he hated that you weren't talking to him."

Georgie sniffed. "I never believed him when he said he was sorry. He was always doing things to tease and torture me."

"I know. But he loved you. He thought you were the best, so tough and determined. He was proud you stood up to him and gave as good as you got."

Georgie's vision blurred. She smiled at Matt. "How come you know all of this?"

Matt shifted back and adjusted his Akubra. "We used

to tell each other everything," he said. "Charlie was the only one I could really talk to as a kid. I don't know what it was, we just connected." He looked so sad Georgie reached out and squeezed his hand.

"I miss him too."

Matt smiled. "I feel him here, all around this land. I reckon his spirit is still here."

Georgie looked at the rich red dirt and small trees. It was a nice thought. Charlie had loved this land.

She moved back to the wall of the well and Matt used a stick to shift the spider into the shrub so they could continue checking for hidden cavities. Georgie gestured to the spot near the shrub. "You can check there."

Matt chuckled. "As you wish."

Georgie's heart wrenched. Did he realise it was a line from her favourite movie, *The Princess Bride*? It was too much to hope he knew the other meaning behind those words. She busied herself checking the rest of the wall, more mindful now of her surroundings.

"How far should I search?" Brandon called.

He'd already scanned a five-metre radius from the well. What they needed was another clue. It was ridiculous to think they'd find a treasure chest which had been buried almost a hundred and fifty years ago in a piece of land this big. Georgie wandered over to Tess and Ed, who were examining the journal. "Anything else?"

Tess shook her head. "It's not clear at all. Maybe the clues relate to an indigenous settlement in the area at the time. Lilian wrote the tribe had helped them find water."

Matt joined them. "I don't know of a camp in this area, but there could have been. My people moved from place to place depending on the season. There aren't any sacred places around here which is possibly why they were allowed to set up the homestead here."

"Maybe we should go to the top of the Ridge and look

from a bird's-eye view," Georgie suggested. "We might see something which stands out."

"Good idea," Ed said. "Why don't you and Matt go?"

Georgie glared at him. Ed was one of the few people who knew how she really felt about Matt. What was he up to?

"Yeah, all right," Matt answered. "Coming, Freckles?"

She scowled and followed Matt over to the old ute.

***

Matt drove slowly towards the Ridge, his attention more on the woman sitting next to him than the track. The powerful urge, no *need*, to stay close to Georgie was uncomfortable. Perhaps it was simply his protective instincts kicking in after her panic attack. It hurt to see her that way. It wasn't often Georgie lost control. But he also felt a little… uneasy. Something weird had happened when Georgie had come back to her senses. There'd been a look, something he couldn't interpret and suddenly he'd realised how soft her skin was. The whole idea set him off-kilter.

He should forget it happened. It would be the easiest solution and he didn't want to talk to her about it in case it was all in his head. That would be awkward.

They didn't speak as they drove to the base of the ridge. It wasn't possible to drive to the top on this side of the valley, so they hiked. The slope was steep enough to make talking difficult.

At the top, Georgie breathed deeply as she looked around. "I never get tired of this view." She spun slowly, arms outstretched, looking like a Goddess bestowing gifts upon her land.

Georgie, a Goddess? He blinked and shook away the thought. Sure, her denim shorts moulded to her butt and her T-shirt pulled tight across her breasts, but it didn't make her a deity. He had to say something. "It's home."

He studied her clinically. She had colour in her cheeks again. She'd been so pale after her fright, so vulnerable. Though he knew how remorseful Charlie had been, he couldn't help disliking his friend for what he'd done.

"Let me read the last page again." Georgie took out her phone and Matt joined her, looking over her shoulder as she flicked to the photo she'd taken of the last couple of pages of the journal. He clenched his hands as the urge to put them on her hips almost overcame him. That would be totally inappropriate.

Georgie frowned. "The only shelter around here is the homestead, or the caves in the canyon."

"Might be some more caves along the riverbed or at the coast." Matt shifted away so he couldn't smell the lemon scent of her shampoo.

She nodded. "And Patrick and Tom might have had their own shelter too."

A good point. "The station hands who replaced Patrick and Tom would have definitely had their own accommodation, but it might have been a tent."

"The shearers' quarters aren't old enough and there aren't any other buildings."

What else then? "Sometimes they had a separate storage cellar from the house."

Georgie grimaced. "How are we supposed to know?"

Matt shrugged. "Let me have a look." He plucked the phone from her hand and smirked at her shout of protest. She was so easy to rile. He read the words and turned in a slow circle surveying the land. Where else would it be? An older watering hole was east of here, but it had to be at least ten kilometres away. Would they have buried the treasure somewhere they couldn't see?

Georgie took the phone back from him. "We should search the caves."

It was the next best choice. The problem was there

were too many possibilities.

"We need the funds. Do you think the treasure is actually still there?" She played with her hair, a sure sign she wanted comfort.

"There's a good chance. Like you said, why would anyone return the journal to the wall if they'd found the treasure?"

She gave him a half smile. "Thanks, Matt."

"Any time, Freckles." He turned his attention north, towards the ocean. He couldn't recall seeing any signs of a building in the area. The only structures were the fences, and the plaque at the gulf which commemorated those who had died in the shipwreck. Or rather those who had died in the mutiny. Lilian's journal had given a whole new history to the Stokes family and the area.

"Could there be more valuables with the shipwreck?" he asked.

Her eyes widened. "Maybe." She slumped. "But I've been to the shipwreck museum. Anything underwater that long is hard to distinguish from coral. Plus, it's illegal to plunder shipwrecks."

"We could still check it out." He wanted to see her smile, and she'd enjoy an ocean-based adventure over a land-based one.

He wandered over to the other side of the ridge and peered down into the gully. His gut clenched. Not so long ago, it had flooded and he'd been stuck on the wrong side, unable to help, not knowing if his friends were alive.

Thankfully no one had died.

Matt checked the time. He still had a couple of hours before he was due to meet Colin at the animal traps. He considered telling Georgie and Darcy about them, but they would want to get involved. The traps were on government land not on the station, though it was likely the smugglers used Ridge land to transport the captured animals.

"See anything useful?" Georgie asked.

"No." He crossed back to Georgie's side. "We might as well go back to the others." In the distance, everyone was gathered around the well and still searching for clues.

Georgie moved down the incline, her steps confident, her butt wiggling.

Matt blinked rapidly. What was he doing looking at Georgie's butt? She was practically his little sister. Though not *actually* his little sister. At some stage over the past couple of years Georgie had grown up. And he hadn't noticed, not until Brandon had come home, and his friend, Sam had flirted with Georgie. But Georgie was off-limits. He shouldn't be thinking about her in any way except as a member of his surrogate family. Anything else would lead to trouble.

He didn't want to betray Darcy's trust, and he wasn't nearly worthy enough for Georgie.

Georgie glanced over her shoulder and called, "Are you coming?"

He'd been standing there staring at her like a fool. He scowled and strode after her. "Just waiting for you to hurry up."

Georgie screwed up her nose and stuck her tongue out. Matt relaxed. This was the Georgie he knew.

"You need more rest than I do being so old and slow," she retaliated and continued down the slope.

He chuckled. Yes, he was definitely more comfortable with the snarky Georgie.

# Chapter 5

Around ten o'clock Matt met Constable Colin Lipscombe at one of the rest stops on the main road. Colin drove the four-wheel drive police van and Matt got out to shake his hand. "Thanks for coming."

Colin grimaced. "Do you realise how mad your sister is? I'm gonna be in the shit for days."

Matt shrugged and chuckled. "She should know better. Follow me."

Matt drove to where he'd found the traps. His skin tight, he waited until Colin stood next to him and then spoke aloud to his ancestors, introducing Colin and explaining why he was here. He felt like a fool doing so, but if he insisted Nhiari didn't come because she was female, he had to follow through with the proper introductions so as not to offend his ancestors or the spirits who dwelled here. Next to him Colin was silent and respectful. Matt appreciated that. Many people were dismissive of his culture.

When he was finished, he took Colin over to the traps. This time a mulga was trying to get out, but the sides were too smooth for it to get purchase. Colin kept a wary distance as he took a couple of photos. "Let me get my things," he said. "These footsteps yours?"

Matt examined them. "Yeah, probably. That's where I stood yesterday."

Matt stood back while Colin documented the scene. The other traps had a couple of little lizards in them, so after Colin gave him permission, he set them free. The venomous snake was another matter. "You got snake catching gear in your van?" Matt asked.

Colin nodded. "But I'm not great with it."

"I'll do it." Nhiari had insisted he learn so he didn't get bitten on the odd occasion he came across a venomous snake on the Ridge which needed relocating.

Carefully he used the long metal pole to lift the aggravated mulga out of the hole and then placed it in the bush away from them. Thankfully it saw its freedom and slithered off in the opposite direction without trying to attack its saviour.

"What happens next?" Matt asked.

"We stay alert and pick up the usual suspects if they come to town."

"Are you going to remove the traps?"

"Yeah, I'll talk to Parks and Wildlife about it. They should be on the lookout as well."

It was all so anti-climatic. He'd been hoping they'd set up some kind of sting operation, but now he thought about it, it could be days or weeks until the smugglers came back and the Retribution Bay police didn't have those kinds of resources.

"Thanks, Colin."

It was almost midday when Matt waved goodbye to Colin. His stomach rumbled and he stopped in the rest bay for a couple of minutes to eat the sandwich he'd brought with him. Since he was halfway to town, he should call Amy to see if they needed anything before starting back towards the Ridge. And he'd been planning to get Georgie something from the evening markets to cheer her up.

He'd left everyone at the homestead going through the journals again, trying to find more clues as to the location of the treasure. Georgie hadn't been as excited as he'd expected her to be. In fact, she'd been a little down all day.

What had brought her to the Ridge in the first place? It was probably Ed. Whenever he visited, she spent as much time as possible there so they could catch up. He lived in Perth over a thousand kilometres away.

But she also came to the Ridge whenever she needed comfort, or if something was bothering her. Georgie said her mother's hugs could instantly make her feel better.

He closed his eyes. She was right. Beth had had a way of including everyone and making him believe everything would be all right. She'd been a second mother to him and he missed her and Bill like crazy.

Perhaps Georgie was worried about the job interview. He'd have to ask her about it when he got back to the Ridge.

He switched on the engine and waited until it coughed to life. As he did so, a small blue car drove past. He frowned at the glimpse of blue hair he spotted through the window. Georgie. Damn. He'd expected her to spend the rest of the day with her family. Maybe he could stop by her unit and find out what was wrong.

Matt stopped at the bitumen and watched as Georgie slowed and then turned right down a road which led to a boat ramp.

Georgie didn't have a boat. What was she up to?

It was bound to be something foolish.

Curious and concerned, he followed.

*** 

They were wasting their time and Georgie had had enough of waiting. They'd read the journals a second time, everybody had put their two cents in, and still they were no closer to finding the buried treasure. Matt's comments about the other shipwreck, the one Reginald had been after, had been circling in her mind for hours. The treasure had come from it in the first place. Not that she would take anything, but to rediscover it would be pretty cool.

Plus she was feeling a little left out. Matt had gone off on an errand, which left her the odd one out. Darcy, Faith and Lara sat on one side of the kitchen table poring over their copy of the journal, Brandon and Amy sat heads together at the end, and Tess and Ed were side by side opposite them.

Alone again.

She didn't have time to feel sorry for herself. The Ridge hadn't brought her the comfort she'd needed, but it hadn't been a wasted trip. And now the idea of finding the Dutch ship had entered her head she couldn't shake it loose. Who knew? Perhaps it would deliver some answers.

To get to the island she needed a boat, and to get the boat she had to borrow the farm's old dinghy and the car to tow it. But if she did that, then her family would want to come too.

She wanted to be alone.

Wanted something that was just hers.

She had a friend in town who might lend her one, and she always kept a beach bag in her car with a spare set of bathers and snorkelling gear in case she got the urge to go swimming. She wandered down the hallway to the lounge and made the call. A few minutes later she had arranged to meet Tony at the boat ramp.

Georgie re-entered the kitchen. "I'm off."

Darcy glanced at her, surprised. "You're going?"

"But we haven't found the treasure yet," Lara added.

Georgie smiled. "I think you guys have it covered,"

she said. "Let me know how you go. I've got a few things to do in town before the girls' night tonight."

Amy glanced up. "What time are we meeting?"

"Six-thirty."

The others nodded and Georgie hugged Lara goodbye. "Thanks for lunch."

Ed studied her and then stood. "I'll walk you out."

Damn it. She could never hide anything from him.

Quickly she jogged down the steps and across to her car. The sun had a sharp sting to it although it wasn't stifling hot.

Ed stopped her from opening the door. "How did the interview go?"

So he hadn't forgotten about it. She shrugged. "All right," she said. "I should know sometime next week."

"Everything OK? The Georgie I know would never miss out on a chance to go treasure hunting."

She raised her eyebrows. "If you get a lead, call me," she said. "But I think we're chasing ghosts."

"Maybe, but the idea is exciting."

Georgie shifted his hand from the door. If she delayed too long, she'd break down and tell him everything that was bothering her, and neither of them needed that. "Yeah, look I've got to go. I'll catch you later before you leave."

Ed watched her as she backed out. She waved, a bright smile on her face, but he didn't buy it. He'd call her later to try and find out what was really going on. But she could hardly tell him she was jealous without sounding selfish.

She turned up the music, hoping the sound would blast any thoughts from her head. Music normally calmed her, made her feel much better.

But not today. Her mind jerked from thoughts about Matt, the treasure and her new job, with more guilt and sadness about her parents thrown in for good measure as she passed the crash site.

By the time she reached the boat ramp, she wanted to scream. At least Tony wasn't here yet.

Quickly she grabbed her bathers from her beach bag and was halfway dressed when she heard a car. Damn it. She ducked behind her door to finish dressing. Not that it wasn't something Tony hadn't seen before, but he was in a relationship now, and she didn't want to put him in an awkward situation especially if his girlfriend was with him.

An old white ute came into view and she jolted, placing a hand to her chest as she gasped. What was Matt doing here?

He parked next to her and got out. "Hey, what are you up to?"

"That was my question."

He shrugged. "I noticed you turn off."

She hadn't seen him at all which was unusual since there wasn't much traffic on the road. "Where have you been?"

"Around." He grinned and her traitorous heart skipped a beat.

He'd been vague when he'd left the house earlier, saying something about having errands to run. "You got a new girl?" She kept her voice light, teasing, but her stomach cramped at the thought.

He chuckled. "No. You got a new guy?"

It would be easy to lie and say yes, but Tony didn't deserve the trouble it might cause. "Nope."

She was saved from any further questions as Tony arrived towing his small fibreglass boat. Matt glanced into her car and spotted the beach bag. "You're going to the shipwreck."

Crap. She nodded, because there was no point denying it.

"By yourself?" he asked incredulous. "We don't know

Stonefish is finished out there. It could be dangerous."

She hadn't considered that. Surely the consortium knew the police had scoured the island. They wouldn't be back any time soon. She didn't answer, just grabbed her bag and walked down the boat ramp to help Tony unhitch.

Tony glanced at Matt behind her. "A romantic outing?"

"No!" If only. She grimaced as she shook her head. "He's a tag along."

"What are you up to?"

"I'm doing observations on the Humpback whales," she lied. "It's volunteer stuff."

"Cool. Listen, the phone reception's crap out here. What time do you think you'll be back?"

"About four."

"Great, I'll be back then."

"Thanks, Tony."

"Not a problem." He waved as Matt came over, carrying a small esky. "Hey, Matt."

"Tony. How's things?"

"Great. I'm glad you're going with Georgie. I don't like the idea of her going out alone."

"Hey, I'm right here," Georgie protested. "I can take care of myself."

"Yeah, but accidents happen." He waved and jumped back into his car before she could defend herself further.

She huffed out a breath, looking at the esky in Matt's hand. "You're not coming with me." She didn't need the extra stress of pretending to be just friends.

"Of course I am. Darcy would kill me if I let you go out on your own."

She growled. "I'm a grown woman."

"It's like Tony said, accidents happen, and we don't know if Stonefish is still around." He placed the esky into the boat. She wanted to be snarky about him always being prepared, but all the men on the station carried extra water and food in case something cropped up. And she hadn't even considered that.

She sighed. They'd be in the water most of the time, and the boat's engine was too noisy for conversation. She could suck it up for a couple of hours. She'd been doing it for years.

They both climbed aboard the small fibreglass boat, and Matt sat in the seat next to hers as she slowly headed out across the gulf. The water was still and glassy, so she pushed the motor faster, which had the additional benefit of being too loud to enable conversation. Not that Matt tried to speak. He stared out at the ocean lost in his own thoughts. When was the last time she'd been alone with Matt?

Last night didn't count because her family were just inside the house, and the same when they went to the ridge earlier.

It must be years since they had travelled into town together or gone horse riding just the two of them. She didn't know what to say, so she said nothing.

It took about half an hour to get to Retribution Island, and she slowed as she approached, knowing the reef wasn't far below the surface. The last thing she needed was to get wrecked on the same reef as both ships. She motored around the back to the eastern side. There was a small chance her family might give up on the treasure hunt and decide to go swimming this afternoon.

Matt threw out the anchor in a clear spot where there was a sandy bottom. Georgie cut the engine and the sudden silence was startling. "You don't have any bathers."

"That never stopped me." The insolent grin he gave shot heat straight to her core.

She swallowed and answered, "You're not worried about getting burnt?"

"I'm fairly sure you'll have sun cream in that beach bag of yours," he replied. "And probably a spare set of goggles."

Damn it, he knew her too well. She slipped off her T-shirt and into a rashie vest, and then handed him the bottle of sun cream.

He removed his jeans, exposing his underwear which were shorts rather than briefs, so not too revealing, but revealing enough.

Georgie focused on the contents of her beach bag, pulling out her set of goggles and digging a little bit deeper to find the old pair she kept for situations such as this when she had an unexpected friend along for the ride. Lara was the only one who'd used them.

"I don't have any spare fins," she said as she handed him the mask.

"I'll manage."

He kept his T-shirt on and rubbed cream into his arms and legs. "Hey, you never told me what your job interview was for."

She glanced at him, surprised. "You never asked."

He rolled his eyes. "What was it for?"

"Parks and Wildlife. They've advertised a couple of positions."

He grinned. "You'd be great at that. Will you deal with the reef and islands?"

His confidence cheered her a little. "Hopefully. One role is land based and the other is ocean."

"They'd be fools not to give it to you." He handed back the sun cream. "Where did the journal say the ship was?"

She blinked at the change in topic. "Somewhere around here, the opposite side of the island from where the Retribution sank."

"How do you want to do this?" Matt asked.

She shrugged. "I thought I'd go swimming and see

what I could find."

"You've never snorkelled this area before?"

"I have, but I wasn't looking for evidence of a shipwreck," she said. "I knew the Retribution went down at the other end. Chances are I swam right past something without knowing what it was."

"All right. How about we go in a line working perpendicular to the island?"

It was as good an idea as any. She nodded. "Let's go." She jumped into the water and the underwater life sprung into clarity; fish, coral, and over there feeding on some weed was a turtle. She focused on the bottom looking for any evidence of a ship. Maybe a canon, an anchor, or even a cup. The ocean was three or four metres deep, but in places the reef was exposed at low tide. The ship would have easily been wrecked if they'd lost their anchor in a storm.

A splash as Matt joined her and they swam away from the boat and the shore until Matt tapped her on the arm. He removed the snorkel from his mouth and said, "You think we've come far enough?"

She had no idea. Lilian's journal had said the divers had dived from a raft, but they hadn't been too far from shore. "Ten more metres."

He nodded without arguing and continued. He wasn't wearing any fins, so she was careful not to kick too hard so he could keep up with her. Despite her reluctance at having him here, it was comforting. A younger Georgie would have made up fantasies about him being there for her, and being her boyfriend, but this older Georgie knew the truth too well. He felt responsible for her, believed she'd get herself into trouble without him. And as a surrogate brother he had to look out for her.

Darcy and Brandon would have done no less. Ed was the only one who saw her as halfway capable, possibly because he was the closest in age to her.

They reached the designated turnaround spot and she took a moment to slowly scan the bottom, before turning back and moving across a few metres from where they had done their last pass.

Perhaps she should simply report this and leave it to the expert maritime archaeologists to deal with. Only problem was, first they needed some evidence the wreck was here; otherwise they would have to explain about the journal.

Georgie and Matt swam laps for almost an hour. Nothing but coral and fish with the occasional bit of rubbish. What a waste of time. Georgie was about to call it quits when she spotted an odd lump separate from the rest of the coral. She frowned. Something about it – the shape, the location – wasn't quite right. She swam over. Kind of T-shaped. Unnatural. Instinct had her diving down to get a better look and she cautiously prodded the large object. The coral was rough on her fingers but even along the long cylindrical surface until it curved away on both sides. Definitely an anchor. She sucked in a breath, forgetting she was underwater and choked, kicking to the surface and spitting the water out. When her coughing fit was over she turned to Matt. "It's an anchor!"

Matt grinned. "Good one, Freckles. You found it."

With renewed energy, Georgie dived and spent some time examining it, Matt diving next to her. She wished she had a scuba tank and a waterproof camera, or had learnt free diving. When she surfaced, she took a bearing from some trees on Retribution Island and the other islands nearby.

"So what do we do now?" Matt asked.

She wasn't entirely sure. "We should contact someone," she said. "Maybe Parks and Wildlife?" She'd have to research where to report newly discovered shipwrecks.

"Are we heading back now?"

It was then Georgie realised how patiently he had explored with her without complaining. Was it any wonder she loved him?

She smiled. "Yeah, thanks for your patience."

"Any time."

Her heart squeezed as he swam back to the boat. When he stopped a few metres away and looked back, she hurriedly replaced her snorkel and followed.

Matt hauled himself up the ladder and then offered a hand to help Georgie up. She ducked her head and handed him her beach towel. It was the least she could do since he'd come with her. Matt stripped off his T-shirt and wrung it out over the side. Georgie stared at his muscled chest, his smooth dark skin making her itch to touch him.

"Take a picture." Matt grinned. "It lasts longer."

Heat rushed to Georgie's cheeks. He'd caught her checking him out. It was mortifying. She shoved him hard and, caught off balance, he toppled over the side of the boat with a splash. Georgie sighed, glad to have a second to compose herself. How was she supposed to face him now? Maybe she could throw it back at him, tell him it was his ego talking.

She turned to do just that, but he wasn't at the ladder. Where was he? "Matt?"

She peered over the side, but he wasn't there. She moved to the other side of the boat. Nothing. Panic filled her as visions of him unconscious and stuck under the hull appeared in her mind. No. She couldn't bear it. She couldn't lose someone else she loved. "Matt!"

Her heart racing, she jumped into the water expecting to see him somehow trapped underneath the boat and drowning. Arms circled her and shoved her further under the water. Georgie fought against them, and she surfaced spluttering. Matt was right next to her, laughing. "Got you."

Fury obliterated her fear. "You idiot. I thought you'd drowned."

"Maybe you shouldn't push a man overboard then."

His flippant attitude only fuelled her anger. She stroked back to the boat and hauled herself back on board, every fibre of her being seething. She trembled as she dragged in the anchor, not caring if he was on board yet or not. He could swim to the island for all she cared. Her vision blurred and her breath came in pants.

By the time the anchor was up, so was Matt. She ignored him as she started the engine.

"Hey, Georgie. It's OK, I'm fine." His gentle touch on her arm was too much. She whirled to him. "I thought you'd drowned," she shouted. The tears came in earnest now, flooding down her face and she was helpless to stop them. Her whole body shook as she tried to take back control.

"Sorry, Georgie," he said. "It was just a bit of fun."

Fun? How could he even think pretending to drown was fun? She shoved the boat into gear, wanting to be away from him as fast as she could. He stumbled back and scowled. "Take it easy."

"Take it easy?" she yelled. She slowed so he could hear her over the engine. "I thought you'd drowned," she repeated. "Don't tell me to take it easy."

"I'm made of tougher stuff than that," he answered. "You should know that."

She shook her head. "Charlie thought that," she shouted. "I can't lose anyone else I love."

Matt stared at her. "I'm not Charlie."

Well, duh. All at once it was too much, the pretending she didn't love him, the hope one day he would realise he would love her. It was time to lay her cards on the table. "I love you, Matt."

He shifted, glancing away. "Yeah, I love you too, Freckles. You're family."

Hurt pierced her. He didn't understand. "No," she said. "I don't love you like a brother or a friend."

He frowned, confusion on his face. God, he was dense. She would spell it out for him, so it was clear, so there could be no misunderstanding. This was her last-ditch effort. She could move on afterwards. She put the boat in neutral. The fear was gone, as were the nerves, all that was left was exhaustion. "I *love* love you — the same way Amy loves Brandon, Faith loves Darcy, and Tess loves Ed."

His eyes widened as his mouth dropped open. She might as well have slapped him in the face with a fish. He said nothing, just staring at her, before shaking his head. "You don't mean it."

Anger returned with a flood. "Don't tell me what I mean."

Devastated, though she'd expected his response, she turned, tears welling in her eyes and her chest too tight for air. She accelerated fast and Matt stumbled back a couple of steps, but not off the boat.

He said nothing, not moving closer to sit next to her, not touching her to comfort her. Instead, he sat in the back corner as far away from her as he could. She increased her speed, letting the boat skim across the top of the water and checked her phone. Three bars. Thank God. She sent Tony a text to say they were on their way back. At least Matt had his own car and would leave as soon as they reached the shore.

She wiped the tears from her face with her hand and got her breathing under control. She could get through this. It wasn't as if his reaction was a surprise.

As they neared the boat ramp, Tony backed his trailer down to the water's edge. Georgie slowed and drove the boat straight on and cut the engine. Matt was already climbing off, esky in hand.

Coward.

Georgie gathered her bag and slung it over her shoulder, forcing a smile.

"Thanks for the loan, Tony," she said.

"Did you get some good information?" He clipped the boat in.

"Yeah." She glanced at Matt. And she'd got closure too. She stood knee deep in water while Tony finished attaching the boat to the trailer.

"I've got to go." Matt's smile was sympathetic, as if she was to be pitied. "I'll see you at the Ridge."

"Yeah, bye."

She watched him go.

"You two have a fight?" Tony asked.

Georgie shook her head. "Nah, he just has to get back." She smiled and walked Tony to his car door. "See you later."

Matt was already driving out of the carpark, but he didn't wave like he normally would.

Her heart broke.

She might know for sure that he didn't love her the same way, but their relationship would never be the same. It was a high price to pay for closure.

# Chapter 6

What the hell was Georgie thinking? Matt slammed his car door, punctuating his thoughts.

She couldn't possibly love him like that. She was Darcy's sister. She had to be confused. Maybe her parents' deaths had her feelings all out of whack.

He threw his hat on the seat next to him and drove away from the boat ramp, too freaked out to wave at Georgie in case she misunderstood the friendly goodbye.

What was wrong with her? There were plenty of guys out there, lots with better prospects than he had. He hadn't finished high school, he didn't own a house, and all his worldly possessions were contained in his small bedroom. Most people would think he was a loser. It was one of the nicer things he'd been called over the years, particularly at high school, though the blatant racist taunts were now more or less only when he was on the football field.

Georgie deserved far better than him.

Maybe he could phrase it that way to let her down gently.

He felt bad about the prank. He hadn't meant to scare her so badly. And watching her sob on the way back had wrenched his heart, but he couldn't risk her taking any comfort he offered the wrong way.

Georgie's words echoed in his head. *I love you. I love you. I love you.* He'd done nothing to lead her on, he was sure of it. They were mates. Half of their relationship was about teasing each other.

He reached the T-junction and tapped his fingers on the steering wheel. He couldn't go back to the Ridge with this tight feeling in his chest. Darcy would want to know what was wrong and he could hardly tell him about Georgie.

Instead he turned right, and headed towards Retribution Bay. What he needed was a stiff drink.

He didn't care what the time was. He had to figure out what this revelation meant for his relationship with Georgie.

How was he supposed to be around her anymore? Would she take a hug or a kind word the wrong way?

No, this was Georgie. She was more sensible than that.

Though she did have an emotional temper.

He reached town but didn't stop, driving straight through. If he stopped, he'd see people he knew and he'd have to chat. He wanted to be alone with his thoughts. He should have gone up to the lookout on the range, but there were always tourists up there. At this time of year there were tourists everywhere.

He turned into the lighthouse drive. At the top he parked away from the other cars. Then he grabbed his hat and moved around the slope to sit and stare at the ocean. The sea breeze was in, and he lifted his face to the cool air and breathed deeply.

Georgie loved him.

Why did his muscles tense and fear shoot through him like he was faced with a deadly snake?

This was Georgie. She wasn't to be feared.

Just because she loved him didn't mean he had to feel the same way.

A vision of her striding down the ridge, her butt wiggling at him, filled his mind.

He shook it away. No, he couldn't lust after her. She was Darcy's sister.

But not his.

The thought was defiant, unfamiliar.

He leaned back, shocked by the strength of it.

No, he couldn't think that way. He didn't like her like that. And he had little to offer her.

So what if he had been unreasonably disappointed when he'd realised he'd missed dinner with her last night.

And the urge to comfort her had been strong, but that was because she was Georgie, he was always there for her. It had been that way since Charlie had died.

But surely it was because she was part of his family.

His gut twisted as he thought of every reason why Georgie loving him was a bad thing. Darcy and Brandon would flip and he didn't want to lose their friendship. They could even fire him if they got mad enough, and he needed his job. And just think of the gossip in town. People would think he was taking advantage of her now Bill and Beth were gone.

At least she wouldn't be going back to the Ridge today. She had the girls' night and then she'd go home to her unit. He wouldn't have to see her until her next day off, and maybe not even then if she didn't come out to the Ridge.

Coward.

Hell, yes he was. He was happy to admit it. Until he understood how he felt, and how he should deal with this situation, he didn't want to see her. She'd mess up his thoughts and he needed a clear mind to work through this.

He exhaled and some of his tension released.

He'd figure out something before he saw her next. He had plenty of time.

The sun was low causing him to shade his eyes to see the ocean. It was almost dinner time. Perhaps he'd grab a bite to eat before he headed back. He stood to walk back to his car.

"Matt, what are you doing here?"

He glanced over. The instinctual gut clench was one he couldn't rid himself of when he saw his high school bully, Jerry. They were football team mates now and occasionally shared a beer with a group of friends. Jerry had apologised for being an asshole, but Matt had too many bad memories to ever completely forgive him. "G'day, Jerry." He smiled more at the tall man with Jerry. "Sudesh. You up here catching the sunset?" He always had time for Sudesh who volunteered on almost every committee in town.

Sudesh nodded but Jerry laughed and lowered his voice. "I'm looking to catch some tourists," he said. "The girls love a sunset and love a guy sensitive enough to know the history of this place."

Matt shook his head, cringing inside at his predatory nature. "No luck today?"

"Nah, it's all the grey nomads," Jerry said. "I'm going to try at the western restaurant in town. You both should come."

"All right," Sudesh answered. "I could do with a night out. You coming, Matt?"

The last thing he wanted to do was pick up a girl, but a distraction from Georgie was welcome.

"Sure."

Maybe after a couple of drinks he could forget all about this afternoon or figure out what he was supposed to do.

***

Georgie did what any self-respecting woman would do when her heart had been broken. She went home to her tiny unit, threw herself on the bed and cried. By the time her eyes were dry, she felt a little better. Who knew crying your eyes out could be so cathartic? She shouldn't be so upset. She had known for years Matt didn't feel the same way about her, but their conversation had quashed that tiny little hope inside that maybe he'd been hiding his feelings.

She wandered into the bathroom to wash her face and grimaced as the mirror displayed her heartbreak in horrible detail; red, blotchy face, bloodshot eyes, and her hair a mess.

Her phone beeped with a text and she couldn't quash the hope it was Matt realising he loved her back.

It was Dot.

*Looking forward to tonight. See you at six-thirty.*

Shit. She'd forgotten all about the girls' night. She could hardly back out now since she had organised it.

Perhaps it was a good opportunity to rid herself of the last feelings of despair. She would have a good time, be the life of the party, and if a guy approached her at the end of the night, maybe he'd help her forget about Matt too.

Determined to look gorgeous, she set herself the task of getting ready. She re-dyed her hair vibrant blue, shaved her legs and under her arms, waxed her bikini line and then soaked in the bath for an hour.

Georgie took her time over her make up and found a killer dress to wear. When the cool, soft fabric slipped over her skin it felt as if she was coating herself in armour. The heels she strapped on as the last item in her arsenal were so high they would be difficult to drive in, but she didn't have far to go.

When she was done, a glamorous vixen had replaced the heartbreak in the mirror. She brushed down the blue dress clinging to her body and nodded to herself. She was going to rock this night.

At precisely six-thirty she strutted into the country music themed restaurant. The walls were covered with posters of musicians and a woman sang about her heartbreak with a country twang. *I hear you, sister.*

Across by the bar Dot spoke with a short stocky man with a shaved head. She looked gorgeous in a royal purple top and blue jeans, but she didn't appear impressed. *Hopefully it wasn't a police matter tonight.*

The man turned and Georgie jolted as she recognised Dot's brother, Mark. It had been years since she'd seen him, but he'd been in Darcy's year at school. Back then he'd had long, thick black hair which often matted together like random dreadlocks.

"Don't you look gorgeous?" the maître d' asked, drawing her attention away.

Georgie flashed him a grin. "Girls' night out," she said. "Are my sisters here yet?"

He gestured to a booth in the corner where Faith, Amy and Tess sat. "Thanks." She strode over, waving greetings to people she knew.

"Georgie, are you trying to stop a guy's heart?" one man called.

Georgie laughed as a feeling of power and control washed over her. "Just dressing for myself," she replied as she continued past to the table.

"You look gorgeous," Amy said as she gave Georgie a hug.

"I feel like I should have put more effort in," Faith joked gesturing to her own jeans and top.

Georgie waved away her comment. "I needed a lift."

A frown crossed Amy's face, but before she could ask why, Dot walked over with Gretchen.

"Hey Gretchen," Georgie said, hugging her. "Any sharks today?"

"Yeah, a couple and some manta rays. The customers were thrilled." Gretchen worked on the whale shark tour boat Sam had just bought.

Georgie turned to Dot. "Catch any bad guys?"

She smiled, any hint of her annoyance with her brother gone. "It was my day off," Dot said. "I had my riding lesson with Faith." Nhiari joined them and Georgie tensed at the reminder of Matt. What would Nhiari think about Georgie pining after her brother? She'd probably laugh at the idea. "Hey, Nhiari."

They settled around the table. "Nice to see you again, Tess," Gretchen said. "Are you in town much longer?"

"Another week before uni goes back. Ed and I are flying home."

A much safer journey than the one they'd had driving here.

Georgie smiled as conversation started around the table. Not too long ago girls' nights had consisted of her, Amy and Gretchen. But with all that had happened in the past couple of months, it had extended to the other women who had a significant role in her life. Dot and Nhiari had investigated the sabotage out at the Ridge, and the other stuff Stonefish was responsible for, and Georgie had come to respect and like both of them.

Georgie paid for the first round of cocktails. It was probably a bad idea to get drunk with her starting work early the next morning and with her emotions all over the place, but she didn't care. Right now she didn't want to be sensible, she wanted to forget.

Georgie was on her second margarita by the time the food arrived.

"Have you booked a date for the wedding, Faith?" Gretchen asked.

Faith grimaced. "We were thinking the end of the year, but it's going to be way too hot, so we might bring it forward to October."

Georgie glanced at her. "I didn't know that."

Faith smiled. "Lara has this romantic notion about a Christmas wedding, and we've been trying to talk her out of it."

It was sweet they both wanted Lara to be involved and she'd taken the role of wedding planner to a new level with her holed up in Beth's craft room making a scrap book about the day. "You need to convince her the date you want to get married has significance," Georgie said. "The six-month anniversary of the first time you met or something."

Faith grinned at her. "Great idea! Now I just have to figure out the first time I saw Darcy."

"Maybe at the gymkhana?" Amy suggested. "I think Beth and I were taking Lara to pony club until then."

"I might have met him at an earlier meeting of the pony club," Faith said. "I'll have to ask if he remembers."

Gretchen stared at her drink, swirling it around with the straw. Georgie knew her breakup with Jordan's father had been nasty.

"Where's Jordan tonight?" she asked.

Gretchen glanced up and smiled. "Sleepover at Cody's. He jumped at the chance. It's not going to be long before he won't want to be at home at all."

"Not all teenagers hate hanging out at home," Georgie said. "Darcy never left."

Gretchen laughed. "Yeah, but home for you is thousands of acres."

"From what I see, some parents are glad for the respite," Dot said.

"Maybe. So what's new with you?"

Dot shrugged. "All I seem to do these days is work."

"Me too," Nhiari said.

Georgie itched to ask them if there was anything new on Stonefish, but they wouldn't tell her, especially not in the middle of a crowded restaurant.

As she finished eating her excellent burger, her phone rang. Quickly she wiped her fingers on a napkin and saw it was Sam. "Excuse me." They'd turned up the music so she stuck a finger in one ear as she answered. "Hey, Sammy, have you found another place you want me to look at?"

His answer was faint.

"Hang on, I can't hear you. Give me a sec." She strode through the restaurant, her heels clicking on the floorboards, and headed outside. "All right, shoot."

"Where are you?"

"At the country restaurant. Girls' night."

"I won't keep you long then. There's a place by the marina which looks good, if you don't mind checking it out."

"Email me the details and I'll call Cindy tomorrow. Are you working out of the office?" The office wasn't quite the right term since Sam worked in the army, but he was about to be decommissioned and so he was training new recruits.

"Yeah, I should be, depending on the time. Let me know when you can make it. I really appreciate this, Georgie."

"No problem. I'm happy to help." Sam had watched Brandon's back throughout the years in the army and she was thankful for it.

"All right, I'll talk to you tomorrow."

Georgie hung up and wandered back inside. Someone wolf-whistled and she turned to see a tourist sitting at the bar eyeing her up. She grinned and waved. Her eyes shifted past him to a table nearby where Matt sat with a couple of his footy buddies. Her steps faltered and she caught herself as he stared unblinking at her. Shit. She didn't need to see him now. What was he even still doing in town? One of the guys with Matt waved and gave her the thumbs up, so she blew him a kiss and continued to her table. Let Matt make what he would of that.

"Who are you blowing a kiss to?" Amy asked.

"Jerry. He's with Matt and Sudesh."

Nhiari turned to look. "My brother, Matt?" Her tone was unimpressed.

Georgie grinned. "Yeah." Had Matt done something to irritate her?

"Excuse me for a minute." She went over to Matt's table. Matt cringed and got up, following his sister outside.

"What's that about? Faith asked.

"Bayungu business." Dot pressed her lips together.

If Georgie was a betting woman she'd say it wasn't just Bayungu business, but police business as well. What had Matt done? And why hadn't he told the others? If she was talking to him, she'd ask.

But she probably wasn't going to talk to him for a while. Not until he'd forgotten about her stupid declaration today.

So maybe never again.

# Chapter 7

How was Matt supposed to forget what Georgie had said with her looking that way? She'd caught his eye when she'd walked out, phone to her ear. The royal blue dress she wore clung to her skin, dipping low to her cleavage and the hem sat mid-thigh, not short enough to be trashy. No, she looked classy, good enough to eat. He hardened, watching the door until she returned.

Some arsehole tourist whistled at her like she was a dog and she'd waved at him.

What the hell?

Jerry waved and she turned, catching Matt's eye. The surprise was expected, but it was the brief glimpse of pain that stabbed him right in the chest.

Damn it.

She walked away and he was mesmerised by the swing of her hips, the power in her shapely calves.

"That is the finest arse I've ever seen," Jerry said. "Have you and Georgie ever…" Jerry nudged him and winked.

Matt tore his gaze away from the person in question and glanced at him. "What?" Since when were his friends lusting after Georgie?

"Come on, don't tell us you've never thought about it," Sudesh added. "A woman that fine practically living with you half the time."

"I'd invite her back to my room," Jerry said.

Matt was momentarily speechless. Why was he the only one who hadn't noticed how gorgeous she was?

"She's so fit, she could go all night."

Matt shoved Jerry a little harder than necessary. "Hey, reel it in. Show some respect."

Both men stared at him. "You've really never tapped that?" Jerry asked.

Matt's hand clenched on the table as he shook his head. "She's family."

"Then you won't mind if I give it a shot," Jerry continued.

Hell yes, he did. He knew how Jerry treated women and Georgie deserved a lot better than him. But what could he say? Georgie was her own person. Besides, she'd just said she loved him. She wouldn't go off with anyone tonight.

Unless she was feeling contrary, and Georgie did contrary better than anyone he knew.

He clenched his teeth and shrugged. "Do what you have to, but don't come crying to me when she turns you down."

Sudesh laughed. "He's got a point."

Matt hoped he was right.

"Little brother, I'd like a word."

He groaned. He'd been so focused on Georgie, he hadn't seen Nhiari approach. From the look on her face she was still mad about earlier. He sighed. "Yeah." He followed her outside, ignoring the jibes from the others.

"What were you doing out by the ranges yesterday?" she demanded.

Not the question he was expecting her to ask, but he could see where this was going.

"Just went for a drive."

She scowled. "You drove through the bush where there are no roads, just for fun?"

He nodded.

"Don't lie to me. You were investigating the trails you found." Her hands went to her hips. "Didn't I tell you to leave it? It's police business. The animal smugglers weren't even on Ridge land."

"They cut through it," Matt answered. "And they were on Bayungu land."

Her eyes narrowed.

"You want me to ignore them and hope Dad doesn't stumble upon the smugglers while doing secret men's business?" Their father would know better than to approach, but it was as good an excuse as any.

"The police are investigating," Nhiari reiterated.

"But you know you can't go there."

She grunted, annoyed. "Promise me you won't go looking for trouble, little brother. These people are dangerous and Lee is still out there somewhere."

He raised his eyebrows. "You think so? I figured he was long gone." Lee had stayed at the Ridge campground and become good friends with the Stokes, but he hadn't been who they thought he was.

She pressed her lips together. "I don't want you taking chances."

Interesting. So the police didn't think this was the end of it. Maybe he should tell Nhiari about the journal and the treasure, but it wasn't his secret. "I won't." He always considered the risks before he did anything.

They wandered back inside. He hugged Nhiari. "Take care of yourself."

She nodded and her expression softened. "You too."

Re-joining his friends he found his dinner had been delivered and they were talking about the football season rather than about Georgie. Relieved, he resumed his seat.

"What do you think our chances are this year?"

"We've got it in the bag," Jerry said with a confidence Matt had always envied and despised.

Sudesh nodded. "We're unbeatable."

Matt tucked into his burger, happy to let both men boast about how the team would win. And if his gaze slid over to Georgie's table more than once, no one needed to know.

It was later than Matt had planned by the time he moved to go. He should have headed back to the Ridge more than an hour ago because he had to be up at first light, but he couldn't bring himself to leave while Georgie was still here.

And she should have left an hour ago as well with her working tomorrow. But she just kept laughing and drinking and having a good time with her friends. He'd counted at least three margaritas, so he wanted to make sure she had a lift home. She wasn't foolish enough to drive, but she was foolish enough to walk. Not that it was far and Retribution Bay was a safe town, but there were still a lot of tourists around.

As the girls' group stood to make a move, he pushed back his chair. "I better head home."

"Yeah, good to see you again." Sudesh stood and he and Jerry moved towards the cash register with Matt. "Looks like Georgie might need a lift home."

Matt scowled. "I'm sure one of the girls will take her."

Jerry grinned. "She might like a better option." He brushed down his shirt.

Not if Matt had anything to do with it. He couldn't let Jerry take advantage of her.

They all gathered around the register to pay, and Matt took Amy by the arm and moved her away from the others. "Are you giving Georgie a lift home?"

"Yeah. Gretchen will give her a lift back to pick up

her car tomorrow."

Good.

When it was their turn to pay, Jerry held up his credit card. "My shout." He handed the card to the wait person. "I know you don't earn a lot, Matt."

Matt ground his teeth. Jerry might have stopped the insults, but he never resisted the urge to one-up Matt and show he was better.

Sudesh clapped Matt on the shoulder and smiled sympathetically as he said to Jerry, "Thanks, mate."

Great, now Sudesh was pitying him as well. They'd both be surprised if he told them how much he had saved in the bank. Still he was getting a free meal, so he wouldn't complain.

Outside he took a breath of the clean air. The girls were waiting so he hugged his sister goodbye.

"Remember, no snooping," she whispered.

"Yes, ma'am," he replied, smiling at her grunt of acknowledgement. "I'll follow you back to the Ridge," he called to Amy.

She gave him a thumbs up.

Jerry stepped forward. "You need a lift, Georgie?"

Georgie glanced at Jerry, surprised and then her gaze flicked to Amy, then Matt, and back to Jerry. She grinned. "That would be great. Thanks." She strutted over to Jerry and tucked her arm into his. "Shall we go?"

Matt's mouth dropped open. She smirked and turned her back, walking away with Jerry. Matt took a half step after her, stomach clenched, gut aching. He turned to Amy. "I thought you were taking her home."

Amy shrugged. "She's a big girl. She can do what she likes." She waved at the girls and headed for her car.

No. This wasn't right. Georgie wasn't herself, but he couldn't tell anyone that without explaining why. And he could hardly demand that he take her home. It would give everyone the wrong idea, and he didn't want to hurt

Georgie more than he already had. He swore under his breath as Jerry and Georgie drove out of the car park together.

Then he stalked over to his car, more pissed off than he'd been in ages and at a loss to explain why.

***

Georgie's hangover punished her for the entire day. Normally a couple of painkillers would fix it, but not today. She'd had to deal with an obnoxious set of customers and the hot Australian sun on top of it. She shouldn't be complaining. Most people would kill to have her job swimming with the biggest fish in the sea every day, snorkelling and seeing turtles and other marine life.

When she finally finished, Gretchen's boat wasn't back yet, so she stumbled down the road to the restaurant where she'd left her car and drove home.

All she wanted to do was take more painkillers and lie down, but she'd promised Sam she'd look at the townhouse and she'd organised a viewing with Cindy in half an hour. She placed the key in her door and twisted, grimacing as the memory of last night hit her. She shouldn't have taken up Jerry's offer to drive her home, but she hadn't been able to pass on the opportunity to show Matt what he was missing. Jerry's parents had recently been on a tour and they'd been so sweet, his mother trying to set them up. She figured it was karma.

Only when she got home, the karma was on her. Jerry had expectations of his own. He'd been insistent about coming inside and she had to stamp hard on his toes to stop him. She'd shut the door in his face with his curses coming in loud from the other side. Not her finest hour.

She had a quick shower, took two more painkillers and grabbed her purse and phone. Cindy was waiting for her outside the townhouse when she arrived.

"Hey, Cindy, sorry I'm late."

"You're not, I'm early." She had the townhouse open so Georgie walked inside.

"Nice," she breathed. She video called Sam. He answered wearing his military fatigues. She grinned. "Good look."

"Don't you know it." He struck a pose, making her laugh. Why couldn't she have fallen in love with Sam instead?

Georgie followed Cindy around as she highlighted the pertinent points of the property. The patio overlooking the canal was one of them. "We could have some great parties out here," Georgie said.

Sam chuckled. "You already planning my life up there?"

She grinned. "Someone has to."

Cindy went to wait outside while Georgie took a slow tour of the townhouse with Sam. It was unoccupied so she poked into all the wardrobes and drawers to show him how much space there was. Three bedrooms upstairs, with a study, living room and kitchen downstairs. Georgie wished she had the funds to afford it.

"How's the location?" Sam asked.

"Well, you could walk to work every day," Georgie said. "It's maybe a two-minute drive into the centre of town and it's got a double garage if you've got a whole bunch of toys. The only thing it doesn't have is a shed."

Sam pursed his lips. "Show me the garage again."

Georgie walked into the enclosed garage, switched on the light and panned her phone around so he could have a closer look.

"There's enough space there for what I want," Sam said. "So what do you think? Should I buy?"

Georgie wasn't totally comfortable about him making such an expensive decision based on her thoughts alone.

"I'd buy it," she said. "But I'm not you. It's very modern and clean, but you could probably make it cosier if that's what you wanted."

"Right now what I want is somewhere easy."

"Well, this is definitely easy. You won't need to paint or fix anything. It'll be move in and start living."

Sam nodded. "Sounds perfect. Let me talk to Cindy."

As Georgie walked to the front door she spotted movement behind Sam as Dobby, his commanding officer, rushed into the room. "Sherlock's been injured!"

Sam whirled around and Georgie couldn't see anything except the floor as Sam asked, "Where? How bad?"

"It's bad," Dobby said. "They're rushing him home."

Georgie's head spun. She'd heard them talk about Sherlock before and she had a feeling he was important. He was part of their team, but not someone who'd come to Brandon's wedding. He'd been called away on another mission. Her mouth dropped open. "Is Sherlock Amy's brother?" she called.

"Who's on the phone? Dobby asked.

Sam swore. "Georgie." He righted his phone, and she could see him and Dobby now.

"Is it Arthur?"

Sam hesitated and then nodded.

"We have to tell Amy," Georgie said.

Amy might be estranged from her brother, but she deserved to know he was injured.

"Not yet," Dobby said. "Not until we know more. All we know is he's on a plane and being medically evacuated to Perth. Anything could happen en route."

Meaning he could die. Georgie's heart clenched as she thought about how she would feel if it was one of her brothers. She'd want to know immediately, but she could understand the sense of not worrying Amy unnecessarily.

"When will you know?"

"By tomorrow morning," Dobby answered.

There was nothing Amy could do between now and the morning except worry. "But you'll call her as soon as you know more?"

Dobby pressed his lips together. "I have to notify next of kin."

"Which is their father?" Georgie guessed.

He nodded.

"Sam, you can tell her, right?"

He sighed. "Yeah. Brandon will kill me if I don't."

Good.

Cindy poked her head in the door. "Is everything all right, here?"

Georgie glanced at Sam.

"Let me talk to her."

Georgie handed the phone over and went outside to overlook the canal while they spoke. Arthur was a few years older than Amy and they'd been estranged since Amy had left home at sixteen. They'd reconnected through Brandon, who was Arthur's teammate, but though the two siblings had spoken a couple of times, they hadn't seen each other in person. Arthur was supposed to come to the wedding, except he'd been called away on a mission. Brandon had been pissed off, but Amy had been more disappointed than surprised.

And now this.

Georgie ran her hand through her hair. She hoped Arthur survived, but what did 'bad' mean? He'd been shot, blown up, beaten half to death? She didn't even know where he'd been.

Cindy joined her and handed back Georgie's phone. "Sam said he'll call you in the morning."

He'd better. Georgie forced a smile. "Is he putting an offer on the place?"

Cindy nodded. "I'll email him the paperwork when I get back to the office."

She hoped the owners accepted. The settlement date should work out perfectly for when Sam got out of the army.

Georgie kept Cindy company while she locked the townhouse and then said her goodbyes. It was a short drive back to her place in the cheaper end of town. As always it felt so quiet when she walked in. Perhaps she should get a dog, but it didn't seem fair with her gone all day. Not much space in her courtyard garden for one to run around.

Her phone rang and she grabbed it, hoping it was Sam with news.

"Hello?"

"Georgie, this is Declan from Parks and Wildlife. We'd like to offer you the park ranger position."

Georgie's mouth dropped open. She hadn't expected to hear so soon. "That's great," she managed. "Thank you. Which role?"

"The land-based one. I know you've got a marine biology degree, but we think with your knowledge of the land, you'll be perfect."

"Oh, OK." Disappointment filled her. Did she want the job if it wasn't around the water? That had been what she'd been working towards.

"We do have someone talking about retiring at the end of the year, so there's opportunity to move into a more ocean-based role in the future."

Right. She had to be logical about this. The tour season would end in a month or two and then she'd be unemployed. This was a good opportunity. She sank onto a chair and tried to force some cheer into her voice. "Sounds perfect."

"When can you start?"

A good question. Jimmy wasn't going to be thrilled with her leaving mid-season. Her contract stated she must give two weeks' notice, but she didn't want to leave him in the lurch. "Ah, I need to confirm that. Maybe two weeks."

"All right, if you could let us know by the end of the week, that would be great."

Georgie hung up and stared at the canvas photo of a whale shark which hung on her wall. She'd got the job. It felt so surreal, but she had to believe it could be the first step towards the career she wanted as a marine biologist. Jobs were few and far between, but she would gain valuable contacts through PAWS. So she had to spend some time away from the ocean, she could deal with that.

She closed her eyes as guilt swamped her. She hated letting Jimmy down. He'd been so good to her, giving her a job and then letting her take as much time off as she needed when her parents had died. It had been hard on the team to cover for her. She needed to find someone to replace her so she wouldn't let him down.

With that in mind, she called Gretchen. "Know of anyone who wants to work on our boats?"

# Chapter 8

Matt swore, the curses coming out as a long stream of profanity, as the bolt finally twisted and his knuckles scraped across the metal. Darcy glanced over. "You OK?"

Matt glowered at him. "Do I look like I'm OK?" He squeezed his knuckles with his other hand, hoping the pain would go away. This was just the cherry on top of another shit day. The ute had finally died after months in its death throes, and he'd spent the past three hours taking apart the gear box and engine trying to figure out what was wrong.

He was fairly sure there was no saving it. The problem was it was thirty years old and had had a hard life.

Darcy looked up and raised his eyebrows but continued working on the motorbike's engine on the bench.

Shit, Darcy didn't deserve his temper. "Sorry."

"You want to talk about what's bothering you?" Darcy asked, not even looking his way.

"I grazed my knuckles."

Darcy glanced at him. "And what about the past week? You're not usually this surly."

Matt pressed his lips together. He could hardly tell Darcy the truth when he didn't want to admit it to himself. He'd been out of sorts since Jerry had driven off with Georgie. He'd tormented himself thinking about what they'd been up to, which was stupid because it was none of his business. He tried to convince himself it was just out of a brotherly concern, but that excuse was growing thinner the more he obsessed over it. It was like a switch had been flicked and all he could think about was Georgie.

She thought she loved him. That in itself seemed farfetched. Surely, he would have had some kind of inkling before now that her feelings were of a more romantic nature. He wasn't that dense, was he?

Though if he thought about it, she always used to sit next to him at dinner or when they went somewhere together in the car. He figured it was just a routine, but others swapped places regularly.

Darcy was still waiting for an answer. Matt shrugged. "I don't know. It feels as if things are about to change." It sounded like a reasonable excuse.

"We haven't got far decoding the journal. It's likely we'll never find the treasure."

It wasn't what he meant, but it would do. "We could do with an injection of funds." Matt twisted off the cap of the radiator and peered into the top. "I don't think we're going to save the ute this time."

"Really?" Darcy asked.

Matt shook his head. "The gear box has more fractures than that crackling nail polish Lara likes to use and the engine casing is worse. A replacement is going to cost a fortune, so it's probably cheaper to buy a new car in the long run. I'll make some calls. The last time I ordered parts for this old girl the guy laughed at me."

Darcy frowned. "Do what you can. At least we've got Brandon's ute and mine."

"Yeah. It's a pity the horses or motorbikes can't carry rolls of wire and a heavy toolbox." Matt wiped his greasy hands on a rag. "I'll be back soon." He headed across the yard to the homestead. A couple of families were sitting in the garden waiting for Beth's famous scones with jam and cream. It was a new thing Amy was trialling to increase the campground income. Not that the café would necessarily bring in a lot of money, but the fact the station had a café would tempt people to stay there rather than other locations along the coast.

Amy was preparing scones in the kitchen when he walked in. She glanced at him, surprised. "What's gone wrong for you to be home at this time?"

"The ute's carked it," he said. "I need to make some calls."

She handed him one of the scones which had just come out of the oven and was slathered in jam and cream. "Take this with you."

He smiled. "Thanks Ames." He wandered down the corridor pausing at the wall of photos that displayed the Stokes family. It started with Bill and Beth's wedding and then showed photos of each child when they were born, their first day of school, their graduation from high school, and in Georgie and Ed's case university graduation. Matt examined Georgie's graduation photo. She was beaming with a grin that always lit up her face and he couldn't help smiling back. Her smile had always made him feel good. He tapped his chest and continued into the office, set his scone on the table and sat in Bill's chair. Across from him was a cabinet full of old artefacts from the station's life. Bottles, keys and knickknacks of past residents. There was history here, maybe not thousands of years, like his, but it was history nonetheless and he didn't want to see the Stokes lose their only home.

He got the address book of their common contacts

out of the drawer and started making phone calls.

An hour later he admitted defeat. His usual go-to guys had nothing, and though they recommended a few other places, none of them were able to help either. Matt then did what any self-respecting person would do and searched the internet. There were a few places in the United States he could get the parts he needed, but the cost of shipping was exorbitant. Was it worth paying so much today when tomorrow something else could go?

He'd taken the whole engine apart and it contained cracking and rust where there shouldn't be any. Really the car was just waiting to fail and he didn't want to be the one driving it when it did. It wasn't safe anymore.

He sipped the dregs of the coffee Amy had brought in earlier and leaned back in the chair. Though Matt wasn't responsible for doing the books, Darcy and Brandon had spoken openly about how bad the finances were. Something had to change. Maybe it was time he got more involved in the treasure hunt. That or winning Lotto seemed their best bet.

He hated relying on chance.

Amy wandered in. "Any luck?"

He shook his head. "Nothing that's worth it," he said. "How are the campgrounds going?"

"We're at capacity most nights," she said.

Good, the money was needed, but it wasn't enough to buy them a new ute. They'd overreached on their credit as it was. "What's the latest on the treasure hunt?"

Amy winced. "It's that bad huh?" She sat in the chair across from him. "It's not going well," she admitted. "Maybe Lilian thought her clues were clear or maybe she wanted it to be obscure enough that not just anybody found it, but either way we've got no idea."

"Mind if I read it?"

"Be my guest," Amy said. "We've made a few copies.

I'll make sure you get one by the end of the day."

"Thanks."

Matt returned to the shed to give the bad news to Darcy. He outlined the cost and then the associated issues he'd found with the ute. Darcy grimaced. "It's had it?"

Matt nodded.

Darcy sighed. "See if you can find a cheap second-hand ute for sale."

Matt hesitated. It wasn't a topic of conversation he was comfortable with, but it had to be asked. "Did insurance ever pay out on your parents' car?" The four-wheel drive Bill and Beth had been driving when they'd crashed hadn't been brand-new, but it had been in decent condition, and if there was money outstanding for that, it could go towards buying them a new vehicle.

Darcy frowned. "I don't know," he said. "Those first couple of weeks were kind of a blur. I'll look into it." Darcy took his hat off and ran his hand through his hair. "Listen, while we're talking about this stuff…"

Matt's gut clenched. Was this where Darcy fired him? They barely had the money for the ute, let alone wages.

Darcy placed his hat back on and stepped closer. "The thing is… I don't want you to feel…" he sighed and took a second to think things through. "Let's face it. The Ridge isn't doing well. There's a chance we'll have to file for bankruptcy."

The resignation on Darcy's face was a new expression for him.

"I don't want you to feel you have to go down with the ship," Darcy said. "If you want to find another job now, before the shit hits the fan, neither Brandon nor I would blame you."

Matt stared at his friend. "You think I'd abandoned you?"

"No, but you've got to do what's right for you. One

day you're going to want your own place, and you're going to need a job to get a mortgage."

Was that a hint? "Do you want me to move out?" Matt asked. "Now you and Brandon have partners I guess it's a bit awkward having me around." He should have considered it himself. Maybe he really was too dense to pick up on signs. He'd spent years not knowing Georgie's true feelings. He was an idiot.

"Fuck off. That's not what I mean. You're part of the family, but when you finally find yourself a partner, she's not going to want to come back to your tiny single bed to get it on."

Relief filled him. Matt rolled his eyes, shaking his head, but froze when it was Georgie he pictured. Shit. He turned away in case his thoughts were somehow clear to Darcy and cleared his throat. "So to be clear, you're not trying to get rid of me because the station is struggling and you want your privacy?"

"No. Hell, if the station was doing well, I'd say build your own house here like I'm planning to."

Wow. It wasn't something he'd ever considered, but he liked the idea. Matt smiled. "OK, thanks."

"But I meant what I said," Darcy insisted. "If you want to find a new job, don't feel like you have to stay."

Matt shook his head. "Stop talking shit. Now, what else needs to be done?"

Darcy chuckled. "One more thing. Do you know what's up with Georgie?"

Matt stiffened. "What do you mean?"

"She hasn't been around lately, and I know you two sometimes talk."

No way was he telling Darcy the real reason. He hesitated. Was he betraying her trust by telling Darcy about their talk the other night? It was better than telling him the truth. "The night she found the journal she was upset. She was missing Charlie and your parents and blaming herself for their deaths."

Darcy put down his spanner and gave Matt his full attention. "What?"

Matt shrugged. "Seems she cursed Charlie for the spider thing and a few days later he died. Then she told that guy from Stonefish that Bill and Beth were going on the tour. She thinks if she'd kept her mouth shut, they'd still be alive."

"That's bullshit." He sighed. "Thanks for letting me know. I'll talk to her."

"No problem." Matt went back to work, ignoring the guilt in his gut.

It was the best for Georgie.

***

Georgie dumped her car keys on the bench and ran a hand through her hair, sighing as she did so. The passengers today had been next level annoying and she was sick of people. First step was a shower, then she'd climb into her pyjamas and binge watch her favourite series on TV. Less than a week to go. With the help of Gretchen, she'd found her replacement, and wouldn't be leaving Jimmy in the lurch.

As she headed for the shower, someone knocked on the door. She stopped, growling. What now? Should she ignore it?

Tempting as it was, she didn't get a lot of visitors.

Unless it was Jerry. She could *not* deal with him today. He'd called her a couple of times since the girls' night and wouldn't get the hint she wasn't interested.

"Georgie, are you home?"

She frowned as goosebumps rose to her skin and she hurried to the door, flinging it open for Brandon. "Is something wrong? What are you doing in town?"

"Nothing's wrong. I had to get a few things and thought I'd drop in."

"You never have before."

"I'm not usually in town at this time." He walked in, causing her to step back and give him room.

She scowled as she shut the door. "Make yourself at home."

"Thanks." He headed for her small kitchen and poured himself a glass of water.

What was going on? Though she was thrilled Brandon was back in the Bay and part of the family again, he never just dropped in, particularly not without Amy. "Where's Ames?"

"Back at the Ridge. She had a late check in." He pulled out a chair and sat. "How was your day?"

She was still salty and wearing her tour boat polo shirt. "Shit. The passengers were a little crazy." Giving in to whatever this was, she poured herself a glass of wine, offering him one. He shook his head and she sat at her small table next to him.

"I guess you've got to take the good days with the bad. When do you start at Parks and Wildlife?"

"Next week."

"It'll be a nice change of pace."

Ugh, what was with this banal conversation? "What gives, Brandon?" she demanded. "And don't give me that bullshit about being in town. Why are you here?"

He rubbed his chest. "I don't want you to get mad at Matt."

The blood drained out of her face. What the hell? Had he told her brothers what she'd said? Was this some kind of intervention?

"He was worried about you. You shouldn't be feeling guilty."

Guilty? Wait. "What are you talking about?"

"Matt told Darcy about your conversation the other night. About you missing Charlie and Mum and Dad. About you feeling responsible for their deaths."

The relief her brothers didn't know of her feelings for Matt was quickly replaced by a sense of betrayal. "He should have kept his mouth shut."

"We've been worried. You haven't been out recently, and you've been brushing off everyone's questions."

Yeah, well, she had her reasons.

Brandon took a long drink of water before putting the glass on the table with a bang. "The thing is, you don't know the whole story behind Charlie's death."

Georgie stared at him. "What?" Had they kept something from her all these years?

Brandon clutched the glass in both hands. "You remember what Charlie was like then. He'd scared all of us with that stupid spider."

She squeezed her eyes closed as the memory returned. Her hand shook as she whispered, "That's why I cursed him."

"Yeah, well I went one step further. I bought a plastic snake and set it up to fling out at Charlie somewhere he least expected it."

The pain in Brandon's eyes made her grip his hand as her brain whirled to connect the pieces.

"The cattle yard seemed like the perfect place."

Georgie's jaw dropped as horror filled her.

"Our old dog, Bertie triggered it instead of Charlie. The cattle stampeded and Charlie was in the way."

She hadn't been there that day, but she'd pictured the stampede a hundred times, pictured her brothers and father trying to get to Charlie in time. The guilt she felt would have been nothing compared to that of Brandon's. "That's why you left."

He nodded.

How terrible for him. She leapt to her feet and hugged him. "It was an accident, Bran."

He held on to her and sighed. "I can accept that now, but I couldn't face any of you."

She slapped him on the shoulder. "You shouldn't have shut us off like that. We could have dealt with it together, as a family."

His chuckle was sad. "Yeah, well we all dealt with it our own ways. I don't want you to feel guilty anymore. Mum and Dad's deaths weren't your fault either. Stonefish were watching the place. They could have easily got that information from a number of people."

She closed her eyes. In her rational moments she knew he was right, but the guilt wouldn't fade immediately. Maybe it would be easier to deal with though. "No more secrets," she said, ignoring the twinge of guilt. Her feelings for Matt didn't count. "If we're going to fix the Ridge, we have to be honest with each other."

"No more secrets," Brandon agreed. He glanced at his watch. "Now are you going to cook me some dinner?"

She laughed. "There's a pizza menu behind you. Order while I go have a shower."

She walked away feeling lighter than she had in days.

It would be nice to spend some time with her oldest brother.

Chapter 9

The next week flew by, and Georgie had little time to obsess over Matt while training her replacement. On her day off, she'd dived on the shipwreck she'd found. The proper authorities had been notified and someone had come up from Perth to catalogue the details, but they couldn't get a team out to review it until later in the year.

Not that she touched it, knowing the archaeologists would want to document everything as it was, but she found evidence of human interaction. Large areas of broken coral and patches of sand where someone had removed something. The damage appeared to be recent.

Stonefish.

She'd avoided heading out to the Ridge, still not in the right frame of mind to see Matt, but she caught up with Ed and Tess before they headed back to Perth.

Finally, her first day at Parks and Wildlife arrived. She exhaled, her breath shaky, and nerves shimmering in her belly, as she pulled into the car park. She could do this. She knew a lot of her new colleagues already. But still it was different from what she was used to, and she'd be largely working on her own.

"Hey, Georgie, good to see you." Her new boss,

Declan shook her hand and smiled widely. "Great to have you on board."

Georgie relaxed. "I'm glad to be here."

"We've got you starting at a civilised time today because we don't want to scare you off," he continued, leading her into a meeting room.

Another woman, maybe in her early thirties, was in the room, someone Georgie didn't recognise, so not a local. She would have noticed her rich red hair, almost the colour of the sand outside. Currently it was tied back in a braid with wisps of curls peeking out from the hairline. The woman's smile was perfunctory, so Georgie gave her biggest smile back.

"Georgie Stokes, this is Penelope Fraser. She's starting in the ocean-based role." Declan turned to Penelope. "Georgie's new too."

This was the woman who'd beaten her to the role she so desperately wanted. Georgie's smile faded as she took a seat.

"Our area of responsibility runs from Red Bluff in Carnarvon all the way to a few nautical miles north of here," Declan began. "We do eight-hour days ranging from six to six depending on what's going on. Georgie, you'll deal a lot with the campgrounds; maintenance, cleaning, making sure the hosts have what they need. Penelope, you'll monitor the whale shark tour businesses and fishing in the area. You'll both need fire training and advanced first aid which I've organised for later in the month."

Georgie took notes as he continued his induction.

"I'm taking Penelope out on the boat today to familiarise her with everything," Declan continued. "We don't have anyone spare to show you around, Georgie, but since you're familiar with the area, I figure you won't have any trouble."

"Sure," Georgie said with more confidence than she

felt. Talk about being thrown in the deep end.

Outside the room, the radio came to life with people calling in updates.

"They're the campground hosts," Declan said. "They check in at this time every day so we can make sure everything's all right. If they need anything, I'll get you to take it out."

There were myriad small, off-grid camp sites along the coast for which PAWS was responsible. Radios were the only way of contacting the town because reception was spotty out there.

It took Declan another hour to cover everything with Georgie and Penelope. "The only other thing you need to keep an eye out for is evidence of animal smuggling." He showed them photos of reptiles bound with duct tape around their bodies and mouths, and some round holes in the ground containing animals. "The smugglers are active in the area at the moment. If you see anything off, call it in."

Georgie stared at the photos, her stomach swirling. Some of the animals were stuffed in socks or hollowed out books. Many of them were dead. "That's horrific."

Declan nodded. "They fetch a high price on the international market from collectors. A large number of the animals die in transit so they send in bulk hoping some will still be alive when they reach their destination."

She wanted to be sick. They didn't deserve to be treated like that. "Do we call the police if we find evidence?"

"Normally we have a Wildlife Officer who takes care of it, but we're advertising to fill the position at the moment. The police are helping us out. They know who the usuals are, because punishment is often only a slap on the wrist and community service. Most of the smugglers aren't dangerous but call it in before you approach anyone."

"Will do."

"That's not good enough," Penelope said, her posture stiffening.

Georgie blinked. "What isn't?"

"The punishment. They're torturing those animals."

Absolutely. Before Georgie could reply, Declan said, "You don't need to convince me, but it is what it is."

Penelope pressed her lips together and as they left the meeting room Declan gave Georgie the keys for one of the four-wheel drives. "You can drive off road?"

She nodded. She'd been four-wheel driving since her feet could reach the pedals.

"What about using a rifle? We have a couple in case we come across injured wildlife."

"I'm not as good a shot as Ed, but I can hold my own."

"Great." Declan grinned at her. "I'll still need to send you on a course, and take you through all the paperwork requirements, but you should be fine."

Georgie turned to Penelope, determined to be nice. "Good luck on your first day."

Penelope gave her an actual smile this time, some surprise in her eyes. "Thank you. You too."

Perhaps she had been nervous at the start. Georgie wasn't going to be bitter about losing out to her. During their meeting she'd asked some intelligent questions and it was clear she knew her stuff.

Georgie loaded her work vehicle and drove out to the campgrounds to take the supplies. She had a checklist a mile long of the places to go and things to do. Part of her role was checking the public facilities in the national park, many of which were long drop toilets. Today she was working the area between the coast and the ranges.

It was a beautiful day with the sky bright blue and the ocean calm and glistening. The perfect day for the boat.

A pang of longing hit her. The ocean was where she

belonged. Hopefully she could prove herself in this role, and when the other ranger retired, she'd get the job and work side by side with Penelope. Georgie would have to invite her for a drink, especially if she was new in town and didn't know anyone.

She would have been miserable and lonely at university if she hadn't had Ed there to support her.

She exhaled, enjoying the quiet of the car. No more dealing with demanding customers. Now she would spend most of the day on her own.

It was lucky she liked her own company.

The morning passed quickly as she visited each campground, dropping off supplies and introducing herself to the campground hosts. The sites were in beautiful locations, only a handful of metres from the crystal-clear beach, with Ningaloo Reef just off its shores. People had to be self-sufficient with no power or water out here, but most loved it. Some even launched boats at the ramp up the coast to fish in areas outside the designated sanctuary zones.

It was nice to do something different, to not have to worry about being overly friendly all the time. She spent a large part of her day in her car, listening to music and enjoying the fresh air coming in her window. Perhaps it would get lonely in time, but right now it was just what she needed.

She had a lot of thinking to do.

Sam still hadn't told Brandon or Amy about Arthur's accident. He hadn't even called her back like he'd promised. It wasn't until she'd messaged him, promising to tell Amy everything if he didn't call her back, that he finally rang.

Arthur was alive but had lost the lower part of his leg under his knee. He'd been medically discharged from the army and would have a lot of rehabilitation. Sam insisted

Arthur didn't want Brandon or Amy to know. He was in a low place, and he couldn't bear to see either one. Sam was worried about his mental state.

Though it galled Georgie not to say anything, Sam had convinced her to stay silent. She'd imagined herself in Arthur's position, struggling to come to terms with the loss of his leg and career, and then having to deal with the guilt of his estranged relationship with his sister. It would be too much. She'd asked Sam to keep her informed of Arthur's progress. She would be Amy's surrogate.

Yesterday Arthur had been moved to the rehabilitation centre at Shenton Park. He wasn't speaking much and didn't want to see his teammates, but Sam visited daily.

Ed continued calling her weekly and he'd rung last night to wish her luck on her first day of work. It was sweet of him, but she could have done without the questions about why she hadn't been to the Ridge lately. He didn't buy her excuse that she'd been busy preparing for her new job and training her replacement.

But the truth was, how could she go home and face Matt? She wasn't ready to sit next to him at the dinner table and pretend everything was as it had been. She could imagine the awkwardness between them and someone would notice. Lara was far too observant for her own good.

Plus it would kill her to be uncomfortable around him.

Georgie reached the end of the road, literally, and went to check the public sites at Yardie Creek. A few groups of tourists were already parked, some waiting for the boat tour, others walking the trail on top of the gorge. A group of four-wheel drives was parked near the entrance to the beach waiting for the tide to go out. The creek could be crossed at low tide, but the sand was soft and people often got bogged.

She cleaned the toilets, made sure there was plenty of toilet paper, and then checked the picnic tables were in good condition. The boat tour was taking on new passengers, so she wandered down to chat to the captain.

When she was done, she headed north and took one of the tracks accessible just to PAWS. The track was rough and she engaged the four-wheel drive as she bumped and rocked her way up the slope of the ranges. She'd always found the Cape Range such an anomaly. In the midst of such flat land, suddenly a range of rock rose up, running parallel to the coast, almost all the way to the tip of the peninsula, an impassable object. It took almost an hour from Retribution Bay to get around to the bottom of the tip as there were no roads passing through it.

If an incident happened out here, she'd be on her own for at least two hours before first response could arrive by road which was why Georgie was booked to do an advanced first aid course later in the month with the Royal Flying Doctor Service. She carried a personal EPIRB and was instructed never to leave the car without her radio. It didn't bother her. Growing up on the station, she knew the risks. Her parents had drummed it into her when she was a child, and she never went out of sight of the homestead without a radio.

She finally reached the top of the escarpment and sucked in a breath. The view always left her in awe. From here Georgie could see all the way along the coast from the tip of the peninsula right down towards Coral Bay. She inhaled deeply and enjoyed the fresh air. It was so silent up here with barely a breeze blowing. All she could hear was the trill of birds singing to each other in the bush. But it felt like home.

Was that how Matt felt?

As kids, she had asked him a million questions about

his Bayungu heritage and though he'd been reluctant to speak of it at first, she'd bugged him until at last he gave in and taught her how to recognise animal tracks and walk silently through the bush. It was difficult for him, balancing the need of a teenager to fit in with the responsibilities and requirements of his culture. Georgie had always thought it romantic he had such ties to the land, and she loved listening to the Dreamtime stories his parents told her of magical creatures who shaped the land and set the laws. As an adult she understood the issues a little better, and wished she'd been more sensitive to Matt's wishes.

She strode over to the monitoring station and took the required readings, then she took a moment to simply take in the surroundings and enjoy the peace. She spotted a little lizard sunning itself on a rock and watched it for a short while as it bobbed its head. The sun was warming now, so she slapped on sun cream and took a long drink from her water bottle.

When her stomach rumbled, she grabbed her sandwich from her bag and bit into the soft bread. Sitting on the back of the four-wheel drive, the door open, she spotted movement all around her as insects buzzed and lizards dashed between hiding places. The idea that a dozen or more could be crammed into a lunchbox-sized container to suffocate or survive was hideous. She shook her head and wandered to the edge of the escarpment and scanned the land below her. She didn't expect to see any traps from this far up, but she would notice a car in an area where it wasn't meant to be.

All was quiet. On the one road that ran down the side of the range, people drove on their way to one of the beach spots ready to spend the day in the water or to go on a boat tour at Yardie Creek.

She frowned as a thought occurred to her. Were the smugglers connected with Stonefish? Darcy and Matt had noticed new tracks when they'd taken a flight over the Ridge. They hadn't figured out why the tracks were there, but perhaps they led to the ranges and allowed the smugglers access to the ocean to ship their illegal cargo.

She'd have to follow it up.

She finished her sandwich and tucked the plastic wrapper in the rubbish bag in her car and then drove back down the range.

Georgie was on her last stop of the day, heading to a remote area of the park to check more monitoring stations. The map Declan had given her was clear, there was only one road in and she couldn't possibly miss it. Georgie slowed her vehicle as she noticed tyre tracks leading off the track. Damn. The tracks crumpled the low grasses and wound to the base of the ranges where trees and shrubs blocked her view.

Declan had told her to report anomalies. A lot of four-wheel drive enthusiasts decided to make tracks of their own just because they could. They didn't like to be restricted. This looked like one of those.

She hesitated. She'd have to be pretty damned unlucky to come across any smugglers. She picked up a radio. "Georgie to base, over."

"What is it, Georgie?" the receptionist, Karen asked.

"I'm out at False Valley," she said. "Someone's driven off the trail heading to the base of the ranges. Want me to check it out?"

A pause before Karen answered. "Yeah, take a quick look," she said. "Let us know what you find."

"Will do."

Georgie shifted into first and turned left, slowly making her way over the bumpy ground, keeping as close to the existing tyre tracks as she could. It wasn't more than about two hundred metres in and she winced as a couple of branches scraped down the sides of the car. If she found nothing, she would feel awful about the scratches.

The road ended in front of a wall of wattle shrubs. Shit. Not enough space to turn. She'd have to back out of here.

Georgie switched off the engine and got out, the car door shutting sounding loud in the quietness. She examined the area for footprints and paths and found a trail of broken branches around the other side of her car. Her skin tingled and she went back to the car to clip the radio onto her belt before she pushed her way through.

She stepped carefully the way Matt had taught her.

Part of her cringed at being overly cautious, but experience with Stonefish made it seem wise.

The wall of wattles was about three plants deep but whoever had been here before had made the way easier. The wattles ended and there were a couple of metres between them and the red rock of the range stretching high above her.

She scanned the area, jolting when she saw a circle of rocks with ash in the middle. A fire. Someone had camped here. Taking another slow look around the area, her gaze drifted upwards to a ledge only a couple of metres above her, but she saw no one.

Walking over to the fire, she crouched down and touched the ashes. They still held a hint of warmth. Her skin prickled. With the range on one side and the wattles on the other, it created a sheltered place to camp.

She clambered up to the ledge to have a better look at the area, pulling herself to standing, and stared into the mouth of a cave. A rattle of stones from inside made her stiffen. Shit.

Probably just a shy wallaby. Still, she reached for the radio on her belt and turned the volume low. Quietly she said, "This is Georgie to base, come in."

Declan answered. "What did you find, Georgie?"

"Looks like someone's camped here recently. The ashes are still warm, but there's no other sign of them." She peered into the darkness of the cave beyond. Heat radiated out.

"Roger that. Take some photos and you can show me when you get back."

She kept hold of the radio as she stared at the cave. The light only penetrated the first few metres. She hesitated. Was it foolish to go further inside? She was alone out here. If someone was in there, they would have heard her conversation, but Georgie didn't want to corner someone who might do something foolish.

Declan had said the smugglers weren't usually violent. And what if the noise was animals waiting to be collected? The images Declan had shown her of the dead and dehydrated reptiles were clear in her mind and anger stirred. She drew her phone out of her pocket and flicked on the torch before stepping into the warm dark interior of the cave. Slowly she panned the light, ready for anything. The cave ran four or five metres back and as she moved forward, she heard that rattle again. Moving more confidently now with images of lizards in need of her help, she took several steps forward, lifting her light so it shone further. A man slipped around the corner. Georgie froze as recognition hit her.

Heart thumping, she debated what to do. The man was not who he seemed.

He'd killed a man.

But he had also shown kindness to her family, and she wanted answers. Gripping the radio tighter and taking a deep breath, she called, "Come out, Lee."

# Chapter 10

Georgie waited, expecting Lee to turn around and make himself known.

For a long moment, there was no response, and nerves raced over her skin. Faking a bravado she didn't feel, she lifted her radio. "You've got two options; you come out and talk to me, or I call it in and the police arrest you."

Her fingers hovered over the button to radio base.

Just when she thought he wasn't going to answer, he called, "Does that mean you won't call the police if I come out?" He stepped forward into the light. It had been a few weeks since she'd last seen him. He'd disappeared one night from the campgrounds at the Ridge just before they'd discovered he was working for Stonefish. He had bags under his eyes, and his face was lined with fatigue. He'd always been neatly dressed, but now his clothes were dirty and wrinkled. He'd been living rough for weeks if he'd been out here all this time.

"I haven't decided," she replied.

He sighed. "What are you doing here, Georgie?"

"I work for Parks and Wildlife now. I noticed the track leading this way and we've had animal smugglers in the area, so I thought I'd check it out."

"Pretend you didn't see it. You don't want to get messed up with this."

"Like you are?"

He said nothing, just studied her.

"You want me to ignore the fact animals are being harmed because people want to make a quick buck?"

"It's more than that and you know it," he said.

So Stonefish was involved. Perhaps Lee didn't care about the lives of animals. He'd shot a man without hesitation. "You killed Tan."

Lee nodded. "Before he could shoot Tess. He would have and been pleased about it."

"You weren't pleased about killing him?"

He pressed his lips together.

Gone was the happy, slightly daggy personality of the landscape photographer he'd pretended to be. This man was lean and hard, with dark eyes that gave nothing away.

She swallowed and took a half step back. "Thank you."

A tiny twitch around his eyes showed his surprise.

"Thank you for saving the woman Ed loves."

"No one would have died if Ed hadn't had delusions of being a hero." His tone was resigned.

"Well, I feel safer knowing Tan isn't out there any longer."

"Tan is the least of your worries," Lee said.

Georgie frowned. "What do you mean?"

He shook his head. "I'm doing my best to move interest away from your family, but you're not helping things by continuing to poke your nose into Stonefish business."

"We haven't done anything."

"You notified authorities about the shipwreck."

Her mouth dropped open. "How do you know about that?" Perhaps he wasn't as isolated out here as she'd suspected. "Why do they care about it? Surely they earn enough from their illegal operations."

"Please just stick to Ridge land and tell Matt to stop investigating the tracks."

"What?" Georgie stared at him. "He's been doing that alone?" The idiot. Hadn't they had enough danger for one year?

A small smile creased his lips. "You didn't know. Does Darcy?"

She had no idea, but she'd be calling her brother the moment she got into reception range.

"You need to go," Lee continued.

She hesitated, uncertain whether to contact Dot and Nhiari. "Are you a bad guy, Lee?"

"Some would think so." He turned to head back into the cave. The tunnels underneath the ranges ran for kilometres and most had never been explored.

"Wait." She wasn't sure what to say. This man said he was trying to protect her family, but what had he done to them in Stonefish's name? "Amy was thrilled you sent the photos of the wedding. Thank you."

He inclined his head slightly. "Your family has been good to me." Then he continued into the darkness leaving Georgie staring after him.

***

Matt had spent the past week discussing the contents of both journals with the Stokes. It had become routine to brainstorm the latest ideas and theories around the dinner table, but everyone was growing more despondent by the day. Only Lara had any measure of enthusiasm now and even hers was waning. He focused on the English translations of the captain's journals trying to figure out how Lilian knew where the treasure was, but so far he'd come up with nothing. The scratchy old-fashioned script was hard to decipher. He'd taken the whole week to read only half the journal and felt like an idiot when Lara had read both journals again in the same time.

Stupid to let it bother him, but it made him conscious of the gap in his formal education. Georgie would have been like Lara and finished them already.

He had to stop dwelling on it and on everything going wrong right now.

Darcy had discovered they'd already received the insurance money for the four-wheel drive and spent some of it on replacing the feed which had burnt, and the rest on other things they'd needed for the station. So they were down one car.

He'd heard nothing more from the police about the smugglers. He suspected there wasn't much they could do aside from keep an eye out for the usual suspects and stop them to search their cars.

And on top of everything, he hadn't seen Georgie in over two weeks. Normally she had dinner at the Ridge weekly, which meant she was avoiding him. She'd even invited Tess and Ed to dinner at her place before they left. He'd stooped to asking Ed whether Jerry had been there because he'd envisioned a cute couples' dinner. Ed had looked puzzled, then amused and told him it was just the three of them.

The relief shouldn't have been so strong.

But damn it if he didn't miss seeing her. He hadn't realised what a constant she'd been in his life.

No, not a constant, a ray of light.

He snorted and shook his head at himself. That sounded so naff.

The phone rang as Matt walked into the kitchen that evening after another long, hot, tiring day. He wanted a cold drink and a seat. Amy was busy stirring dinner on the stove. "Can you get that?"

He picked up the phone. "Retribution Ridge."

A sharp intake of breath and instantly he knew it was Georgie. His muscles tightened.

"Matt."

"Georgie." He waited for her to say why she'd phoned. When the pause was in danger of becoming ridiculously long, she blurted, "Why are you investigating the tracks on your own? Does Darcy know you're doing it?"

He blinked. "How did you know?" Damn. He shouldn't have admitted it.

Another long pause before she said, "I have my sources."

He'd been certain no one had seen him, and his parents wouldn't have mentioned it to her. He'd been cautious because he hadn't wanted to run into the smugglers. So how had she known?

"Are you going to answer?"

Matt stepped down the hallway and into the lounge. "I wanted to see what was there." Maybe someone had been on top of the ranges, but in that area there weren't any public trails.

"On your own?"

"Darcy doesn't need the trouble."

"And you do?" Her voice rose. "You could have been hurt, and no one would have known where you were."

He almost asked her why she cared, but then he remembered. She did care and that's why her voice held so much concern. He cleared his throat. "We all do things we shouldn't."

"Not dangerous things."

"So borrowing a boat and going out to the island by yourself wasn't dangerous?"

"Stonefish knew the police had found their base. They weren't likely to be back."

"You don't know that. You seem happy to take risks you wouldn't want your family to take." Anger simmered at the thought of what might have happened to her had she run into a Stonefish employee on her own.

"I'm an adult. I can make my own choices."

"Yeah, Jerry was very appreciative of your adult status the other night." He regretted the words as soon as they left his mouth. What the hell was he thinking?

Georgie's gasp of outrage made him wince and he held the phone away from his ear, waiting for the shout, but her voice was quiet, hard as steel. "How dare you?" She took a breath, about to start her tirade, but all she said was, "Tell Darcy to call me when he gets in." She hung up, leaving behind echoes of her pain.

Matt swore and ran a hand through his hair. He'd stuffed that up. He'd hurt Georgie and now he felt like shit. It wasn't her fault he still didn't know what to do about her declaration of love. It didn't give him the right to try to unsettle her as well.

He was jealous and the fact he was jealous about Georgie shook him. He stared at the phone. Should he call her back and apologise? He typed her number in, but his finger hovered over the call button. What could he possibly say? Sorry wasn't good enough. He'd need to explain his feelings and didn't understand them enough to do that yet. He sighed and walked back to the kitchen.

Amy glanced up from setting the table. "What did Georgie want?"

"To speak to Darcy." He put the phone back on the cradle.

"Did you two have a fight?"

He scowled. "Georgie was just being Georgie."

Amy studied him. "You mean cheerful and happy?"

His scowl deepened. "Annoying and stubborn."

"That doesn't normally bother you."

"Yeah, well she was particularly annoying today." He went to the cupboard and pulled out the water jug, filling it with ice.

"She hasn't been around much over the past couple of weeks," Amy commented, as she placed salad dressings on the table. "Not since the girls' night. Do you know if anything is up with her?"

He didn't like the way she examined him. He turned to fill the jug. "Georgie doesn't tell me much."

"I thought you two were good friends."

The way she said it, slightly suspicious, slightly probing, made him look up. Had Georgie said something to her? Did Amy know how Georgie felt about him? "I'm not Georgie's keeper."

"But you do care for her."

Startled, he turned from the sink and water sloshed over the side of the jug. He swore, turned off the tap and got some paper towel out to clean up the mess. "I care for the whole family."

Amy said nothing, just raised her eyebrows. Before he could ask what she meant by that look, Lara raced in, wearing an 'I love horses' T-shirt and dressed in jeans and riding boots. "Hi, Uncle Matt. Hi, Amy." She strode over to the sink, nudged Matt out of the way with her hip, poured herself a glass of water and proceeded to gulp it down. When she was finished, she placed the glass on the counter and wiped her mouth. "Ahh, that's better."

Matt smiled, relieved at the interruption, some of his annoyance fading. Lara could cheer up anyone.

Just like Georgie.

The realisation hit him hard. Georgie had lost her shine. During their conversation she'd been wary and unsettled. Normally a conversation with Georgie was enough to brighten his day no matter how shit it had been.

And it was his fault.

He needed to figure out how to fix it.

And bring back Georgie's shine.

# Chapter 11

Georgie had never been so pleased to work alone as she was the morning after Matt had insulted her. She was in one cyclone-sized mood and all she wanted to do was be alone. Her mind had snarled and taunted her all evening, first taking her anger out on Matt, imagining all the torturous things she could do to him, then turning inwards and telling her she wasn't worthy of love. She wanted to scream. Better to head out somewhere isolated before she released her crazy.

But first she needed to stop at the office to pick up supplies.

She waved a greeting at Karen. "Morning." She was almost at the corridor when the receptionist answered.

"Declan wants to see you before you head out."

Damn it. "All right." She kept moving down the corridor. She was almost at her office where she could close the door and give herself a minute to get her shit together when Declan appeared. With him was Helen Roe, Matt's mother.

"Georgie, good timing. Come into the meeting room. I want you to be part of this discussion. You know Helen, don't you?"

She forced a smile, not wanting the reminder of Matt right now. "Of course." She hugged Helen. "I don't think I've seen you since the wedding."

"Matt tells me you've been busy. It's good to see you."

Georgie's throat tightened and to her horror, tears blurred her vision. "I'll join you in a second." She dashed for the bathroom, not caring what anyone thought. Locking herself into a stall, she pressed her hands to her eyes, desperately trying to stem the flow of tears. What was wrong with her? She shouldn't be upset. She loved Helen. Whenever Helen had come to pick up Matt when he was younger, Georgie would sit at the table while her mum and Helen had a cuppa and caught up. Helen always asked her about her day or her horse-riding, and taught her a few Bayungu words. She'd felt like she was being let into a special, secret world. Now however, after a night of feeling unloveable it was all too much.

Get a grip.

Declan wouldn't be impressed with her for being a weepy female. She took a couple of long, deep breaths and pushed away the self-pity. She could do this. She was strong, a woman who could achieve anything. Unlocking the door, she stared at herself in the mirror. *I am woman, hear me roar.* Determination swept over her. She nodded at herself and then smiled. It wasn't quite her usual smile, but no one would notice that it didn't quite reach her eyes.

On the way to the meeting room, she grabbed her notebook from her desk, and joined Helen, Declan and Penelope.

Declan smiled at them. "PAWS has been working with Helen and the Bayungu to jointly manage the area between here and Coral Bay. We acknowledge the Bayungu are the traditional owners of the land, and we want to work with them to ensure its sustainability."

Georgie nodded. Helen had mentioned it when

Georgie had run into her at the supermarket the other day.

"At the moment, we're working on branding. The traditional colours of the Bayungu are red and white. We want to ensure future signage reflects this, and also contains Bayungu terminology where we can. You may have already noticed the Bayungu words in some places."

"I have." She thought it was a great way of showing respect and educating people.

"I'd like you to work with them to review our current signage and discuss what needs to be updated."

For the first time that day Georgie felt a glimmer of happiness. "I'd love to." She smiled at Helen. "When would you like to start?"

"I'm heading out to the islands with Penelope today," Helen said. "We're just waiting for—"

Matt rushed into the room. "Sorry I'm late." He drew up short when he spotted Georgie.

Shit, shit, shit. Georgie stared at him. He wore a clean checked red long-sleeved shirt which he wore for his 'dressier' occasions, and a pair of clean blue jeans. Helen must have told him to make an effort otherwise he would have turned up in his work gear. Helen cleared her throat. Matt glanced at her, removed his hat and sat in the spare seat next to his mother, across the table from Georgie.

She dragged her gaze away and gritted her teeth to control the desire to burst into tears.

"Oh, good, you're here," Helen said to her son. "I was just telling Georgie you would be working together."

"What?" The word came out sharper than she intended.

Declan nodded. "Helen will be working with Penelope and we thought you and Matt could work together on the signs on the west of the ranges."

Matt looked as horrified by the suggestion as she felt.

She'd be stuck alone in a car with him for hours, maybe even days. "Has Darcy given you leave for this?" Georgie asked.

He nodded, but he didn't look pleased at the situation.

"Great," Declan said. "Now that it's sorted, let me go through the details."

Georgie clicked her pen, staring down at the blank notebook in front of her. She could do this. She had to show Declan how capable she was, and that included working with the man who'd broken her heart. She forced herself to focus on her boss's words. So what if the roar of earlier was down to a pathetic mewling.

She could do this.

***

Matt barely heard what Declan was droning on about, but at least Georgie was taking notes. His mother had asked him to attend this meeting weeks ago, before he knew Georgie was working for Parks and Wildlife, or that she loved him. He'd thought they would be talking strategy, but it appeared all the details had been worked out ahead of time.

His mother squeezed his hand and when he glanced at her, he saw concern in her eyes. Her gaze shifted to Georgie and then back to him in an obvious question. He shook his head and smiled as if nothing was the matter, but he didn't fool her.

Georgie sat across the table only a couple of metres away, looking pale. The dark circles under her eyes and her ragged nails were a sure sign she'd been upset. Between taking notes, she twisted a short strand of her blue hair around her finger. The blue had faded since he'd seen her in town, but it still looked good. Georgie could pull off any look.

Somehow he had to work with her, but he still hadn't figured out how he felt, let alone what to say to her. All he knew was he had to make things right.

Around him people gathered their notes. "Everyone on the same page?" Declan asked.

Matt nodded though he had no clue what he was agreeing to.

"I'll get my keys." Georgie dashed out of the room.

Matt walked with his mother back to reception and they said their goodbyes to Declan. When Penelope arrived with her gear, Helen said, "I'll be with you in a moment. I just need to speak to my son."

Matt sighed as they exited the building and went to stand in the shade of one of the gum trees.

"Are you and Georgie fighting again?"

He hated how obvious it was to everyone. He'd never even had to think about his relationship with Georgie until now. Sure, they occasionally argued, but they were always mates.

Until now.

"We'll sort it out." It wasn't until he said the words that he realised how much he needed them to be true. He hated this uncomfortable tightness in his chest when he saw her. He wanted things to be normal again.

"You'll have plenty of time today to do so." She kissed his cheek and joined Penelope at her car.

Georgie was already waiting by one of the four-wheel drives. He got into the passenger seat and the silence as they drove out of town was bizarre.

"Did you pay attention to anything Declan said?" Georgie's voice made him jump, but her wry tone was so familiar and welcoming.

He exhaled. If she was going to pretend things were normal, then he could too. "Something about signs and Bayungu terms."

She shook her head, but her snort of laughter gave him hope. "At least one of us was taking notes." She explained the branding exercise and then said, "I figured we'd start at the far end and work our way back towards town."

"You're in charge."

"Yeah, I am," she murmured, her tone a little odd.

It was overcast today, the clouds forming a grey patchwork in the sky. They shielded the sun making it a little cooler, but the humidity was still high. Georgie had the air-conditioning cranking.

"Any progress on the treasure hunt?" she asked.

"None. All we're doing is decreasing our options."

"I'd count that as progress. How's Lara taking it?"

"You'd know if you'd visited in the past couple of weeks." OK, so maybe he wasn't quite as prepared to pretend things were normal. Eventually they'd have to address the humongous whale shark flipping about on the shore.

Her glare was laser sharp. "You know why I haven't."

"People have noticed. Amy's been asking whether we've fought."

"Amy should mind her own business."

It was the first time he'd heard her say anything even slightly negative about her new sister-in-law. "She's worried."

Georgie hummed but said nothing further.

Frustration simmered in him. He wanted to discuss this, but he also wanted her to look at him so he could see her warm brown eyes and tell what she was really thinking. He'd wait until they stopped.

Georgie turned on the radio and music he recognised as her favourite playlist filled the cab. OK, so she didn't want to talk, but at some stage today they would.

Yardie Creek was busy. Tourists gathered, waiting for their boat tour and while they waited, they read the signs about the area, giving Matt no chance to talk to Georgie privately. Georgie wasn't the slightest bit perturbed. She greeted the tourists, answered questions about the area as if she'd been working in Parks and Wildlife all her life. Her knowledge was impressive. While she spoke, she took photos of the signs, and then when the boat tour called for boarding, she pulled out a notebook and added notes. "What do you think we can add to this?" She gestured to the sign.

Matt blinked. He'd been so busy watching Georgie, he'd forgotten his reason for being here. His mother wanted their culture to be shared.

Quickly he reviewed the details which spoke about the rock wallabies and bird life living in the area. "We could talk about the irukandji," he said. "The jellyfish head for the creek in numbers whenever a cyclone is due. It's one way of knowing to prepare for a storm."

She wrote it down. "What about Bayungu names for animals? There's *bigurda* for kangaroo."

"How do you know?"

She gave him an incredulous look. "I do listen," she said. "You've been teaching my brothers the correct names for over a decade."

And she'd remembered. He'd always felt a bit foolish when Charlie had asked him this kind of stuff. He'd never been able to tell whether it was because Charlie was genuinely interested or just testing Matt's knowledge.

A warmth spread through Matt's chest. "Thanks, Georgie. It means a lot."

She smiled and moved to the next sign, but she murmured, "I know."

The words hit him like a dumper, dragging him to the bottom of the ocean and holding him down. She meant what she said. She understood how much his heritage meant to him and therefore had paid attention all these years.

She really did love him.

His lungs constricted and he struggled to breathe, fighting to the surface so he could figure this all out.

Georgie was already at the next sign down by the creek. She glanced back. "Are you coming?" The defensive snark in her tone had him moving towards her without even thinking. He had to say something, had to make this right. He stopped next to her and she frowned, one finger curling around her hair. "What's wrong?"

There it was again. She knew him, just like he knew she was nervous and upset with that one raised finger.

The truth hit him.

Why he'd been so jealous of Sam and Jerry.

Why he knew her every movement.

Why he'd missed her so much.

He loved her.

"Matt?" Concern crossed her face. "What's going on?"

He stepped closer, his gaze not leaving her face. She had the cutest dusting of freckles sprinkled over the end of her pert nose. Her brown eyes could warm him like a hot chocolate on a cold night, or make him feel like dirt if he'd upset her. Her thick blue hair fell around her face highlighting how unique she was, and her lips... he'd avoided focusing too much on her lips in the past. They were plump and pink and so, *so* kissable.

They parted slightly as if she was about to speak, but no words came out. Her eyes widened and he was lost in the depths of them.

"Georgie." He slipped his arms around her waist and pulled her against him. Damn, she felt good. It was like receiving something he'd been starving himself of for years. Famished now, he bent his head and his lips touched hers.

Paradise. Like diving into the cool ocean after a particularly hot and dusty day's work.

She sighed and he tasted her sweetness, and all the

tension in him released. This was what he'd been denying himself, this was what he'd been missing. He touched his tongue to her lips—

Suddenly he was shoved away.

He stumbled back, taking in Georgie's flashing eyes and her outrage.

What?

"How dare you!" The tremble in her voice made his brain kick into double time. He'd upset her. But wasn't this what they both wanted?

When he continued to stare at her trying to figure things out, she advanced on him, poking her finger in his chest.

"Don't—" Poke. "you dare—" Poke. "use my feelings for you—" Poke. "to scratch an itch."

"Georgie." He grabbed her hand before she could poke him again. It hurt.

She tried to shake him off, but he held tight. Her eyes flashed fire. "No. You don't get to kiss me. Don't you see how cruel you're being? You don't love me." She was near to tears and it killed him.

"But I do."

She stilled in his arms, staring at him with shock.

"You said the other day that I was slow." He smiled. "I've kept my feelings for you hidden even from myself. Since you told me how you felt, I've been so messed up." He rubbed her arms, soothing her. "I've missed you. I've been so used to having my weekly fix of you, but then you stopped coming. Darcy will tell you what a rotten mood I've been in." The words kept tumbling out. "And I've been so jealous of every guy who's shown you any interest. I nearly punched Jerry when he said how hot you looked the other night."

"He didn't come inside. I only accepted his offer to make you jealous."

"Well it worked. I've been obsessing over it ever

since." He kissed her again because he couldn't help himself. "It's taken me a hell of a long time to realise it, Georgie, but I love you too.

"Really?"

He nodded. Before he could say anything, she flung her arms around his neck and dragged him closer, kissing him. He smiled against her lips as a hunger took over him. This was where he needed to be, this was where he belonged. He'd been a fool not to see it sooner.

A car horn beeped and a guy yelled out of the window, "Give it to her."

Matt backed away, glaring at them, and Georgie laughed, waving at the car full of young guys.

The interruption was timely. They had work to do and all he wanted was to have Georgie to himself. The faster they got this done, the faster that would happen.

Georgie slid her hand into Matt's and turned back to the sign she'd been studying. "Maybe we should talk about the seasons in this one."

Just like that he was forgiven, and everything was all right. Was it no wonder he loved her?

He nodded, marvelling at the way she went from being kissed to focusing on the sign. But her hand was in his and it was so easy, so normal. He squeezed her hand and agreed.

They continued their tour, making notes of where things needed to be added or changed, and though everything with Georgie felt right, there was a voice in the back of his head asking how Darcy would react. He glanced around the car park to make sure no one from town was there.

"What are you looking for?"

Right now he wished she wasn't so in tune to him. "Nothing." When she continued to look at him, he sighed. "I'm worried about how your brothers will react."

She frowned. "About us?"

Us. He liked the sound of that. He nodded. "You're their little sister and they've always been protective of you."

"It's none of their business," Georgie said.

She didn't get it. "Your family has been good to me," he said. "I don't want them to think I've taken advantage of you."

"Why would they? It's not like I'm sixteen."

She made it sound so simple. "You've never heard Darcy's concerns. He was so worried about you going to university and men taking advantage of you."

Her expression grew incredulous. "I bet he never had the same concerns about Ed."

"Ed's not gay," Matt joked.

Georgie scowled. "You know what I mean. Darcy wasn't concerned about women taking advantage of Ed."

"You're so trusting and he sees your happy nature as naïveté rather than optimism."

"So what?" she said. "You believe Darcy will think you're the big bad wolf tempting me away? Lying in wait for all these years?"

It sounded ridiculous when she put it that way. "It might come as a shock to them," he said. "We should break it to them gently." He tugged her closer. "Please."

She sighed and nodded. "All right. Come on, we've got a lot more sites to visit before I can have you to myself." She grinned.

He liked the sound of that.

# Chapter 12

Over the course of the day Georgie changed her mind. Working alone had been a nice change, but it was a hundred times better working with Matt by her side. Her dream come true.

He loved her.

She couldn't believe it. After all these years of hoping and wishing, he'd finally realised it. As she parked at the next stop, she glanced at him, just to make sure she hadn't imagined the whole thing. He grinned back at her. "Ready?"

Was she ever. She seriously wished she could ignore work and drive them both straight to her place, but it wouldn't be fair to Declan or to Matt. What they were doing was instrumental in keeping the Bayungu culture alive. "Always."

Matt slipped his hand into hers as they walked over to the beach carpark signs and Georgie had to resist the urge to shout in happiness. In front of the sign, she slipped her arm around his waist and kissed him. Easy. Comfortable. Right. She didn't want to let go, but she had to take notes.

With a sigh she shifted away from him to take photos

and write down what could be added and changed.

When she was finished Matt held her hand again. "I can't seem to stop touching you," he said.

"I love it," Georgie answered. "Don't stop." She tugged him closer and they kissed again, her heart singing at the rightness of it all. Except the kiss soon deepened and her core throbbed. When they broke apart, both were breathing heavily. Georgie glanced at the bonnet of the four-wheel drive. How strong was it?

Matt laughed. "While I'm totally on board with what you're thinking, there's a car coming."

Damn it. She'd have to wait to get him home, alone and naked.

It was mid-afternoon when they drove into False Valley. Matt gestured to the tyre tracks Georgie had checked out yesterday. "That shouldn't be there."

"I know. I reported it yesterday."

"Has anyone checked it out?"

"I did. Someone's been camping there." Matt would flip out if she mentioned Lee.

"You went to investigate on your own?" He turned to her, his 'Georgie's been naughty' expression on his face.

She held up a hand. "It's my job. I called it in before I went in, and I spoke to the office while I was there."

"There are smugglers around."

She glanced at him. "How do you know?"

He muttered a curse. "I saw the traps when I went to investigate the tracks the other day. I reported them to the police."

Georgie was still cross at him for going alone, so she could understand why he was so upset now. "I was careful." No way was she telling him about Lee now. They both knew Lee had a gun and wasn't afraid to use it.

"How far in do those caves go?" Georgie asked, hoping to sound casual.

"The caves in the ranges?"

"Yeah."

"A fair way. Some people in town have explored them, but there's no official record. It gets hot in there."

"Can you get from one side of the ranges to the other?"

Matt shrugged. "Probably. I don't really know."

She was hoping he might have a Dreamtime story or ancestry knowledge about it. "I guess they'd make a good place to shelter in a cyclone."

"Yeah, I imagine that's what my ancestors did."

So there was a possibility Lee had figured a way through the caves. He had to park his car somewhere and he had his tent with him, so aside from food and water, he could easily live out here for weeks and no one would see him. "Did you ever teach Lee any of the bush tucker stuff?"

It was the wrong question to ask. Matt shot her a glance as she quickly got out of the car. The slam of the car door echoed.

"Why are you asking, Georgie?"

She shrugged. "Just curious. No one has seen him for a month."

"He's probably gone back to Singapore."

"He's not from Singapore."

He waved her comments away. "To Stonefish or wherever that is."

"Do you think he'd be welcome there after shooting Tan?"

"Ed said Tan had made a mistake."

Georgie was sure Lee had unfinished business here, otherwise why would he stick around? There were better places to disappear. Matt joined her over by the final sign. "Why all the interest in Lee?"

She shrugged as she took photographs. "All the talk about smugglers made me think it might be part of

Stonefish's operation, and that made me think about Lee."

"Promise me you'll be careful," he said. "I don't like the idea of you out here on your own with them around."

"I get that, but it's a bit like looking for the treasure. Chances of running across it in all this land are slim."

"Yeah, but we've seen the tracks and the traps nearby."

She squeezed his hand and then kissed him, thrilled she was able to. "I promise I'll be careful."

He pulled her closer and deepened the kiss. "Make sure you are," he said when they broke apart. "I don't want anything to happen to you."

"You're not getting rid of me that easily." She smiled and tugged him back towards the car. "Come on. That's everything finished for the day." She glanced over her shoulder and smiled. "Wanna come to my place for dinner?"

He grinned. "I'd love to."

***

Georgie stopped by the office to drop her notes and change vehicles and then Matt followed her back to her place. Nerves shimmered over her arms as she pulled up outside her small unit. Matt had been here before. He'd helped her move in, though she hadn't had much furniture then. But he hadn't been here for months, not since she'd redecorated. And not as more than a friend.

Matt had borrowed Amy's car to come to town, and it was a little comical watching him unfold himself from the small vehicle. He was so… Matt. Tall and lean, with understated muscles. He didn't need a gym to be strong, he just was. He kept his thick dark hair short, not that she could see much from under the Akubra he always wore. Then there was the slow, sexy smile, just an upturn of his lips at the sides as his dark eyes stared at her with focused intensity.

Finally.

He stalked towards her and when she reached for him, he nudged her inside the house, shutting the door behind them. Alone, at last.

His mouth met hers and she moaned. The kisses they'd shared all day had kept her in a constant state of arousal. He pressed her against the door, his erection hard against her as he deepened the kiss, his hands running all over her body as if he needed to touch all of her.

"Georgie," he murmured, trailing kisses along her chin down to her neck. He scraped his teeth against her sensitive skin and she gasped. "Do you like that?"

She nodded, her words lost.

"I want to learn everything you like." He tugged at her shirt, pulling it out from her pants, and his warm hand touched her stomach, sliding up to cup her breast.

This was Matt and somehow his touch was a hundred times more erotic than any other man she'd been with. She was a puddle of desire. If his other arm hadn't been holding her, keeping her upright, her legs wouldn't hold her.

Normally she wasn't so passive, but his hands on her made her lose all reason. She couldn't think.

His fingers made fast work of her bra and then his thumb circled her nipple and she moaned again. Her fantasies had been pathetic by comparison.

Matt groaned. "I need you naked. I need to see you and touch every inch of you." He tugged her towards the bedroom and the short reprieve was enough for her mind to kick back into gear. When he drew her close again, she went straight for the buttons on his shirt, her fingers a little uncoordinated as she desperately undid them, needing to see him too.

Matt swore and stepped back, stripping off his shirt,

and she did the same. She reached for him, but the intensity in his gaze made her hesitate.

Reverently he pulled her closer as his hands brushed her breasts, his dark skin contrasting against her white. "You're so beautiful."

She felt like a goddess as she unbuttoned her pants and slid them off.

Only to get to her boots. Crap.

They both looked down and as one, they laughed.

Before she could bend to undo the laces, he pushed her back, and she tripped, falling onto her bed with a shriek. "Matt!"

He was already crouched, busy untying her laces and in moments she was fully naked. He stayed low as he undid his own boots and undressed.

Georgie shifted further onto the bed and watched as he slid off his jeans and his penis sprang free. Her mouth watered.

"My eyes are up here."

She didn't need to look to know he was grinning that smug smile of his. "I've seen them before," she replied not lifting her gaze.

With a chuckle which was half growl, he joined her on the bed and captured her lips with his.

More.

She ran her hands over his lean muscles, feeling the tension in his shoulder blades as he held himself above her. His mouth plundered hers and she met him passion for passion. She'd waited so long for this. His erection pressed against her skin and she opened her legs wider.

He groaned as he shifted and swept a hand down her side, finding her core. "Georgie."

She was ready for him, more aroused than she'd been in her life. She wanted him inside her. "Matt, condom."

He swore. "I don't have any."

Georgie pushed him away and reached over to her

bedside table to grab the box. She was on her stomach and Matt squeezed her butt, and then proceeded to cover her cheeks with kisses. Holy yes. She squirmed, as he slipped his hand under her to touch and she forgot her mission as her body celebrated. She felt like an instrument being expertly played.

"Georgie, you going to get that condom?" Matt murmured against her skin.

Right. That's what she'd been aiming for. Her hand flailed, hitting the box and she managed to extract what she needed. She held it up in triumph and Matt snatched it from her, flipping her on to her back.

She desperately wanted to touch him, but she also desperately wanted him inside her. Torn, she reached for him as he finished rolling on the condom. He pushed her hand aside, pinning her to the bed.

"Ready?"

"Yes." Almost before the words left her mouth, he pushed inside her. She arched her chest, and he caught one nipple with his mouth and sucked. Stars exploded as he began to move and she wrapped her legs around his waist, urging him on.

This, all of this.

It was hard, and fast and just what she needed. Her arousal built and her breath came in gasps.

"Come for me," Matt ordered.

"You first," she challenged.

His expression was half scowl, half grin. "Together."

"Together," she agreed. The orgasm hit her and she moaned as the waves took over her body, and Matt came with her shouting in triumph.

When they were both spent, he collapsed next to her, holding her tight. Matt's satisfied sigh made her smile. "I can't believe we waited so long to do that."

"I did say you were a bit slow." Her laugh was stopped by his mouth on hers.

"I'll show you slow."

And he proceeded to do so.

***

Matt followed Georgie into her kitchen, slightly dazed, but all the way satisfied. He'd been an idiot, that much was certain. Why had it taken him so long to realise how he felt about Georgie? The sex had been out of this world, but it wasn't just that. It was the comfort, the friendship on top of it. He'd never laughed while having sex before. If he'd caught his pants on his boots like Georgie had, he would have been mortified. But this was Georgie. Trust and laughter came hand in hand with the best sex of his life.

Georgie stood at the fridge, door open, wearing only a singlet and undies. She glanced over her shoulder. "I was planning to make spaghetti tonight. Is that all right with you?"

She could have served toast or boiled eggs for all he cared. He slid his hands around her waist, kissing her neck. "Whatever you want."

She chuckled. "I'll hold you to that later."

Hell, that promise had him hard again. He turned her to face him and captured her lips with his. She melted into him, her arms stretching around his neck and pulling him closer.

How sturdy was her kitchen table? He broke the kiss and assessed it. She'd picked up the cheap flat pack thing in a garage sale and it had to be at least twenty years old.

"The bench will be stronger." Georgie grinned.

He loved where her mind was at.

Matt lifted her, ignoring her shriek of laughter and sat her on the bench. "Want to test it?"

"Absolutely," she said. "But if we don't eat now, we'll never eat and I could do with the sustenance."

He kissed her again. "Spoilsport."

"Animal." She pushed him away and hopped down. "Do you want to get the pasta from the cupboard?"

So easy. Had anything been so easy and so right as cooking dinner with Georgie in her kitchen after mind-blowing sex?

His gaze caught on a framed photo on the bench. A family photo of everyone at Brandon's wedding. Guilt punched him.

He'd just had sex with his best friend's sister.

He stepped back, inhaling deeply, shaking away the feeling.

No.

He'd just made love to Georgie. He had nothing to feel guilty about. It was consensual and they loved each other. The Stokes brothers were going to have to deal with it. Darcy probably hadn't considered Georgie a candidate when he'd spoken about Matt settling down.

Matt got the pasta out of the cupboard, frowning at how little was in there. "Where's your food?"

"I don't cook much," she said. "Lunch was provided on the boat, and then I'd buy what I needed for dinner on the way home."

"You should be taking better care of yourself."

She shrugged. "It's hard cooking for one."

He'd never considered it. When he got home from work he had the Stokes family to eat with. First Beth, then Amy, always cooked dinner, with them helping out if there were still things to do when they got home. If he needed a change, he'd visit his parents. "Do you get lonely living alone?"

She didn't look at him as she answered. "There's usually someone in town who's free for a drink if I need company." Her tone was upbeat, almost flippant, but the fact she didn't look at him told him there was more to it.

"Georgie, look at me." He placed the pasta on the table and touched her shoulder.

She shrugged him off. "Yeah, of course I get lonely, but it made sense to live in town so I didn't have to get up so early to get to work."

No wonder she'd spent her free day out at the Ridge. "I'm sorry. I never realised."

"I didn't want anyone to feel sorry for me. I made my decision."

"So what about now?" he asked. "You can choose your starting hours."

"Brandon and Amy don't need me moving home," she said. "And I don't want to be there when Darcy and Faith finish their house and move out. It would be too weird."

The conversation with Darcy came back to him. He understood how Georgie felt, as if he no longer belonged there. He'd figured one day he'd build or buy his own place, but there never seemed any urgency.

Now he wished he'd bought months ago. "What if you built your own place out there like Darcy?"

She shrugged. "I don't know if they would want me out there."

Matt frowned, stopping her from lighting the stove, and turned her to face him. "Your brothers would love to see you more often. Darcy said I could build a house on the land the other day."

Her eyes widened. "He did?"

Matt nodded.

"Well you're his best friend, so of course he wants you hanging around."

Where was this lack of confidence coming from? This wasn't the Georgie he knew. Before he could ask, she said, "Besides, my lease doesn't run out until the end of the year."

They had a couple of months to sort out what to do next and hopefully by then, the situation with Stonefish would have been resolved.

He stilled. Already he was thinking about the future, a future with Georgie. It wasn't scary, it was comforting, joyful. Shouldn't he be freaking out? Everything was happening so fast.

"Are you all right?" Georgie asked, turning from the stove where she was cooking the mince.

He smiled. "Yeah, I am."

He kissed her and held her in his arms where she was meant to be. "What can I do to help?"

# Chapter 13

Georgie resisted the urge to send Matt a text message before she left the PAWS office the next morning to say she was thinking of him. There was no point, he'd be somewhere out on the station without reception. If she sent him half a dozen texts throughout the day like she wanted to, he'd get them all at once when he got home and it would make her seem needy.

Which she wasn't. She was just so thrilled about them being together.

She smiled and hummed along to an upbeat pop song as she drove out of town. Matt had stayed far later than he should have, considering his early start, but she hadn't had the strength to tell him to go.

Georgie giggled. Matt loved her.

It was as if she'd finally been rewarded for doing something right. Last night had been better than even her most vivid imaginations. After dinner they'd chatted about the treasure hunt, then they'd tested out the sturdiness of the kitchen bench. She grinned.

When he'd finally left, she'd stayed awake until he'd sent her a text to say he'd arrived safely at the Ridge, and then she'd fallen asleep dreaming of him.

There'd been no post sex awkwardness, no wondering whether he would call her again, no stress at all. It was as if it was meant to be.

She slowed, searching for the track she needed. Today she was at the bottom end of the ranges on the eastern side not far from where the Ridge bordered the national park. She'd fallen into a nice rhythm, stopping at the office in the morning to catch up, and then heading out to do her work.

In the distance a tell-tale dust cloud told her somebody was driving where they shouldn't. Tourists. Declan had warned her about this part of the job on Monday. Not all of them appreciated being given a Lawful Direction to move on. She sighed and found the track, turning off and heading towards the dust. It settled before she could reach it, but she noted the direction. What was the bet she'd drive up to find the car bogged and a couple arguing about coming this way in the first place while kids screamed in the backseat?

She grabbed her radio and called it in. The most she could do as Parks and Wildlife was fine them for being in a prohibited area, but a lawful direction should be enough. She'd take the number plate and their details in case they became a repeat offender.

The track wound close to the base of the ranges and she slowed as she reached the area where the dust had settled. She rounded a bend and braked, finding the white four-wheel drive directly in front of her, with no people around. She radioed the office. "Karen, I've found the car. It's an old white Land Cruiser with a dented back bumper." She read out the licence plate number. "No one is here, so I'll take a look around."

"Roger. Take your radio with you."

Most four-wheel drive enthusiasts didn't park unless they were near the beach or were bogged, but this sat on top of the red dirt.

She scanned her surroundings, her skin prickling. Small shrubs and straggly trees populated the area but it was difficult to see far. To her right the ranges stretched above her, overlooking her. She sniffed for a fire though it was unlikely whoever it was had driven all this way just to cook breakfast. All she smelled was the fresh air and red dirt. Georgie circled the four-wheel drive. The windows were covered with makeshift curtains so she couldn't see in the back. That wasn't unusual as some people camped on the cheap, sleeping in the back, putting up curtains for privacy.

The keys were still in the ignition and on a hunch, she retrieved them, tucking them into her pocket.

The red sand was soft, and she made out two sets of footprints which led off into the bush. Toilet stop? Whoever it was must have heard her arrive. Maybe they didn't want to get into trouble being somewhere they shouldn't. She followed the footsteps, cautious now and quiet.

She moved slowly, constantly scanning for a hint of colour from their clothes.

"We should get out of here," a man murmured close to her right.

"Shhh, they haven't left yet," another man responded.

Her skin prickled. Moving back the way she came, she angled further right to come around behind them. The trees were more like shrubs, but they gave enough cover, and her khaki uniform ensured she blended in.

The two men still faced the direction of the cars when she saw them. Both in their early twenties, dressed in jeans and scruffy T-shirts, one with a blond mullet, the other in a blue baseball cap. They stood by a couple of holes in the ground and had a pile of plastic containers. Bastards. She took out her phone and photographed them with their smuggling gear.

"Let's go." The panic in blond mullet's voice gave her

confidence.

"Stay still," hat guy said.

Neither was holding a weapon and there were no guns tucked into the back of their jeans. What should she do? She couldn't let them get away with it, but together they could overpower her.

Her radio squawked and all three of them jumped. "Georgie, can you report?"

The two men spun to face her, eyes wide. She smiled with fake bravado as she reached for her radio. "I've got two animal smugglers here." She watched them closely, waiting for a reaction. "Can you call the police?"

"Will do. Be careful."

Mullet guy glanced around as if undecided which way to run. Hat guy was defiant. "What are you talking about? We aren't animal smugglers."

She looked pointedly at the traps and the plastic containers. "All evidence points to it."

"Where did you even come from?" Mullet guy asked.

He wasn't the brains of the operation, but hat guy was also struggling to come up with a decent excuse. Neither were men she recognised, so they had to be from out of town. "I guess the police will go easier on you if you tell them who you're working for."

Mullet guy gestured to his friend. "Lance knows. I'm just helping out."

Lance glared at him. "Shut up, Jay. Run."

Lance took off towards the car with Jay taking only a second to follow. Georgie smiled and tapped the keys in her pocket, moving to see inside the traps. A few lizards and a couple of snakes. Georgie wasn't entirely sure what the process was now. It would take the police at least an hour to get out here, maybe more if they were on other business.

"Where are the keys?" Lance shouted.

"You drove," Jay responded.

As they argued, Georgie relaxed and moved back towards the car. They weren't the cutthroat smugglers she'd been envisioning. Her radio came to life again. "Georgie are you there?" It was Dot.

"Yeah and I'm looking at two animal smugglers. You got the details of their car from Karen?"

"Yeah, we're on our way. Are they giving you any trouble?"

Georgie raised her eyes at the two. Jay slumped in defeat and shook his head. "I'll tell you everything I know."

Lance scowled at him but didn't say anything. He was the one to watch. He was already starting to sweat. "They shouldn't if they know what's good for them," Georgie replied.

"I'd take her seriously, gentleman," Dot responded. "We won't be long." Then she was silent. The men exchanged a glance, but otherwise didn't move.

Lance narrowed his eyes. "You took my keys."

Georgie felt a twinge of concern. "There's no point trying to run," she said. "There are only a couple of roads out of here and the police have your car details. They'll catch you before you reach the Coral Bay turn off."

Lance kicked the tyre and swore.

She exhaled and moved closer. "Have you been doing this long?"

"This is my first time," Jay said. "Lance has been doing it for months."

Lance punched Jay in the arm. "Shut up!"

Jay rubbed his arm and glared at Lance. "You said it was easy money. You said we wouldn't get caught. My parents are going to have a fit."

"Don't blame me. You knew the risks."

"You made it sound like the biggest risk was a snake bite."

To be fair, that was a real possibility and a mulga was

in one of the traps, so Jay had a point. Georgie retrieved a bottle of water from the car while they argued.

Maybe she could get some information from them while they waited. They might be less cautious speaking to her than talking with the police. She pulled out her phone and hit record on the voice app. "Who's your contact in town?" It was a guess, but Jay glanced at Lance, his mouth open. "Yeah, I figured Stonefish had someone local." Another guess and this time Lance's eyes widened in fear. Bingo. "With Tan dead you must have a new boss."

"Tan?" Lance frowned, but it was genuine confusion.

That was interesting. Maybe someone else ran this part of the operation. Lee had admitted to Ed there were more players in the game. "Tan must be the guy above your guy," she said. "Why don't you give me a name?"

"You're not the police," Lance said.

"Didn't you say his name was Matt?" Jay asked.

Georgie gasped. He couldn't possibly mean her Matt. There was no way Matt would get involved with this, no way at all. Besides, Matt was a common name, and he'd said he'd reported it to the police.

"I'm not saying anything. They'll kill me," Lance said.

Jay paled. "What?"

"They're dangerous guys. You don't want to get on their wrong side."

"You never said—"

Lance cut him off. "It's a massive operation, probably some kind of crime syndicate, what the hell did you think?"

"I didn't."

A flash of light caught Georgie's eye in the range above them. It came from about halfway up and Georgie scanned the area looking for another flash. She hadn't brought her binoculars with her. There it was again. Definitely something moving up there, and not an animal of the four-legged variety. She stiffened, suddenly feeling very exposed. From that angle the trees wouldn't shelter them. The men were still arguing, but she interrupted them. "These people you're working for, are they likely to keep watch on you—make sure you're doing things right?"

Lance turned to her. "That's what they said, but we're in the middle of nowhere."

Lee. It had to be. "For argument's sake, what if someone was watching us now? What would they do if they knew the police were on their way?" Whoever was up there had a clear shot of all three of them.

Lance whirled around, checking every direction. "What did you see?"

"Someone's up on the range. Get behind the cars." Georgie moved around the back of her car, while the men went in front of it. No point giving them an easy opportunity to tackle her. She ducked low, the solid metal providing welcome protection. "Sit down."

They both sat in the shade of their four-wheel drive. Georgie grabbed two water bottles out of her esky and threw one to each of them but didn't sit. She crouched, keeping enough distance that she'd have warning if Lance chose to attack.

"What the fuck have you got me involved in?" Jay asked.

Lance shrugged, miserable. "I've almost got enough to buy a house. I was going to stop when I did."

"They approached you?" Georgie asked.

"Yeah. I was up here on holiday and had been mouthing off at the pub about how expensive housing was and that I'd be renting forever. Someone approached me as I left that night."

"This Matt?"

"Mark. His name is Mark."

Relief filled Georgie.

"Said it was easy money. All we had to do was come up here every month, check the traps and bring anything we found to them."

"Where?"

"The gulf. They'd ship the animals out."

Interesting. Declan had said most animals were smuggled in the mail. But if they had enough animals, maybe it was more cost effective to ship them together—or they were shipping something else as well. "How long have you been doing this?"

"Six months."

"This is my first time," Jay said.

Sucks to be him.


It was another half an hour before the police arrived. Sergeant Dot Campbell drove and with her was her constable, Colin Lipscombe. She parked next to Georgie's car. "Is this where the other traps were?" she asked Colin.

He shook his head. "They were another five kilometres south."

Dot studied the two men on the ground. "Did they give you any trouble?" she asked Georgie.

Georgie shook her head. "But I think someone might have been watching us from the ranges."

Dot gave her her full attention. "Why?"

"I saw a flash of light up there, like the reflection off glass. It happened twice, so we moved behind the cars so we were out of view."

"Good idea." Dot turned to Colin. "Get Georgie to show you the traps but keep an eye out."

Georgie grabbed her binoculars from the car and then led Colin through the bush, keeping low to the shrubs. Before stepping out into the open, she said, "The light was about halfway up." She used the binoculars to scan the range where she'd seen the light. Nothing but red dirt, rocks and shrubs.

She expanded her scan but saw nothing out of place. "I can't see anyone."

Colin nodded and moved forward to take photos of the traps. "Did Matt teach you to move like that?"

She frowned. "What?"

"The way you placed your steps and moved was just like Matt did when he showed me the other traps."

She smiled, liking the comparison. "I tagged along when I was a kid and took note."

"It's impressive. I might have to get him to teach me." After Colin had the evidence he needed, Georgie set the lizards free. She got her snake catching kit from her car and moved the brown snake carefully to the bush. By the time they returned, Lance and Jay were in the back of the police car and Dot was documenting what was in the back of their four-wheel drive. Georgie peered over her shoulder. "What's in there?"

"More animals," Dot said. "Lance says they're from further south."

There were several dozen plastic containers inside, most containing myriad reptiles. They'd have to be released where they came from and it would take time to remove the duct tape from their fragile skin. "Want me to take them and arrange for their release?" Georgie asked.

Dot nodded. "That would be great. They're all still alive."

Georgie reported to the office and let them know she'd be bringing in the animals, then carefully transferred them into the back of her car.

"Lance told me the guy he reported to was called Mark," Georgie said. "They take the animals to the gulf." Using Ridge land.

Dot scowled. "Can you stop by the station when you're done so I can get your statement?" she asked. "It's probably best to take care of the animals first."

"I will."

Georgie climbed into her car and headed back to town. What a morning. She still had a lot of work to do, but the animals took precedence.

In the rear-view mirror, the ranges soared into the air. Had it been Lee there or someone else?

She sighed.

At least they hadn't taken a shot.

# Chapter 14

"You've been in a better mood today," Darcy noted as he and Matt walked towards the house at the end of the day.

Matt's half smile vanished as he stiffened. He couldn't tell Darcy he was thinking about Georgie. Not when he hadn't figured out the best way to broach the subject. He could hardly blurt it out with no warning. He shrugged. "Nothing broke today."

Darcy studied him as they took off their boots on the verandah. "Did the stuff with your mum go well yesterday?"

"Yeah." He hesitated. "It was at Parks and Wildlife. I spent the day with Georgie reviewing the signs in the park."

Darcy smiled. "How's she going? I was going to call her today."

Crap, he wasn't ready for that. He had to tell Darcy about the change in their relationship himself. "She's a natural," Matt said with a smile. "But she mentioned she had a busy week. She pretty much went straight to bed yesterday." His body warmed at the memory.

"How do you know?"

"She told me that was her plan." OK, so it wasn't totally a lie, but he moved inside to avoid answering more questions. "Hi, La La."

Lara sat at the kitchen table doing homework, still wearing her yellow and brown school uniform. She looked up and pouted. "Hi, Uncle Matt." She twisted her head so Darcy could kiss her cheek.

"Hey, pumpkin. How was school?"

"I have to work with Natasha on a project." The disgust on her face was clear. Natasha was Lara's nemesis, just like Jerry had been Matt's.

"What's the project?" Matt asked.

"We have to pick a topic and then write a report and do a presentation on it to the whole class."

"Have you chosen a topic?" Darcy asked.

"I want to do the shipwreck of the Retribution," Lara said. "But Natasha thinks that's lame. She wants to do it on a K-Pop band."

"Perhaps you can find a compromise," Darcy said.

Music and history. The girls had to have something in common. "Doesn't Natasha do horse-riding with you?" Matt asked. "Maybe you could do something related to that."

Lara brightened. "That's a great idea! I could bring Starlight in for the presentation."

Darcy laughed. "I'm not sure your horse will fit inside the classroom."

She waved him away. "Then we'll do it outside. Maybe we could do it on correct posture, or techniques, or taking care of a horse." She shoved her chair back and strode towards the corridor calling, "Faith! I need your help."

Darcy handed Matt a beer from the fridge. "Good suggestion. I wonder why her teacher paired them. She knows they don't like each other."

"Maybe it's an attempt to make them get on. In sixth

grade Mr Naughton made me do a project with Jerry." Matt shuddered.

"Jerry..." Darcy pursed his lips. "From football? I didn't realise you didn't like him."

"I don't hate him," Matt said. "But as a kid he was a racist prick and never missed an opportunity to insult me."

"So how did your project go?"

"It came close to an all-out brawl," Matt admitted. Jerry had taunted him at every occasion. *Abo. Dumbass. Salvo.* "If it hadn't been for Charlie, I probably would have been suspended." Charlie always had his back. They'd balanced each other.

Darcy swore. "I hope Lara has a better time of it."

Amy and Brandon came into the kitchen, both smiling, hair damp from a shower. Brandon looked particularly smug. Matt didn't want to know what they'd been up to.

"Can I help with dinner?"

"No, it's been in the slow cooker all day," Amy said. "It's ready when everyone wants to eat."

Matt checked the time. Georgie should be home. Should he call her now? It might be better to wait until later, when he'd gone to his room. Then he could take his time and not be interrupted.

"I'm taking a shower first," Darcy said.

Matt placed his beer on the table. "Good idea."

"OK, let's say dinner in half an hour then," Amy said.

Matt went back outside and crossed the yard to the shearers' quarters. As he clomped up the stairs to his room it suddenly hit him how small his room was. He'd been living here for years and about the only changes he'd made since he'd first moved in was taking down the posters on the wall and buying a new dark green bedspread for his single bed. In the corner sat a small desk and his few clothes hung in a wardrobe next to the desk. Aside from that all he had was a laptop he used as a TV on the nights when he didn't feel like hanging out with the Stokes.

It wasn't much for ten years.

He couldn't bring Georgie back here, make her dinner, seduce her.

Buying a house hadn't seemed worth it. Not when his work was here, and he'd had the run of the shearers' quarters with its communal kitchen and living area. If he'd bought a house in town, he'd have to travel over an hour each morning to get here.

Even Georgie who had only graduated from university at the beginning of the year had moved out and got her own place. He didn't have anything to offer her.

He groaned at himself, grabbed a change of clothes and went into the bathroom.

With Georgie in his life he should think about his future. He wanted her part of it, but it would be a challenge. One or both of them would have to travel to work in order for them to live together. And could he offer her the type of life she deserved?

He shook his head. He was thinking too much. It had been easy to be with her.

Matt turned on the shower and stepped under the spray. He had to tell Darcy about their relationship by the weekend when Georgie would be out here. Darcy would be shocked. This would all seem like it was happening so fast and he might think Matt was taking advantage of Georgie's feelings for him.

Though Darcy didn't often play the protective brother, Matt had seen it a time or two when someone in town hadn't taken no as no.

Would Matt's relationship with Georgie ruin his friendship with Darcy?

With a sigh he twisted off the taps and dried himself,

dressing in shorts and T-shirt. His phone beeped on the way back to his room.

*How was your day? xx*

Georgie. He grinned, his concerns pushed away for the moment.

*Better now. What did you get up to?*

He hung his towel over the hook in his room and waited for her reply.

*Captured two animal smugglers.*

His heart stopped and he swore. She had to be kidding. His fingers dialled her number before he could even finish the thought.

"I'm fine," Georgie said as she answered.

"Are you serious?"

"Yeah, I came across them this morning. They didn't give me any trouble."

He sat on the bed, his heart racing. "Tell me everything."

"It wasn't a big deal." She spoke quickly as if wanting to reassure him. "Spotted a car somewhere it shouldn't be, and when I confronted them, they didn't resist. The..." Her voice trailed off.

She was leaving something out. "What Georgie?"

"I think someone was watching from the ranges, but I moved everyone behind the cars when I saw the glint."

Shit. "Did the police check it out?"

"I told Dot about it."

Maybe he should head that way tomorrow and see if he could find any evidence someone had been there. Or he'd call Nhiari and find out what the police were doing. "I don't like this."

"Neither do I, but I didn't go looking for them. I thought they were tourists in the wrong place."

He bit his tongue. Now wasn't the time to suggest she'd made a mistake about her new career path. It wasn't her fault these people were there. She had a right to do her job safely.

But maybe he could convince her and Darcy to let him ride along for a few days until they caught the guy in the ranges. Darcy wouldn't have a problem with Matt protecting Georgie, and if he could phrase it to Georgie as wanting to spend more time with her, she might go for it.

"How about I accompany you tomorrow?" he suggested.

Silence.

He winced, waiting for her response.

"Don't you think I can handle myself?" The hurt in her voice was unexpected.

"No." He swore. "I know you can, but I'd feel better knowing you weren't alone."

"I reported in with the office before I even followed the car," she said. "I'm following all the protocols."

"They won't help if the next guy has a gun."

"I know that, Matt, but there's no reason for them to seek me out. I'm not going out of my way to find them."

"Stonefish don't care about intentions."

"You think it's them?"

"Yeah. Those trails I followed the other day led straight to the traps and we know Stonefish knew about the trails."

She sighed. "I'll talk to Dot. She'll tell me if I'm in danger."

"All right." It was the best he could hope for at the moment, but he'd call Nhiari and ask her opinion. He checked the time. "I've got to go to dinner. I'll call you later?"

"Yeah. Say hi to everyone for me."

He hung up without promising and rang Nhiari.

"Little brother, what have I done to warrant a call mid-week?"

Shit. He hadn't thought how to phrase this. "How

dangerous are the animal smugglers?"

She was silent a moment. "What makes you ask?"

"I spoke to Georgie today."

She swore. "Dot should have told her to stay quiet."

"Is she in danger being out there all alone?"

"She's in as much danger working alone as you are," Nhiari answered, which wasn't really an answer as far as Matt was concerned. He regularly worked alone, but he always had a radio with him and he stuck to Ridge property.

"Did they have weapons?"

"I can't tell you that."

"What about the guy watching from the ranges? Are you going to look into that further?"

Nhiari sighed. "Matt, I understand you're worried, but I can't discuss details with you. All I can say is, we've spoken to Parks and Wildlife and they know what to do."

Not good enough. "I need to know Georgie will be safe."

"Have you finally admitted you love her?"

Matt's mouth dropped open and then flapped without any words coming out.

Nhiari chuckled. "You still there, little brother?"

He swallowed. "What?"

"Matt, I'm a cop. I've seen the way you look at her. I know how much you care for her."

Words failed him.

"Am I wrong?"

He shook his head. "No, but it's new. Only Georgie knows."

"She's the only one who counts." A pause. Nhiari cleared her throat, clearly unsure about continuing and then said, "Are you keeping it a secret?"

This was weird. He didn't discuss things like this with his sister; she didn't like to share feelings. "Yes. No... I haven't figured out how to tell Darcy."

"He'd be a hypocrite to have a problem with it. You're his best friend." The aggression in her voice hinted at bad experiences of her own.

She was right, but it didn't stop his concern. "Thanks. Will you keep your eye out for Georgie?"

"Always, little brother." She hung up.

Her words calmed him. He could always rely on Nhiari to have his back.

Now he just had to figure out how to tell Darcy he was in love with Georgie.

***

Finally it was the weekend and Georgie had two days off. Absolute bliss. To make things even better, she was going to the Ridge and seeing Matt.

They'd spoken every night, sometimes video-calling, but it wasn't enough. Georgie had offered to drive out to the Ridge, but Matt still hadn't told her family about them. She was trying to understand his concerns, trying to keep the uncertainty in her head quiet. Matt loved her. He wasn't ashamed about them. He was simply waiting for the best moment.

If he hadn't found it by now, she'd tell her family. She'd waited her whole life for this to happen, and she wasn't pretending they weren't in a relationship.

Georgie had bitten her lip to prevent herself from telling Faith when she'd called earlier this morning to invite her out for the weekend. If it had been Amy she might not have been able to resist. Amy knew how Georgie felt about Matt.

Soon everyone would know.

Georgie grabbed her overnight bag and jogged out to her car. A quick stop at the supermarket to get the few things the Ridge needed, and then she was on her way home.

Home.

It was the first time the Ridge had felt like home again since her parents had died. Was it due to Matt being there? His comment about Darcy saying he could build his own house had been thought-provoking. There was plenty of space. She hadn't really considered moving back, not with her work on the boat, but with her new job and relationship with Matt, it had got her thinking.

Faith drove into town three days a week to work in her law office. She never complained about the hour-long drive.

Declan said her work hours were flexible. On the days when Georgie had work on this side of the national park, she could go straight there instead of heading into the office. That would save her time.

She sighed and smiled. So many things to think about. She and Matt were early days still.

She drove into the yard at dusk and parked near the shearers' quarters. Darcy would wonder about her sleeping out here, rather than in the house, but it would give Matt an opportunity to break the news, if he still hadn't. She carried her bag to the porch and before she could put it down, Matt's door opened and he dragged her inside, shutting the door behind them. "I've missed you." He pressed her against the door and kissed her.

Yes.

She kissed him back, tugging his shirt from his waistband and popping the button on his jeans. Three days since she'd last touched him. Too long.

She lowered his zip and slipped her hand into his underpants, feeling his hard, warm erection. He groaned and dragged his lips from hers.

"We can't do this now."

"Why not?"

"Someone might hear."

Her arousal vanished in a puff of disappointment. "You haven't told them?" She withdrew her hand and slipped past him, further into the room.

He didn't look at her. "There was never the right moment."

Her insecurities pummelled her. "Are you ashamed of us?"

"No!" He stepped forward, reaching for her.

She put her hand on his chest. It would be too easy to forgive him if he held her. They needed to work this out. "So why haven't you told them?"

He ran a hand through his hair. "I don't know."

She waited, studying him.

He met her gaze. "You deserve better than me."

What? "Are you serious?" Where had this come from? She hadn't seen this insecurity from him since they were kids.

He nodded.

Her own concerns were brushed aside as she stepped forward, holding both his hands. "How can I deserve more than an amazing man who loves me?"

Matt frowned, confusion crossing his face.

"You are everything I deserve; a sexy, hardworking man who loves his friends and family, and who challenges and loves me."

He shifted away. "Look around, Georgie. All I own is right here. You deserve someone who can give you the world."

Georgie snorted. "I don't want the world. I want you. I don't have much either, but we can build on that together."

He fidgeted so she cut him some slack. "Is that what you're worried about—that Darcy will think you can't provide for me?" It was such old-fashioned thinking.

He shrugged. "It's got to be confronting for him."

She could work with this. "OK, let me call Faith and Amy over. You do up your pants." She smiled as she dialled the house number and Amy answered. "Can you and Faith come out to the shearers' quarters without the boys?"

"Sure. What's up?"

"I'll tell you when you get here." She hung up and glanced at Matt. "Ready?"

He nodded and pulled her close. "I'm not ashamed about us." He kissed her. "I want to be with you."

And she wanted this too much to let his reluctance to tell her brothers ruin what they had.

"Georgie?" Amy called.

Matt squeezed her hand. "I've got this." He opened the door. "She's in here."

Amy and Faith moved inside and Matt shut the door behind them. It was a bit of a squeeze with them all in the small room, but Matt slipped past them to stand next to Georgie.

"What's going on?" Faith asked.

Matt slipped his hand into Georgie's and she grinned. Amy's mouth dropped open. "You're finally together."

Georgie nodded, and Matt said, "Yeah."

Amy squealed and hugged them both. "I'm so pleased for you."

Faith shook her head. "I had no idea. How did I not know?"

"I didn't know until this week," Matt joked.

"We're a little worried about how Brandon and Darcy will react," Georgie said when the hugging was done.

Faith and Amy exchanged a glance. "I can't see why they'd be upset," Amy said.

"Darcy was always really protective of Georgie," Matt answered. "Especially when she went to uni."

"But they love you both," Faith said. "If Darcy can't see how you feel about each other, I'll talk to him."

Matt's grip on her hand relaxed and Georgie could have kissed Faith. "You ready?"

"Yeah." Matt answered.

Amy opened the door and they filed out, Georgie hand in hand with Matt. He froze on the porch and Georgie glanced at him. He stared across the yard at the house where both Brandon and Darcy were waiting on the verandah, Brandon with his arms crossed.

They must have seen Amy and Faith leave and wanted to know what was happening.

"Come on," Georgie murmured and tugged Matt down the steps. Darcy frowned and folded his arms across his chest.

They had to be kidding. Since when did they care about who she dated?

Both Faith and Amy said something to their respective partners as they walked past and the men uncrossed their arms but didn't stop frowning.

Nerves skittled over her skin. This was way more awkward than she'd thought it would be. Maybe Matt had been right to be worried.

Georgie moved onto the verandah, so her brothers didn't have the advantage of height on her. "Matt and I are dating."

Matt coughed and cleared his throat before slipping his arm around her waist.

"Since when?" Darcy asked.

"Tuesday."

Darcy raised his eyebrows. "That explains your good mood this week."

Matt nodded.

"Congrats," Brandon said. He raised his eyebrows at Georgie. "What about 'no more secrets'?"

Georgie blushed. "No more from now."

"I'll hold you to that." He grinned and wandered inside.

Georgie relaxed a little but kept her gaze on Darcy. He was the one Matt was most worried about.

"Can I have a word to Matt alone?" Darcy said.

"No," Georgie said. "Did you take Tess aside and have a word to her?"

"No, but you did," Darcy answered.

Shit. How did he know that?

"Go on, Georgie," Matt said. "We won't be long."

Men. She kissed his cheek and moved into the kitchen, pleased when the flyscreen door shut with a bang behind her. Lara hugged her. "I'm so happy! Matt will be my real uncle now."

"Slow down, La La." Georgie grinned. She glanced towards the door, hoping they wouldn't be long.

Lara tugged on her hand and whispered, "Why didn't you tell me? I told you about Jordan and you said you didn't like anyone."

Georgie couldn't ignore the slightly hurt expression on Lara's face. She drew Lara down the corridor away from the others. "Because I didn't think he liked me, and I was embarrassed."

"So what changed?"

Georgie smiled. "I got mad at him, and I just blurted it out."

"Really?" Lara was delighted.

"Really, and he was so shocked he was speechless."

"Then did he sweep you into his arms and kiss you?"

"No. It took him a couple of days to realise he felt the same way."

Lara shook her head and tutted. "Men."

Georgie laughed. "You've got that right. Come on, let's go check on them. I'm worried your dad might be upset."

"Why? He loves you both."

"Because he's a man."

Lara thought about it a moment and then nodded. "Good point."

They headed back to the kitchen.

# Chapter 15

"Let's walk," Darcy said, moving away from the house without waiting for an answer.

Matt cringed. He couldn't read Darcy's expression, didn't know if he was angry or upset. He had to make this right. "I'm sorry."

Darcy turned and raised an eyebrow. "You're sorry about dating Georgie?"

No, he'd never be sorry for that. He shook his head.

"Good. What I want to know is, why didn't you tell me sooner?"

Matt stared at him, surprised. Of all the reactions he'd envisioned, it hadn't included this. "I didn't know how you'd react. You've always been protective of her."

"Won't you treat her well?"

"Of course I will."

"Then what?"

Matt was silent while he sorted out his emotions. "Because I'm not good enough for her."

Darcy stepped back, eyes wide. "Why would you think that?"

Matt shrugged as all of his insecurities from his childhood battered him. Of being other, being poor and dumb.

"You're my best friend," Darcy said. "Do you think I'm that bad a judge of character?"

"You don't have a lot of options out here," Matt said, trying to make a joke, but it fell flat.

Darcy stared at him in the take-no-shit expression his father had sometimes worn. "You kept me sane," Darcy said. "When you started working at the Ridge I was on the verge of a breakdown."

Matt frowned. "What?" He didn't remember that.

"Sofia was pregnant, Mum was still lost in her grief over Charlie, we barely saw Dad, and I was trying to finish school and keep the family together. You helped remind Mum there was a world out there, and you helped with all the chores. It was a relief."

Matt stared at him. "I had no idea."

"Life got easier when you arrived, not just with the station work, but at home. I could talk to you without worrying about saying the wrong thing."

Matt remembered a couple of times when Darcy had spoken about getting Sofia pregnant and how he'd been worried about being a teenaged father. "I'm glad I helped. The Ridge was always a haven for me." Somewhere he could be with no judgement.

"You helped keep this place together," Darcy said. "I can't think of a better person for Georgie than you."

It was Matt's turn to gape. "Really?"

"Yeah. I had no idea you felt that way about her."

"Neither did I."

At Darcy's raucous laugh, heat rushed to Matt's face. "I buried my feelings deep because I didn't want to ruin things here." He sighed. "And I had no idea she loved me."

"She had a massive crush on you as a teenager, but I didn't realise she still cared," Darcy said. "I'm happy for you both." He clapped Matt on the shoulder. "Let's go eat."

Matt smiled and followed him. Just like that, everything was all right. He shouldn't have doubted.

Everyone was sitting at the kitchen table, and he sat in the free seat next to Georgie. He kissed her cheek.

"No black eye," Georgie observed.

"It's all good," he murmured.

"It had better be." She glared at Darcy who spoke to Faith.

"I'll tell you about it later," Matt promised and poured her a glass of water. Happiness filled him at her smile, and he squeezed her knee.

She grinned wider. "You want to play footsies under the table?"

He tensed. "Not with the family around." But now she'd put those thoughts in his head, "I'm feeling pretty tired though. I might have to go to bed early tonight."

She faked a yawn. "Now that you mention it, I'm pretty exhausted as well."

Brandon groaned. "Oh, please spare me. You're both sleeping in the shearers' quarters tonight, right?"

"Yes," Georgie answered.

"Hey, you can't complain." Matt glanced down the table to make sure Lara wasn't paying attention. "I recall you and Amy weren't anywhere near as subtle in the beginning."

He grinned. "It's one of my fondest memories." He passed Matt a bowl. "Salad?"

Matt relaxed. "Thanks."

Everything was fine.

***

Georgie woke and groaned as her muscles spasmed around her. She was squashed between the wall, Matt's leg wrapped around hers and his arm covering her waist.

Spending the night sharing a single bed was not

something she'd recommend. Not that they'd done much sleeping. She shifted, trying to lift Matt's arm off, but instead it tightened around her. She glanced at his face.

His dark eyes were slightly unfocused. "Where do you think you're going?" he murmured.

She smiled, unable to help herself. "I'm trying to get some feeling back in my body."

He shifted, running his hand up and down her side. "You feel fine to me."

"You're hilarious." But his hands were making her feel a lot better. She stretched, pressing her body into his and suddenly she was on her back and he was on top of her, his whole body awake.

She forgot about her aching muscles as desire pooled between her legs.

Matt kissed her neck. "You said you were on the pill, didn't you?"

"Yes."

His hand moved to touch her core and she shuddered at the wave of desire.

"Now," she agreed to his unasked question.

He slipped inside her, and they both sighed. She would never get tired of this. He moved slowly as he kissed her neck, murmuring her name over and over. His fingers caressed her breasts as if they were fragile and precious and she arched into him, the desire building. "Faster," she whispered.

He kissed the side of her mouth. "Don't be so impatient. I like taking my time with you."

His words aroused her further and she moaned in protest, but he kept up the slow, sweet torture as he moved inside her and covered her neck and face in kisses. She was drowning in sensation.

"We'll have to go back to your place tonight," he said. "There are so many things I want to do with you and this bed isn't big enough." His pace increased slightly and she tilted her hips, wanting more.

He groaned as she encircled her legs around him, and thrust.

"More, Matt," she begged. "I need more."

"Georgie." He shifted and his thrusts were deeper, faster, stronger.

"Yes." She gripped the sheets as her orgasm washed over her like waves on a shore, over and over and over. Matt thrust faster and then he shouted her name and slid down on top of her, still part of her. He kissed her neck as he whispered, "I love you."

Georgie bit her lip as she squeezed him against her, not wanting this moment to end. "I love you more."

He chuckled. "Not possible." He shifted off her and sat to clean up. Georgie joined him, not ready to be so far away.

"What time is it?" he asked.

She glanced at her phone and her eyes widened. "Nine." She hadn't slept this late in a long time, but they hadn't got to sleep until the early hours of the morning.

"I'm surprised Lara hasn't woken us," Matt commented.

That's right. They were going through the journals again today. "Maybe they started without us."

Quickly they showered and dressed before heading over to the house for breakfast. Everyone sat at the kitchen table and there was the strong scent of bacon and coffee. Lara glanced at them. "Finally! I didn't think you would ever wake."

Georgie swallowed her smile. "We've been working hard."

Brandon snorted.

"Why didn't you wake us?" Matt asked.

"Dad wouldn't let me," Lara said. "Said you needed rest."

Georgie was by the coffee machine. She mouthed *thank you* at Darcy while Lara spoke with Matt. He nodded with a smirk.

"So what's the plan for the day?" Georgie poured two coffees and gave one to Matt.

"We need to share our notes," Faith said. "You haven't been around to hear our theories, and Matt hasn't told us what he's found."

Georgie glanced at Matt. "You've found something?" She hadn't known he was still involved. She'd thought it was just Lara and Faith who were searching.

"Amy made me a copy the other day. I've been going through the Dutch journal."

"It can't be too far from the house," Faith insisted. "It would have been difficult to carry."

"They split the treasure with the other two Fenians," Darcy reminded her. "It might not have been a lot at all."

Georgie picked bacon from the plate in the middle of the table and then handed some to Matt. "Lilian doesn't strike me as a foolish woman. She would have known a cyclone can change the landscape, so she would have chosen somewhere lasting."

"Like the ridge?" Lara asked.

She nodded, smiling. Lara had always been convinced treasure had been buried somewhere on the ridge.

"What about the island?" Amy asked.

"Would she have hidden it where she knew the pearl divers would look?" Brandon asked. "They had the Dutch version of those journals."

"What do the clues say again?" Matt asked, staring at a spot in the middle of the table.

"Where shelter, food and water collide, you will find the treasure hide," Lara answered.

"Could she mean salt not fresh water?" He looked at Faith. "We've been assuming fresh water because shelter, food and fresh water are what you need to survive, but maybe she meant the ocean. They would have eaten a lot of seafood during the early years as it was more what they were used to compared with kangaroo and goanna."

"So we're looking for shelter along the coast?" Georgie asked.

"Maybe." He shrugged. "There are a few inlets with salt water as well."

"Or she could be referring to the river or the ridge canyon," Faith argued. "Water definitely collides there after a storm."

"Let me get the map," Darcy said.

They cleared the table while he went to get it. "Let's assume for now they kept the treasure within view of the homestead," Darcy said. "We can expand our search after we've covered that." He pointed to places on the map. "That leaves us the riverbed, the wetlands and the ridge."

"There's no shelter near the wetlands," Brandon said, glancing at Matt for confirmation.

Matt nodded. "And they probably would have dried before Lilian and Reginald arrived."

"I've never noticed any shelter near the riverbed," Amy said from near the pantry where she was putting together backpacks with snacks and drinks for their expedition. "We gathered a lot of rock from there when we made the new sites for the campgrounds."

"We should walk it again though," Lara said. "Just to be sure."

Georgie smiled. "We've all explored the ridge as kids and found every cave there."

"Yeah, but we never really looked for treasure," Brandon said. "Plus there's the coin Ed found as a kid."

"He still can't remember where he found it though," Georgie argued. "It could have been anywhere." They'd covered this ground already. She studied the page of the journal and then gasped. "Maybe Lilian meant a different type of hide," she said. "We've assumed she means it's hidden in the shelter, but maybe she means a camouflaged hide, you know the types used to look at animals."

"So it's a hidden shelter?" Lara asked.

Georgie shrugged. "Maybe."

"That puts a different spin on things," Brandon said.

Lara jigged in her seat. "This is so epic!"

"How about we do one more pass along the ridge and riverbed today?" Amy suggested. "For all we know, she might have hidden the treasure in a termite mound."

Brandon laughed. "That would be clever. Hidden in plain sight."

"We can't dig up every mound," Darcy said, glancing at Lara sternly.

She pouted but nodded.

Matt squeezed Georgie's hand. "We can do the riverbed."

"Sure." It would give them time together alone.

Amy handed out the backpacks full of water, sun cream and snacks. "Grab a radio on your way out." It was just the way Georgie's mum had done.

Georgie smiled through the pinch of sorrow, and on a whim hugged her. "Thanks, Ames. You're just like Mum."

Amy squeezed her. "I was taught by the best."

Matt waited for her by the door and when they stepped outside, the others had already piled into Brandon's ute. Amy jogged over to join them. Georgie waved and took Matt's hand. They walked to the riverbed which lay half a kilometre from the homestead. It had been a while since she'd been this way. She closed her eyes listening to the sounds of the insects buzzing through the shrubs and the birds calling around them. Peaceful. Like the home she remembered. Speaking of which… "What did Darcy say to you last night?"

They hadn't done much talking when they retired early to bed the night before. She smiled at the memory.

"He wanted to know why I never said anything about how I felt."

"He didn't give you the third degree about your intentions?" Georgie was surprised.

"No. He said he couldn't think of a better person for you." Matt shook his head as if he couldn't believe it.

Matt's words filled her with warmth towards Darcy. He'd been one of the constants in her life and she wanted him to approve. "Finally, one of my brothers got something right," Georgie joked, and kissed Matt's cheek. He caught her in his arms before she had a chance to step back and deepened the kiss.

So much passion.

"I can't get enough of you," he said when he finally stepped back.

"Me neither." She glanced around. Not a lot of cover and the fine red dirt would stick to their clothing.

"Georgie, while I like the direction your mind is going, we should focus on the search, at least until we get bored, or far enough from the camp sites that we're not likely to run into any of the campers."

He was right. Her family might be able to see them from the ridge and Lara had packed binoculars. This wasn't the type of education she wanted to give her niece.

"Should we go south or north when we get to the riverbed?" she asked.

"Let's head south first."

A few small gum trees clung to the edge of the dry riverbed. It only had water in it after a storm and it lasted only a few days before sinking below the sand. They hadn't had any rain since the storm which had almost killed Lara and Faith.

Georgie shivered.

The trees shaded the riverbed and there weren't too

many rocks. What remained after Lilian and Reginald had settled here had been used when they marked out the campground bays.

"Do you know of any shelters along here?" Georgie asked.

"No."

Lilian sounded like an intelligent woman. "I can't imagine they would bury anything so close to the river. They wouldn't want it washing away."

"Perhaps they hadn't seen it full of water when they buried it."

"But they would have known it was a riverbed. It's obvious."

"Should we expand the search to a few metres either side of the river?" he asked.

No rocky outcrops along here, only small sand dunes, but, "What would they have used to build a hide? Surely anything organic would have broken down by now."

Matt shrugged. "Wood. Mud. Maybe sheets of tin if they'd brought some with them."

A hide should be obvious on this mostly flat landscape. "The river's our best bet for the water element. We can bring the horses back later and explore further afield."

"As you wish."

Those words again. Georgie turned to Matt. "Why do you say that?"

"What?"

"As you wish."

He frowned, thinking about it. "Aren't they from the movie you like so much? You made me watch it over and over again after Charlie died."

"In The Princess Bride they mean I love you."

Matt's eyes widened. "Oh. Did I know that?" The second part was said more to himself than Georgie. "I don't know. Maybe sub-consciously I did." He squeezed her hand. "You're so wrapped up in almost all my memories of this place."

She understood that. "My first clear memory of you was when I was about seven. You caught the bus home with us, because you were staying the weekend with Charlie."

"I'd been to the Ridge before then."

"I know, but this memory is crystal clear. Charlie was going on about wanting you to teach him how to track animals, and both Ed and I wanted to join you. Charlie didn't want us tagging along, but you said, 'They can come. They're part of this land too.'"

Matt raised his eyebrows. "I don't remember that."

"It was a pivotal moment for me. Usually Mum ordered the boys to let me tag along, and here you were allowing me to come of your own free will. I thought you were the best." She grinned. "After that, I pestered Charlie to invite you over more often."

"You're why he invited me out?" Matt asked.

"No, he was going to ask you anyway, but I did bug him a lot. Mum had to tell me to stop."

"At the time I thought you were adorable. I always wanted younger siblings, because Nhiari was already a teenager and thought she was cooler than me."

"Charlie reached that stage far earlier." Georgie sighed. "I still miss him though. He was always so thrilling, just a little bit naughty, but he almost always had time for me."

"He wanted to make sure you could do all the fun stuff— be the best motorbike rider, shoot a gun, ride a horse. He found the girls at school weak and hated how they screamed at spiders and snakes."

Georgie grimaced. "Well he failed in that regard."

"You don't scream." Matt slipped an arm around her waist.

"Maybe I should do something about it," she said. "I

hate that I freeze."

"I think Jerry has a pet tarantula," Matt suggested.

Georgie shivered. "I knew there was a reason Jerry wasn't right for me."

Matt chuckled. "You would have been bored in an hour. Jerry likes to hear himself talk."

"Then why are you friends?"

"We're team mates more than anything. I hated him at school."

"Wait, was Jerry the bully?"

Matt nodded.

Georgie stared at him. "Wow, I didn't realise that. I never would have got a lift with him if I'd known."

"It was a long time ago."

She shook her head. "He was a troll of the worst kind. Ugh, I can't believe you can even speak to him after what he did."

"It's not worth my time hating him anymore."

So mature. She hugged him. "I'm glad." They reached the wetlands where the river ended and the rocks were much more sporadic. "Shall we search the other direction?"

"Yeah. Do you want to go out to dinner tonight?"

Georgie jolted and glanced at him. "You mean a date?"

He smiled and tipped his hat. "Yeah. I figured we haven't done anything normal yet."

She loved the idea of going out in public with him. "What about the treasure hunt? We're supposed to search the gulf tomorrow."

"We can come back. I'd much prefer to sleep in your bed tonight."

"Absolutely." She stretched, shifting some of the kinks. "Where do you want to go?"

"How about the brewery?"

"Sounds good."

They retraced their steps. Along the way a racehorse goanna trundled down the slope and into the riverbed in front of them. They both stopped to watch. Goannas generally weren't aggressive, and they looked so slow with their careful steps, but they could run fast when provoked.

Georgie sighed. "Those smugglers had dozens of reptiles of all sizes in the back of their car. I can't understand how anyone can look at one and only see a pay check."

"Not everyone respects nature," Matt replied. "What are the police doing?"

"Like Dot would ever tell me." Georgie snorted. "Why don't you ask Nhiari?"

"Same reason. Did Darcy ever tell you we found signs of a camp on Retribution Island?"

"No." She'd have to ask Amy and Faith if they knew.

"It was packed away in one of the caves. Looks like they leave supplies there for when they need to use the island."

So Stonefish could be out there at any time. She hated the thought. Her family often went swimming at the gulf and the idea someone was spying on them gave her chills.

"It's why I went with you when you were searching for the shipwreck," Matt continued. "I didn't want you going on the island alone."

"I'm glad you did." It had led to this moment.

"Me too."

# Chapter 16

Another hour went by as Matt and Georgie searched the riverbed. It was a little shaded which kept the heat down. Nothing around them could be the shelter Lilian spoke of and Matt hadn't seen any evidence of a camouflaged hide. They were probably wasting their time in terms of the treasure search, but being with Georgie, alone, was never a wasted opportunity. As they navigated around a particularly rocky section, half a dozen stacked rocks on the riverbank caught his attention. "What's that?" Matt pointed and his pulse raced as they both scrambled over. The rocks were piled in too orderly a fashion for them to be natural.

"Anyone could have piled them up," Georgie said.

He nodded. "But it looks like a directional cairn. Take some photos from each angle." She always had her phone on her.

Georgie did as he asked and then they both examined the pile of rocks. "So which way does it point?"

"North." He looked west and in the distance he saw the homestead almost directly across. It was luck Amy and Lara hadn't destroyed the cairn while they'd been gathering rocks for the campgrounds. Or maybe Lara had built it when she'd grown bored.

That was the most likely scenario.

Georgie slipped her hand into his and a rush of affection swept through him. "Do you think anything is buried underneath it?"

He studied the base of the cairn. "Looks like it's on more rock."

"You didn't build it with Charlie as kids?" she asked. "Charlie went through an explorer phase."

"Not that I remember, but Charlie might have built it on his own." And if he had, he would have thought it a hoot they were following it.

"So we head north?"

"Yeah." He was fairly sure it couldn't be as old as they hoped. There'd been too many cyclones over the years for the rocks to stay in place.

"Do you think there'll be any more?"

He had no idea. "Might not be another one until we have to change direction. The river's a clear path."

They followed the riverbed until the main road intersected it. They both stared at the bitumen. "Well, this wouldn't have been here in Lilian's time." Georgie swung the backpack off and sat under the shade of the last tree along the riverbed. She passed Matt a bottle of water and then opened one for herself, gulping it down before wiping the sweat off her brow.

Disappointment curled in Matt's gut. "I never realised the road cut the river in half."

"They probably didn't even notice it," Georgie said. "It's dry most of the time."

During the last storm, the water pooled on the edges of the road but hadn't washed it out. "I'll let the others know we're crossing to the other side." Matt got the radio out and spoke briefly with Darcy.

"You found anything?" Darcy asked.

"We found a stack of stones which could be a

directional cairn. Anyone your end know anything about them?"

Silence for a moment before Darcy came back on. "No. None of us built it."

That was something. "We'll keep following the river then. Any luck there?"

"Nothing. Let me know when you're ready to turn back and we'll pick you up," Darcy said.

"Thanks." He finished the bottle of water and handed it back to Georgie. Then he held the fence open so she could slip through. She rolled her eyes as she did so. "You know I fit through easier than you do." She held the wire open for him.

"I know." But he wanted to do little gestures for her. Things that showed her he cared.

The other end of the river picked up about twenty metres from the road.

Matt scanned the bank but saw nothing out of place.

"Your mum is coming in on Tuesday to finish reviewing the signs at the national park," Georgie said. "She seems really happy with the progress."

"It's nice to be acknowledged," Matt said.

"Yeah, it's far too long in the coming," Georgie agreed.

Matt understood how important this was to his mother. Their people had been stripped of their land, their identity and their family, and were now struggling to reclaim their language and their culture. A lot of progress had been made in terms of recognising land ownership over the past decade or so, but it was difficult to reclaim culture and language when people had been beaten if they tried to practise it. A lot of knowledge had died with the elders who had come before them. "How long will it take for the signs to be made?"

Georgie shrugged. "I imagine it'll be a month or more. Then we'll need to erect them."

"Mum's thinking about running cultural tours." It wasn't common knowledge but he wanted Georgie's reaction.

She turned to him. "You mean sharing Bayungu language and culture?"

He nodded.

"That's an awesome idea. I bet heaps of people would love to learn. Tourists are always asking what else there is to do around Retribution Bay."

Her enthusiasm made him smile and relax. "I'm trying to help her, but I've got no idea."

"I can help. She could start with one or two options, build a website and then advertise. Are you going to run any of the tours?"

He shrugged. "Mum's asked, but I'm busy on the Ridge."

"Darcy would give you time, if you want to."

She was right, but he'd spent so much of his life at odds with his culture, it was hard to get enthusiastic about it. Jerry's words were always clear in his head as were those of others like him. "Maybe Amy can help with the website."

"Absolutely. She did a great job on the Ridge's site." Georgie stumbled on the uneven ground and Matt grabbed her before she fell, holding her tight. Her face was red and sweaty and it was getting close to midday.

"Good reflexes." Georgie took her hat off and wiped the sweat from her brow. "Have you had enough yet?"

"It's definitely time for a lunch break." He radioed Darcy to pick them up and then got the multi-purpose tool from his pocket and made a mark on the trunk of one of the nearby trees. "We'll have to mark the beach track as well so we don't lose our place." He slipped his hand into Georgie's as they headed towards the track that led to the gulf. He made a few more markings in the trees so they could easily find their way back. Georgie dug around in the backpack when they reached the road and with a shout of triumph, she pulled out one of Lara's scrunchies. "I knew there'd be one in here," she said. "Lara has them all over the place." She twisted the bright yellow band around a branch on a tree.

It didn't take long for Darcy to arrive. "The others are getting lunch ready. Find any more cairns?"

"Not yet," Matt answered. "How did you go?"

"Nothing," Darcy answered. "If there were any clues at the bottom of the Ridge they would have washed away long ago. I can't imagine them lugging a potentially heavy chest up the Ridge."

He had a point. The Ridge had quite a steep incline and though the horses could make it up, a cart wouldn't.

"Lara wants to check out the plaque so let's go swimming this afternoon." Darcy said. "It's hot enough."

"Good idea," Georgie said.

Matt smiled. Georgie never passed the opportunity for a swim.

They got back to the house and the table was spread with makings for sandwiches. The others had already started, and Matt took the plate Brandon handed him and sat next to Georgie.

"Did you find anything?" Lara asked, her eyes wide and hopeful.

"Only the one cairn," Matt answered.

Lara gasped. "Tell me everything."

Matt chuckled and on Georgie's gesture, told them about the cairn they'd found. When he was finished, he glanced at Brandon and Brandon said, "I've never noticed it."

Georgie was typing a text on her phone, probably asking Ed the same question.

"We should follow the river to see if we can find more," Lara said.

It was a decent distance to cover to get to the ocean. "How about we each do a section? Someone can drop the others along the river and we can meet up. If anyone spots more cairns that point in a different direction, we can radio it in."

"Good idea," Georgie agreed. "We'll cover more ground."

Darcy got out the map again and measured the distance. It was about ten kilometres so if each couple did a few kilometres, they could finish it in a couple of hours.

With a new plan and Lara encouraging them all to hurry, it didn't take long to finish eating and head back out again.

As they crossed the road, Georgie's phone beeped. She read the message and grinned. "Ed says he remembers where he found the coin!"

"Where?" Matt asked, excitement rising.

"Near one of the tidal inlets, not far from the plaque."

"Should we go there now?"

"There are lots of inlets. Let's focus on the cairns first. They might point us to the right one."

She had a point. Matt helped Georgie down from the back of the ute when Darcy stopped next to the yellow scrunchie. Georgie untied the hair tie and waved as the ute continued down the track. Darcy would drop the others at intervals and then pick them up later. Lara had been concerned her father was missing out, but Matt was fairly sure he'd got the best gig, sitting in an air-conditioned car while the rest of them searched for potentially non-existent directional cairns which may or may not be pointers to treasure.

"Honestly," Georgie said, when they'd stopped for a drink break. "There'd better be something at the end of this."

Matt grinned. "Isn't the journey supposed to be the

reward?"

She snorted. "No, a chest full of treasure is supposed to be the reward." She sighed. "How bad are the Ridge's finances"

He glanced at her. "We can't afford to replace the ute."

"Are we likely to lose the station?" Her voice was soft and full of concern.

"I don't know." He pulled her into his arms. "The campgrounds are bringing in enough for day-to-day needs."

"For the house, not the station."

"We'll get a boost of funds after shearing."

"My father could be so stubborn at times," Georgie said. "We should have made adjustments far sooner than this."

He wasn't going to speak ill of Bill, but Georgie was right. Dingoes and wild dogs had been attacking the flock for years and taking away their revenue and the droughts throughout the country hadn't been great for the price of feed. They should have moved to cattle and tourism.

They continued walking until they met Brandon and Amy coming from the opposite direction. Matt didn't have to ask whether they'd found anything, it was clear in their glum expressions. He radioed Darcy to pick them up.

As they drove towards the gulf to join Faith and Lara, the radio crackled. "We found something!" Lara called.

Georgie squeezed Matt's hand as Darcy answered, "Where are you, pumpkin?"

"Not far from the beach. We're heading to you."

They all scanned the bush as they neared the beach, looking for Faith and Lara. Lara raced out, waving her hands and Darcy stopped, winding down his window. "What did you find?"

"Another cairn, and it's pointing east."

Not a lot out this way. No shelter that he knew of, just the ocean and mangroves. They spread out and walked in a line moving away from the beach. A termite mound stuck up above the ground, making him at first think it was a rock.

After about ten minutes Faith called, "Over here."

They all congregated around a cairn on top of a larger rock.

They were only about twenty metres from the beach and the grass was flattened by tyre tracks.

Georgie sucked in a breath as Matt exchanged glances with Darcy and Brandon. The sheep had been moved from this area months ago when Stonefish had killed a bunch of them, but this was still Ridge land. Someone had been trespassing.

Bushes and shrubs surrounded the area, shielding it from the ocean.

"Where to now?" Lara asked.

Darcy placed a hand on her shoulder. "I don't think this is a treasure marker, pumpkin."

"What is it then?"

Matt studied the mound. A hollow metal tube was stuck between a circle of rocks. If someone stuck a flag in it, it would be high enough to be seen from Retribution Island. Maybe this was where Stonefish met. The tyre marks led towards the track they'd discovered about a month ago. That had led them to take a flight over the Ridge where they discovered more tracks crossing Ridge land.

"I don't know, pumpkin. How about we go swimming, and Matt and Brandon can look?"

"Something's wrong." Lara narrowed her eyes and studied the area. "Are the tyre tracks not ours?"

Darcy sighed. "No, they're not. We'll give Dot a call after we've gone swimming."

Lara slipped her hand into his. "OK. Let's go." She knew how dangerous Stonefish was.

Faith and Amy joined them while Matt studied the ground. "The tracks don't look new. Some of these plants are already brown and dying."

"But they've been here more than once," Brandon said.

Matt nodded.

"Assholes," Georgie said. "I bet this is where they ship out the animals."

"Animals?" Brandon asked.

She bit her lip and Matt grinned as Brandon said, "Spill it, Georgie."

"I caught some animal smugglers the other day in the national park. Dot arrested them."

"And you didn't tell us because…"

"It was work business and not on our land," she said.

Brandon glowered. "You promised no more secrets."

"You don't talk about army stuff."

"Dot and Nhiari will want to know," Matt interrupted, hoping to stop an argument. "There's nothing we can do now, so how about we join the others? I could do with a swim."

Georgie nodded and took his hand, not waiting for Brandon's agreement.

Brandon growled but followed.

The tide was heading out giving them a small strip of sand on which to lay their clothes. Darcy had driven the ute closer and unpacked the bag of towels and the esky of drinks.

Georgie grabbed a tube of sun cream. "Will you do my back?"

Matt took the cream as she stripped off her T-shirt. Wow. He must have avoided looking at Georgie in her bathers in the past because there was no way he could have not realised how sexy she was. The tiny bikini left very little to the imagination and although he'd already seen her naked, the bikini was a complete tease. "With pleasure," he murmured and proceeded to slowly rub the sun cream into her back making sure he didn't miss a spot. By the time he was done, everyone else was in the water and all he wanted to do was drag Georgie behind the dunes and have his way with her.

"I need to cool off in more than one way" Georgie said.

Matt chuckled. "Me too."

But he'd have to wait until they were alone.

# Chapter 17

After swimming, Georgie wrapped her towel around her waist and wandered away from the group to stare across at Retribution Island. It looked no different than usual, but it was creepy to think Stonefish Enterprises had set up a camp so close to them. If the smugglers she'd caught had been bringing the animals here, then surely there was a boat nearby. She sighed. Maybe the boat was only here at the designated rendezvous times. Lee had indicated that Stonefish wasn't finished with them yet.

"What's wrong?" Matt asked, sliding his arm around her.

She stopped twirling her fringe. "I'm wondering when Stonefish is going to surprise us again."

He kissed her forehead. "Yeah, it sucks not knowing. Did the guys you caught mention when their next rendezvous was?"

"No, but it's got to be soon," she said. "But that might change if Stonefish knows they were caught."

"The police don't have the resources to keep watch."

So more animals would be lost. She scanned the beach. "You want to go for a walk?" Maybe she could find a clue and she was curious to look for the inlet Ed had mentioned.

He nodded. "Sure. We looking for anything in particular?"

She shrugged and put a couple of new water bottles in her backpack and slipped on her bright blue Ningaloo T-shirt and her shorts. "Maybe there are more tracks on the other side of those we found."

The others were talking about the treasure, and Faith and Lara were rereading the plaque which listed the names of people who were on the Retribution. "We're going for a walk."

Brandon raised a hand in acknowledgement as he finished drying himself. "Be careful."

Georgie slipped her hand into Matt's as they wandered along the sand. "There's got to be some kind of staging post, right? Somewhere they gather the animals from all their smugglers and then take them out to the island."

"You think it's more than just the two you caught?"

She nodded. "Definitely. Their area was south of the ranges. Surely an operation like Stonefish would have more lackeys getting animals from all over."

"They wouldn't hang around for long though."

He was right. "So maybe they all deliver on one night, but at different times."

They reached one of the inlets and waded across. At low tide it would be easy to cross in a four-wheel drive, but there were no tyre marks. This way led to the new track they'd discovered recently. The one Lee had used to flee the scene after he'd shot Tan. "Did you and Darcy investigate the track Lee escaped on?"

"Yeah, but only to see where it came out. We knew it ended at the beach."

They reached the track with deep tyre grooves in the sand. Matt frowned. "That's made by more than one car."

Georgie tensed. "So someone has been here regularly?"

Matt nodded and unclipped the radio on his shorts. "Darcy, have you or Brandon been on Lee's track?"

Georgie held her breath until Darcy replied, "No. What gives?"

"Looks like it's been used since then. We'll take a look."

"Be careful."

They followed the track almost a kilometre back to where they'd found the cairn. This had to be the rendezvous point. Georgie avoided walking in the tyre tracks in case the police could get a mould. She moved through the bush towards the beach. Gouge marks in the sand at the high tide mark proved a boat had been there recently. She scowled. "They've been here since the police searched the island."

Matt nodded and crouched to take a closer look at the sand. "There's a good footprint here." He radioed Darcy. "If you guys are finished, do you want to head back to the house and call Nhiari?"

"You found something?"

"Some tracks. The police might be able to get something useful."

"You two got enough water?"

Georgie nodded at Matt's questioning glance. "Yeah. If the police are going to be too long, you can pick us up."

"Roger that."

It was a short boat ride to Retribution Island and a few smaller islands dotted beyond it. "Did you guys check out the other islands as well as Retribution?" Georgie asked.

"No. We didn't have time."

The police might have, but Georgie was curious what was out there. "After Dot and Nhiari arrive, maybe we should bring Dad's dinghy down and look."

Matt looked incredulous. "You think Dot and Nhiari will be cool with that?"

Georgie grinned. "All right, after they leave."

"We shouldn't get involved, Georgie. These guys are dangerous."

Georgie studied him. "If it was Darcy suggesting it, would you answer differently?"

Matt at least had the grace to look her in the eye. "Fair point. I don't want you to get hurt."

"But you don't care about Darcy?" She was pushing him, she knew it.

"He can take care of himself."

Georgie just raised her eyebrows at him.

Matt drew her close. "The thought of you on those guys' radar gives me chills. I've seen what they can do, what they can make average people do in order to save their loved ones." He kissed her. "The day the Ridge flooded was terrifying. I didn't know who was alive, and I kept imagining seeing Faith's or Lara's bodies floating past me." He stiffened in her arms and Georgie stroked his back. She'd never considered what it had been like for him. He'd been stuck on the other side of the flood waters unable to help.

"Then we won't investigate the other islands."

He kissed her again. "Thank you."

It was an easy promise knowing how much it scared him, and Lee's words niggled in the back of her brain. *Tan is the least of your worries.* She didn't want to get too close, didn't want anyone to come after her or her loved ones. "What do you want to do while we're waiting then?"

His hands dipped lower. "I can think of a few things to keep us occupied."

She grinned. "Do tell."

And Matt proceeded to show her exactly how creative

he was.

***

Matt almost didn't hear the police car arriving. If it hadn't been for Georgie pushing him away, he would have missed the rumble of the engine through his haze of desire. Georgie clambered to her feet and tied her bikini top back into place, brushing the sand from her body before replacing her T-shirt and hat. Such a shame to see her clothed. She combed her fingers through her hair. "How do I look?"

"Like you've been making out on the sand." He grinned and adjusted himself, staring off into the bush trying to ignore his rock-hard boner. If his sister was in the car, he didn't want her to see him like this.

Yep, the thought of Nhiari did the trick and he got to his feet, brushing the sand off Georgie's back. He checked the time. Less than an hour since Darcy and the others had left.

Not enough time for the police to get here.

His heart leapt as he scanned the surroundings for somewhere to hide. There weren't a lot of shrubs. "Georgie, it can't be Dot."

Her eyes widened, but immediately she headed away from the turnaround spot and into the bush. They moved to what little shelter there was behind the low trees.

Georgie's Akubra hid her blue hair, but her T-shirt was too bright. He stripped off his darker shirt. "Put this on." While she did so, he did a quick sweep to ensure no animal traps were in the area.

Clear.

He crouched next to Georgie as the vehicle pulled to a stop and cut its engine. They were too far away to see anything. He switched off the radio in case someone tried to contact them and scanned the area behind them, mapping out their escape route.

Two car doors shut and then voices raised. "Are you sure they're gone?" a female asked.

"You saw the ute drive away," a deep male voice answered. "The drone followed it back to the house. They won't be back today."

Matt's skin prickled. The male voice was familiar, but he couldn't quite pick it.

"How long do we have to wait?"

"He should be here within ten minutes if he knows what's good for him."

Matt exchanged a glance with Georgie. They had to be the smugglers, and higher on the chain than the two Georgie had caught. Getting a look at them would help Nhiari. He leaned closer to Georgie and whispered, "Have you got your phone?"

She nodded and slipped it out of her pocket.

He held out his hand for it and she shook her head.

Like hell she was taking the photos. "I blend better." She sighed, handing him the phone. He passed her the radio and then made sure her phone was on silent. "Move further back. Radio Darcy and tell him what's happening."

Georgie kissed him. "Be careful."

Matt nodded and waited until she'd moved another twenty metres away and he couldn't see her. Then he moved forward, muscles tense, keeping an eye on where he stepped. The pair had stopped speaking, but he smelled cigarette smoke. Idiots could start a bush fire if they weren't careful.

He peered through some bushes and spotted the sleek, brand new black Dodge RAM. Matt almost laughed. No way they would blend in with a car like that. He took a photo of the car, making sure to get the licence plate number and then sent it to Nhiari's phone. No signal, but it would send when there was one.

He crept around the clearing, trying to spot the two people. He followed the cigarette scent and found the peroxide blonde woman looking bored, waving her hand to shoo flies next to the passenger side of the car. "Can't we wait in the aircon, Mark?"

Mark moved around the back of the car. "No, I want to hear them coming." He was short and stocky with thick crooked fingers as if they'd been broken a time or two. His head was shaved, and the bright Hawaiian shirt and board shorts screamed tourist, but he wasn't. He was Dot's brother.

He lived in Carnarvon now, but still had plenty of friends in town. Matt had played him in the football finals last year and he'd spoken to Jerry at the restaurant the other night.

Dot was going to be devastated.

"Them? I thought it was one guy."

"You're here as my cover, not to ask questions, Tory. If anyone catches us, I say I'm looking for a good fishing spot and what do you say?"

"I told him not to come this way. He never listens to me." Tory sounded bored. She flicked her cigarette butt into the bush.

Matt cringed. He couldn't see where it landed, but she didn't seem to care.

"Jesus, Tory are you trying to start a fire?" Mark strode over and stomped on the butt and then picked it up. "We leave no traces."

Tory rolled her eyes.

Mark moved over to her and grabbed her chin, forcing her to look at him. "This is not a game. The people who fund your lifestyle can rip it away before you can blink." He let her go and she stepped back, rubbing her chin, eyes concerned.

"You said it was nothing for me to worry about."

"It's not, as long as you do what I tell you." Mark

swore. "I knew I shouldn't have brought you along."

Matt took a couple more photos and sent them to Nhiari. In the distance he heard an engine.

Mark stiffened. "Here he comes."

Still too soon to be the police. Matt glanced in the direction Georgie had gone. She'd start to worry if he was too long, but he wanted to get a photo of whoever they were meeting. Hopefully Georgie would be patient.

The thought made him shift to leave, but the four-wheel-drive pulled up. Too late.

Matt's jaw dropped as the man climbed out. What the hell was Jerry doing here?

Jerry saluted Mark. "Good to see you." Without waiting for an answer, he went around the back of the car and opened it.

Mark did the same with the back of the ute, rolling back the cover. "What have you got for me today?"

"Everything on the list, though the goanna gave me trouble."

Matt stared. So this was why Jerry had money to burn. The bastard. He clenched his teeth. Jerry hadn't changed from the sneaky asshole he'd been at school. He didn't care who or what he hurt as long as he wasn't caught. Matt squeezed his hands into fists, fighting the urge to burst forward and confront him. No, it would be far sweeter to have the evidence he needed so Jerry would finally pay for his crimes.

He exhaled at the thought and took a few more photos as the men transferred the containers of reptiles to the ute. Through the clear plastic he spotted several snakes, various lizards and in one large cage a very unhappy racehorse goanna.

"You were supposed to tranquilise the big reptiles," Mark complained.

"I did. I mustn't have used enough."

Tory watched from a safe distance, a frown on her

face.

Matt should get back to Georgie. She'd definitely be worried by now. Just as he was about to move, another noise reached his ears. An engine, but a boat not a car, and he was between the gulf and the parked cars. Time to move.

Mark swore. "He's early. Tory, go see if it's a silver dinghy. Should be one guy on board."

Tory did as he asked, walking right past Matt. Shit. If she turned around she'd see him crouched by the bush.

He checked to ensure Mark and Jerry were busy moving animals and shifted across to the next bush, then the next, keeping a close eye on all parties, his pulse racing.

He wanted to get a photo of whoever was on that boat too.

A hand clamped onto his arm and he flinched, spinning to find Georgie right next to him looking pissed. "I thought you'd been caught," she murmured into his ear.

"Sorry," he whispered and then motioned for them to move further away.

Georgie followed and when they were far enough, she said, "What's going on?"

"Transfer of animals. Someone is coming from the ocean to get them."

"Did you get photos?"

He nodded. "Did you get through to Darcy?"

"Yeah. He and Brandon are talking to Dot and Nhiari. They'll go down one track and the police the other. That way the smugglers can't escape."

The boat engine died and Matt gestured for Georgie to follow him. They crept back to the beach where a large silver dinghy was pulled up against the sand. Matt crouched behind a clump of mangroves and snapped a photo. The tall man who got out pulled his hat low over his face and moved fast with a lethal grace, scanning his surroundings, his hand resting on his hip.

No, on his gun holster.

Matt's blood ran cold. "We need to get out of here."

"This way." Georgie moved away, darting from shrub to shrub, and Matt followed keeping an eye behind them. Not much cover, but the dark shirt she now wore made her more difficult to see. He heard voices but couldn't make out the words until an unfamiliar voice shouted, "Go!"

Matt expected to hear the cars' engines but instead he heard the crash of people moving through the bush. Shit.

Georgie dragged him into one of the inlets and they moved along the muddy bottom, leaving a clear trail. As he was about to point it out, Georgie crossed to the other side and climbed out moving through a gap in the mangroves. "Can you see where they are?"

Matt ducked, dragging Georgie with him as he spotted Jerry bumbling his way towards them.

"I found a T-shirt," Tory called.

Jerry reached the inlet and looked down, spotting their footprints. He scanned the far side of the bank and Matt ducked his head.

"This way," Jerry called.

"What the fuck is Jerry doing here?" Georgie hissed.

"Later," Matt said. "Somehow they know we're here. Come on."

Georgie moved with him as they sneaked further away from the inlet. He glanced over his shoulder and spotted Jerry as he pushed his way through mangroves and stood on their side. Jerry's mouth dropped open. He glanced back and then forward again his indecision clear. Matt shook his head and placed a finger to his lips.

Jerry screwed up his face and in that moment Matt knew Jerry was going to rat them out. "Run!"

Jerry yelled, "They're here."

"Georgie, go!" Speed was more important than stealth. He followed Georgie, keeping behind her to make sure no one could get a clear shot at her. Georgie grabbed the radio from her belt. "We need a little help here."

A gunshot cracked over their heads and dust kicked up in front of them.

Fuck. Fear lent him speed as he pounded along the dirt behind Georgie.

"They're shooting at us," Georgie called into the radio as she darted in the opposite direction, putting a couple more shrubs between them.

Almost immediately a police siren echoed through the air. It was still some way off, but hopefully it would be enough to have the animal smugglers scurrying back to their cars and making a run for it.

Another shot rang out, followed by a grunt, and Matt checked behind him. No one was there.

Georgie circled around, heading towards the track.

"Slow down," Matt called. They were far enough ahead to hide now. He flinched at the third gunshot, but it was further away. It was quickly followed by a fourth.

Georgie gasped for breath next to him. "Which way?"

He nodded in the direction she'd been leading them. Brandon and Darcy would come down the new track.

In the distance was the whine of the boat dinghy. Was the guy with the gun leaving or had someone else stolen the dinghy to get away?

He heard no one behind them, but he kept checking. They reached the track as the sound of an engine grew louder, but the siren was still at a distance.

Please let it be Darcy.

Georgie radioed in. "You're about to reach us."

The ute tore around the curve with Darcy behind the wheel. Matt had never been so pleased to see anyone.

Darcy braked and Brandon leapt out of the passenger

seat, rifle raised, scanning the bush behind Matt and Georgie.

Georgie threw open the back door and jumped in, Matt right behind her.

"What's going on?" Darcy demanded as Brandon climbed into the tray of the ute and hit the roof of the cab twice.

As Darcy drove forward, he grabbed the radio. "We've got Georgie and Matt."

"Hang back," Nhiari replied. "We'll take care of this."

Darcy ignored the instruction and kept driving.

"Where are you going?" Georgie demanded. "Turn around."

Darcy's expression was grim. "We have to stop them."

Matt shook his head. "The guy with the gun is dangerous. He moves like he's had military training." Brandon would be a clear target on the tray of the ute.

"Someone's already taken the dinghy to escape," Georgie added.

The police sirens grew louder, coming from the west.

Brandon tapped the roof. "Faster!"

Darcy did as he was told, bumping over the rough track.

"What was Jerry doing there?" Georgie asked, not as breathless now.

"Delivering the animals he trapped," Matt told her.

"Ugh, asshole. He's never taking me home again."

"He'd better not. I might have to shoot him." The man who had professed that he would never hurt Matt again had turned on him. Jerry could have pretended he hadn't seen them. Though Matt had never really liked him, the betrayal still stung. It would be a pleasure to watch Nhiari arrest his ass.

Darcy pulled to a stop as they reached the parked cars. Brandon jumped down. "Stay in the car and stay low."

"Be careful," Georgie called.

The police sirens were coming from the direction of the ocean. They must have taken a track from the main road and be driving along the shore to get here so quickly. The sirens cut off and the silence was all encompassing.

Brandon moved around the site, rifle raised, ready to react.

Matt's heart lodged in his throat as he thought about Nhiari doing something similar on the beach. She'd be the closest to the person escaping. He'd never seen her in action before, never really realised how dangerous her job was.

Georgie squeezed his hands. "They'll be fine." Her voice wasn't steady.

Matt swore. "I didn't warn Dot about Mark." She should be prepared.

"Her brother Mark?" Darcy asked.

Matt nodded. "That was the other guy."

Georgie looked horrified as Darcy reached for the radio. Matt grabbed his arm. "Don't. You'll give away their position." Make them an easy target. "I should go." He moved to get out of the car.

Georgie grabbed him. "You can't. Do you want them to shoot you accidentally?"

"We're sitting ducks here."

"I don't think so," Georgie said, her voice dull. "How many gunshots did you hear?"

"Four. The first one only just missed us."

"And how many people were there?"

Matt felt sick as realisation dawned. "Four."

Had the guy in the dinghy killed everyone before leaving?

He definitely needed to warn Dot. As he reached for the door handle Nhiari strode over to the car and yanked open the door. She dragged Matt out, hugging him.

Matt gaped at her as she trembled in his arms. Nhiari didn't do emotion. "*Gunyjan*, are you all right?"

She stepped back and cleared her throat. "Fine. I need to know exactly what happened."

"Where's Dot?" Georgie asked as she climbed out.

"She needs a minute."

Shit. "Are they dead?"

Nhiari nodded once and spoke into her radio. "We need to get forensics up here and get someone in the air. I want that dinghy tracked."

Matt pulled Georgie to his side and angled his body so she was between him and the car. "What happened?"

"I asked you first," Nhiari said.

He opened his mouth to protest and she cut him off. "From when you heard the car."

Her voice trembled and she blinked rapidly. Clearing her throat she said to Darcy, "You might as well get out too."

"Georgie heard the engine first," Matt said.

Georgie took up the story. When she got to the point where the dinghy guy arrived, Dot walked into the clearing, Brandon by her side. Her face was pale, eyes red.

Brandon crushed Georgie in a hug. "You're OK?"

She nodded.

Brandon let her go and hauled Matt forward, hugging him. "Thanks for protecting her."

"Always," Matt said.

Georgie smacked Brandon. "Hey, maybe I protected him."

Matt smiled and slipped his arm around her shoulders. "We kept each other safe."

"The man in the dinghy must have been monitoring the radio," Dot said.

Nhiari nodded. "It's the only way he could know Matt and Georgie were here. Georgie mentioned Matt was taking photos."

"That's why he shot them all," Dot said.

Matt flinched. "I'm sorry."

"Not your fault. Show me the photos." She was all business, but her tone was dull.

Matt handed over the phone.

Dot and Nhiari studied the photos. "Animal smuggling," Dot murmured. "Why?"

Nhiari squeezed her arm before handing Georgie's phone back. "We need those photos sent to the station *immediately.*"

"Are we in danger?" Georgie asked.

"The guy is likely long gone, but the sooner we can get his photo circulating, the safer you'll be."

Georgie nodded. "What about the animals?"

Nhiari sighed. "Take a look. Tell me what needs to be done."

Georgie crossed to the back of the Dodge RAM with Brandon.

"I'll document it," Dot said.

"I'll get the gear," Nhiari said, her shoulders slumped.

Georgie would be safe with Brandon. Matt followed his sister across to where the police car was parked on the shore. "You all right?"

She sighed. "I will be."

"That was Dot's brother, wasn't it?"

"Yeah."

"How's she holding up?"

"She'll get through it." Nhiari handed him a bag of equipment and took one for herself and they returned to the other vehicles.

"All these animals are from around here," Georgie said. "We can probably release them now if we can get the tape off."

"We need to document the scene," Dot said. "Darcy, take Georgie's phone and go find some reception. Send the pictures to the station."

Darcy nodded. "What about the others?"

"They can stay to help with the animals. When you're done, come back to pick them up."

Darcy handed out bottles of water from the esky in the ute and then drove off. Matt pulled Georgie into the shade and they sat while Dot and Nhiari worked the scene.

"I don't know how they can do it," Georgie said. "It's horrific enough without knowing those who were killed."

"Nhiari's always been strong," Matt said. She'd had to be.

"Dot's superwoman," Brandon said. "But she's going to need help."

About half an hour later, Dot crossed to them. "You can free the animals now." She turned to Nhiari. "Let's go deal with the rest."

Matt's heart twisted at the ache in her voice. Brandon stood and moved towards her, and Dot held up a hand. "Don't."

She strode into the bush.

# Chapter 18

Georgie got to her feet, her eyes filled with tears. If only she could take Dot's pain away.

Nhiari nodded in acknowledgement of Brandon's attempt to help and then followed Dot.

Georgie trembled as the realisation hit her that it could be Matt lying on the dirt. They'd nearly been killed.

She'd run as fast as she could, knowing Matt could run faster and she was holding him up. It had been terrifying.

"Come on, let's take care of those animals," Matt said, heading over to the black ute.

She exhaled as she followed him.

These animals were in worse condition than the last lot Georgie had freed. She was horrified at the number of them all squashed in together in tiny containers. Right now she wasn't all that sorry Jerry was dead.

He'd ratted them out.

They worked quickly to free the non-dangerous animals first, the small geckos and lizards which hadn't been taped, just crammed together in lunch boxes and take-away containers. The larger lizards had been wrapped in masking tape which didn't have quite the hold as the duct tape of the last lot, but would still damage the scales as it was taken off.

"Get me some water," Georgie said.

Matt fetched a bottle as Brandon carried the first container with a snake away from the area.

She showered the first goanna in water, letting it soak in before she carefully peeled back the tape. It came back fairly easily. "Looks like Jerry used cheap tape."

"Sounds like something he'd do," Matt answered as he started on the next one.

They spent the next half an hour removing tape from agitated lizards. Georgie filled one of the containers with water and placed it away from the ute so the lizards could drink if they wanted to.

Brandon had freed the rest of the snakes and helped with the remaining lizards. Soon all that was left was the racehorse goanna, about a metre and a half in length.

The goanna had stopped hissing and was eyeing them warily. "Is it likely to attack?" Georgie asked.

"I reckon we've got a fifty-fifty chance. Hopefully it'll be happy to have its freedom," Matt answered.

"Georgie, you want to radio Dot and Nhiari to warn them?" Matt asked as he and Brandon lifted the cage to the ground.

"All right." She took the radio Brandon handed her and walked away from the cage, scanning the bush for a glimpse of the police officers. It didn't feel real that Jerry and Mark were dead. She wanted to see it for herself.

She followed the low murmur of the officers' voices and saw the blue of their uniforms through the gaps in the shrubs. She moved around a bush, opening her mouth to call out and stopped short when she almost tripped over Jerry's body. Shit. A bullet hole was in the middle of his chest and a pool of browning blood covered his T-shirt. His eyes were open, dull, and his body crumpled on the ground where it had fallen.

Dead.

Dead because he got involved with the wrong people, because he wanted a quick buck. Part of her felt sorry for him, but a stronger part of her wanted to kick him for ratting them out. He'd pretended to be Matt's friend, he'd tried to sleep with her, but all he cared about was saving his own ass.

"What are you doing here?" Nhiari strode towards her. Behind her, only a few metres away, Dot was bent over the bodies of Mark and a woman, studying them clinically. Nerves of steel.

They must have all converged when Jerry had spotted them. Nhiari moved to block her view. "Georgie?"

They were all dead. Seeing them lifeless on the ground, flies swarming around them, put it into sharp perspective.

"Georgie!" Nhiari barked.

She flinched and shook her head, bringing her gaze to the senior constable.

"We're releasing the goanna and wanted to warn you in case it's aggressive."

"You were supposed to radio them." Matt walked into the clearing. "It's gone now."

"Glad to hear it," Nhiari said.

Georgie turned. They'd let it loose while she wasn't there. Though it made her feel all warm inside that Matt wanted to protect her, she would have preferred him to be upfront about it. Matt pointed to Brandon who had followed him. "It was his idea." The cheeky smile which followed the statement made her swallow her complaint.

Brandon pushed him. "Tell tale."

The touch of humour was just what she needed. She exhaled and moved to hug both of them.

In the distance a car engine broke the silence. Her radio burst to life. "Just about back."

Darcy.

Dot joined them. "We're going to be here a while," she said. "Go with Darcy and we'll drop into the Ridge on our way back to town. Make sure Darcy's sent those photos to the station. I want that man identified as soon as possible."

Lee could probably identify the man, but Georgie doubted he would still be at the cave.

"Will do," Matt promised. He glanced over Dot's shoulder, flinched and then back at the sergeant. "How are you?"

"We've had better days." Dot's tone was clipped. Her gaze hard, she didn't really look at them, but beyond them. She was holding it together, just.

"We'll let you get back to work. Be careful," Georgie said. Maybe with them gone, Dot would release her pain.

"Always are."

Matt hugged Nhiari. "Take care, sister."

Georgie held Matt's hand on the way back to the cars, needing the comfort. When Darcy pulled up they got in and Matt placed his arm around her shoulder. She leaned into him. Protected.

"You sent the photos?" Brandon asked.

"Yeah, and called to confirm they got them," Darcy answered. "What now?"

"We've freed the animals. Dot will drop by the house when they're done here."

Darcy turned the car around and drove them back to the house. Georgie closed her eyes but all she could see were the bodies of the dead. That could have been her and Matt. If Jerry had had a gun, or the man hadn't missed them, they could have been lying on the ground baking in the sun. She trembled.

"We're safe," Matt murmured and kissed her forehead.

"He's still out there."

"There's no reason to come after us."

She shook her head. "Lee said they're unhappy about us poking around." What if they wanted revenge?

Matt stiffened. "When did you speak to Lee?"

Shit. She bit her lip as Darcy slowed and glanced in the rear-view mirror. "What's this about Lee?"

Hell, they were going to be so mad. Georgie sighed and sat up, brushing the hair from her face. "Can this wait until we get back?"

"No." All three men answered in unison.

Of course not.

"I ran into Lee on Monday when I was working."

"Where?" Matt demanded. "Why didn't you call the police?"

"Because he would have been long gone," Georgie answered.

"Did he threaten you?"

"No, he tried to hide, but I called him out." Matt growled and she held up a hand to speak. "He warned me to stay away from the animal smuggling. Asked me to pretend I didn't see the tracks and to tell Matt to stop investigating."

"So that's how you knew," Matt said.

She nodded. "He knew we'd notified authorities about the shipwreck and said he was trying to move interest away from us, but we kept poking our noses into Stonefish business."

"He could have killed you, Georgie," Brandon said.

"I got the feeling he's trying to protect us. He said we'd been good to him. I thanked him for saving Tess and for sending the wedding photos."

Brandon swore under his breath. "You need to tell Dot about this."

She didn't want to. If they had someone working for Stonefish on their side that had to be a good thing.

"He's right," Matt said. "They need to know he's still in the area. Lee might not feel so protective of the police."

She couldn't argue with that. "I'll tell them when they drop around."

"You want to tell me what you were investigating?" Darcy asked Matt.

Georgie smiled. Now it was Matt's turn to get into trouble.

"I followed the tracks towards the ranges and found some animal traps. I reported them to the police."

"You both should know better. No one is to go off alone."

"My job is working alone," Georgie pointed out.

"Maybe Matt can go with you," Brandon answered.

She almost laughed. What was it with the men in her life? She'd had this argument already. "Declan's going to think I can't handle myself."

"Declan will do what the police ask him to do," Brandon said.

"Can you spare Matt from the station?"

"We can if it keeps you safe."

"And how would having Matt by my side keep me safe?" She squeezed his hand. "Neither of us have guns. It just means both of us would be killed."

"It's an extra set of eyes."

"I'm all for it," Matt said. "Think about it. We can spend our days together, hanging out, just the two of us."

He painted a nice picture, and in any other circumstance she'd jump at the chance, but she wasn't putting him in harm's way. "Let's talk to Dot about it."

She patted his knee and they drove in silence the rest of the way home.

As they pulled up outside the house, Lara burst out and raced across to the car. As soon as Georgie and Matt were out she flung her arms around them. "I was so scared! Are you all right? What happened?"

Georgie smiled at Lara buried between their arms. She stroked her hair. "We're fine, La La."

"We'll tell you the whole story when we get inside," Matt added.

Georgie glanced at Matt who was smiling at Lara with deep affection, and something in Georgie's heart pulled. Matt would be a wonderful father. She could picture it clearly probably because she'd seen him with Lara as a baby. Though she wasn't ready for kids yet, she had no doubt she wanted kids with him.

"Come on," Brandon called. "Everyone will want to hear what happened."

Matt pulled away and patted Lara on the back. "Let's go, La La."

Lara slipped her hands into theirs and together they walked into the kitchen where the others waited.

Amy strode over to her. "I'm so glad you're safe," she said as she hugged Georgie.

"Me too." Thanks to Matt. She might not have considered the car coming towards them wasn't the police.

"They were watching, waiting for the ute to leave," Matt said. "They mustn't have seen Georgie and I walk off."

"How could they get so close without us hearing?" Brandon asked.

"They had a drone," Matt said. "Must have been high enough that we didn't see or hear it."

Amy held up a bottle of water and one of beer. "Drink? Or something stronger?"

Georgie sank into a chair. She was hot and tired, and a beer would only make her more emotional. "Water please."

"For me, too." Matt sat next to her and handed her the plate of biscuits on the table.

"So what happened?" Faith asked.

Georgie let Matt tell the story since he was the one who had heard most of it.

"Dot thinks the guy who shot them had his own radio and was listening to us," Matt concluded. "He must have heard Georgie radio the house and report the smugglers which is how they knew we were there."

"Jerry spotted us and raised the alarm." Georgie still wanted to smack him. She couldn't imagine how Matt felt. She squeezed Matt's hand. "I'm sorry."

"Me too."

"How's Dot?" Amy asked.

"Holding it together," Georgie said.

"She's pretty stubborn, but maybe you can all help her," Brandon said.

Amy nodded. "We'll do our best. She doesn't like to get emotional."

Brandon smiled and kissed her. "So we've got two men to watch for," he continued. "This guy and Lee."

Amy gasped. "Is Lee still here?"

Brandon gestured for Georgie to tell her story. When she was finished, she said, "I get the feeling he's trying to protect us."

"Even if he is, there might be a time when he has to make a choice," Brandon said.

Georgie passed her phone around so they could see the photo of the murderer.

"I'll increase the size and see if I can get a better image of his face," Amy said. "Print a few copies if I can."

The photo wasn't great as the guy had done his best to hide his features.

"The boat doesn't have a registration number on it," Faith noted.

"Do you think he's staying on one of the islands?" Amy asked.

"No," Matt answered. "Georgie and I went looking for the shipwreck a couple of weeks back. If he'd been there then, he had the perfect opportunity to get rid of us."

Goosebumps rose to her skin. They'd been focused on the seabed, not their surroundings. Even if they'd heard a boat coming, they wouldn't have thought it brought danger.

"No more investigating," Brandon announced. "No looking for smugglers, or for treasure."

Lara made a sound of protest.

"He's right, pumpkin," Darcy said. "Until they're caught, it's too dangerous. Georgie and Matt have been lucky so far. If the smugglers they caught had been higher up the chain of command, they could have been in worse trouble."

"But we're so close," Lara whispered under her breath.

Georgie smiled at her optimism.

"We should buy some drones," Amy said. "Use them to check the areas we're working in before we go in. That way we won't accidentally run into them."

"Do we have the funds?" Faith asked.

"I know a couple of guys," Georgie said. "They'll lend theirs to me."

"Of course you do," Matt said, squeezing her hand and smiling.

"Not jealous anymore?" she teased.

"Not when you're next to me."

Georgie kissed him and stretched. "I'll chat to Declan about the danger on Monday. They might have some contingencies." The events of the day were beginning to catch up on her. She felt sweaty and dusty and vulnerable. She stood. "I need a shower before Dot and Nhiari get here."

Matt nodded. "Have a nice soak."

He wasn't joining her. Maybe he wasn't quite comfortable with the situation, or maybe he wanted to speak to her brothers privately. "No discussing what's best for me without me here."

Matt grinned. "I wouldn't dare."

As she left the house, she took a moment on the verandah and scanned her surroundings. A grey nomad couple were setting up their caravan across the way, Bennett lay sprawled in the shade of the sheds panting, Maggie was hiding from some kids underneath another caravan and they were trying to tempt the kangaroo out, and Flotsam and Jetsam grazed around the horse yard. It was a normal Saturday afternoon, so why didn't she want to step off the verandah?

There were plenty of places for a gunman to hide. Inside the machinery shed, behind the tack shed, hell he could be lying wait in her room or if he had a long range rifle, perched on top of the sand dunes behind the house.

She was letting her imagination get the better of her. He would be hiding waiting for the police to clear the scene.

Taking a breath, she trotted down the steps and across the red dirt to Matt's room where she'd left her bag. Her muscles were tight, waiting to hear the loud crack of a gunshot. She threw open his door and hurried inside, slamming it behind her.

Safe.

She rubbed her arms and quickly got some clothes from her bag. Maybe Matt should move into the homestead. There was a spare room and he'd be surrounded by family, not on his own out here. It would be safer.

With her things prepared, she rushed over to the small bathroom and shut herself inside, and then checked the cubicle to ensure it was empty before locking the door.

She let out a shaky breath and turned on the water. It was ridiculous. Would the man really come after them now? The damage was done. He'd shot three people in cold blood. He wouldn't hang around.

She stripped and stood under the cool spray, letting the water wash away the dirt and the sweat. As she closed her eyes she saw Jerry's body lying bleeding in the dirt.

She shook the image away. It seemed surreal that only a few weeks ago he was trying to charm his way into her apartment.

Now he was dead.

His parents would be devastated.

Her eyes stung and her throat ached as she thought of all the heartbreak. No one should have to lose someone they loved in this kind of circumstance. It wasn't fair. It wasn't right.

As the emotion overwhelmed her, she slid down the shower wall onto the floor, hugging her knees to her chest and sobbed.

Stonefish had threatened too many people she cared for. They had to be stopped.

"Georgie, can I join you?"

Georgie shrieked at Matt's voice and held a hand against her rapidly beating heart, her sobs evaporating in the shock. "How did you get in?"

"I used the key. Sorry, I didn't mean to scare you."

Matt was here. He was safe. "He killed them all." Georgie pulled the shower curtain open. Matt's eyes widened at seeing her on the floor.

"Oh, honey." He stepped into the shower, clothes and all, crouching next to her and pulling her into his arms. "Nhiari will catch him." The tears began again as he held her, murmuring nonsense while he stroked her back.

It felt so good to be held and soothed by him, as if everything would be all right.

After a minute, she wiped her eyes and pushed her wet hair from her face. "Your clothes are wet."

"They'll dry." He kissed her. "You want to talk about

it?"

"Why shoot them all because the police were close?" she said. "Why didn't he order them into the dinghy?"

"Because he knew we had photos. They'd be caught at some stage."

"They must have known enough to identify him. Maybe we're getting closer to the one in charge."

"Maybe the police are getting closer," Matt corrected. "We're not chasing them remember?"

She sighed. "Yeah, I know." She wanted Stonefish stopped but she understood the danger.

"Try to put it behind you."

Easier said than done when she kept seeing Jerry's dead body when she closed her eyes. She climbed to her feet.

"Do you still want to go out tonight?" Matt asked as he stripped off his wet clothes and wrung them out.

She shook her head. "Why don't we get takeaway and stay at my place?" She'd be vulnerable in public and she didn't want to stay here in case the man came after them. She'd protect her family any way she could.

"That works for me." He took the soap and washed her back.

Now she just had to figure out how she could protect Matt too.

# Chapter 19

Matt refused to let Georgie see how shaken he was. She needed him to be strong and he would be, but he kept replaying the moment the bullet had hit the ground just next to them. If Georgie had zigged instead of zagged it might have been her body he'd stared down on instead of Jerry's.

His hand shook as he soaped her back, and he exhaled quietly to regain his control. They were both alive, uninjured, safe.

He'd do his best to ensure they stayed that way.

Darcy had taken him aside and told him he didn't want Georgie on her own, a sentiment Matt heartily agreed with. He'd suggested Matt move in with her for a while. The station could manage with him working a few less hours.

It suited Matt perfectly, but Georgie wouldn't like to be handled. Still after finding her sobbing in the shower, he might not have to work very hard to convince her it was a good idea.

As he handed Georgie her towel he asked, "How are you feeling?"

She shrugged as she wrapped the towel tightly around

her torso. "Everything about the situation sucks."

He couldn't stand to see her so upset. "I want to move in with you," he blurted. "At least until this guy is caught."

"All right."

Matt closed his mouth on his argument, surprised. "I thought you might be harder to convince."

Her smile was a little sad. "I've wanted to live with you for years," she said. "And right now, I'm not foolish enough to want to be contrary about the reason."

Good. It would be a good way to test living together, and hopefully Nhiari and Dot would have an update when they arrived.

He didn't want to be in limbo for long.

It was late afternoon before Dot and Nhiari dropped in to get their statements. They looked exhausted and sweaty. Amy poured them both a glass of iced water and Matt pulled out a seat for his sister.

Nhiari raised an eyebrow but sat.

"What did you find?" Brandon asked.

"No sign of the dinghy," Dot said. "He must have somewhere to hide it because my guy flew over the area for more than an hour without spotting anything."

The dinghy couldn't have gone far before the plane was airborne which meant the guy knew the area well. Damn it.

"He's dangerous, so if you see anyone even remotely resembling him, you call it in. Do not approach him." Nhiari looked pointedly at Brandon.

"He won't," Amy said, squeezing Brandon's hand. He sighed and nodded.

"Declan said animal smuggling doesn't carry a heavy sentence," Georgie said. "Why kill everyone?"

Dot shook her head. "Might be animal smuggling is only one of their activities or maybe one of them knew too much."

Matt studied her, but aside from the exhaustion both officers showed, he'd never guess her brother had just been murdered. She was one tough cookie.

"We need to speak with you and Matt again," Dot continued. "Review your statements."

"Use the lounge room," Brandon said.

While Georgie went with Dot and Nhiari, Matt went back to his room to pack some things. He glanced around the room. Pretty much everything would fit in a single duffle bag. How sad was that?

With a sigh, he threw clothes, toiletries and his laptop in and lifted the bag over his shoulder.

He should have more to show for his life.

Matt returned to the house and when it was his turn, he rehashed what had happened.

"Be on your guard," Dot said as they walked back into the kitchen.

"We will be." Darcy placed his arms around Lara and Faith.

"Good. We've got to go." Dot headed straight outside and Nhiari took Matt aside. "Maybe you should stay in the house for a while."

It wasn't often Nhiari looked so concerned. He felt a punch of worry. "I'll be staying in town with Georgie."

"What's the security at her place like?"

"Locks are solid." He and Darcy had made sure of it when she'd moved in.

"Might be worth installing a couple of cameras just in case."

He jolted. "You think he's going to come after us?"

"I don't know what he'll do, but no going off alone without telling someone where you're going and how long you'll be."

"I won't. Have you identified the guy yet?"

"No. He hid his face too well, but we're checking with

the AFP and Interpol as well." She raised her eyebrows and he nodded. He got her meaning.

"Report anything that feels off, no matter how small," she continued.

"I will. Might help if you chat to Declan, get him to keep Georgie in the office if he can."

"I'll apprise him of the situation. His people will need to be on the lookout as well."

"Thanks, Nhiari." He hugged her.

"Just keep out of trouble." She climbed into the police car and she and Dot drove away.

Matt moved over to Georgie. "You ready to go?"

She nodded.

"You're not staying for dinner?" Darcy asked.

Matt smiled. "I owe Georgie a date. Do you think fish and chips is fancy enough?"

The others laughed, but Georgie said, "That sounds perfect."

They said their goodbyes, and then he followed Georgie into town. When they arrived at her place, he went straight through to put his bag in Georgie's bedroom, checking the other rooms as he went.

"Everything all right?" Georgie asked.

"Just checking for surprises," he said.

She bit her nail and he went over to her, taking her hands in his. "I'm probably being overly cautious."

"Did Nhiari tell you to be?"

He nodded.

"I hate this. I hate that these people seem to have a thing for the Ridge, and we get blamed for getting in the way when it's our place."

"It sucks," Matt agreed. "Let's go pick up dinner and then we can watch a movie."

"The brewery delivers pizza."

"Perfect. What do you want?"

While they waited for their order, they sat on the

couch and flicked through Georgie's subscription service.

"Did Darcy talk to you about me?" Georgie asked.

"Yeah, he told me it was fine to work fewer hours if I wanted to stay with you."

"Do you want to stay?" She glanced at the ground. "I mean, I know you said you wanted to move in, but is it just because of the danger?"

He placed the TV remote on the table and took her hand. "It's a weird situation, but I want to stay… for as long as you'll have me."

"That might be a while."

"Fine by me." He grinned. "I feel as if I've been starving myself of you for years." That wasn't quite right. "Now I can hold you, I want to feast on as much as I possibly can."

Georgie laughed. "Feast huh? I'm not sure how I feel about being likened to food."

He squirmed. He'd never had a way with words. He brought her hand to his lips and kissed each finger. "You didn't have any complaints when I feasted on you last night."

She fanned herself. "Good point. How about we have an appetiser before the pizza arrives?"

Matt was more than happy to oblige. "As you wish."

***

Georgie didn't want to go to work on Monday morning. She'd spent a blissful twenty-four hours cocooned in her unit with Matt and she wasn't ready to emerge yet. She scowled as she made them both sandwiches while Matt washed their breakfast dishes.

"You keep poking your bottom lip out like that and I'll suck on it." Matt patted her bottom as he reached for the tea towel.

"Promises, promises." She rolled her eyes even as her

215

body heated. "Want to play hookey?"

Before he could answer, her phone rang and when she answered, Declan said, "Can you come straight to the fire station?"

Georgie frowned. So much for playing hookey. "Sure. What's up?"

"Training. The whole department is doing a refresher. Fire-fighting is one of the tasks of a park ranger."

He'd mentioned that, but the timing of the training was a little suspect. "Do we train often?"

"A couple of times a year."

She glanced at Matt. "Is it a full day?"

"Yeah."

Convenient. "I'll see you soon." She hung up and turned to Matt. "Looks like I'm staying in town today. Training at the fire station."

He raised his eyebrows. "Fire fighting?"

"Yeah." Surely if it had been planned, Declan would have mentioned it last week. "Did you have anything to do with this?"

"No." He sighed. "But Nhiari might have. She was going to have a word to Declan so he could tell his team to keep an eye out."

She didn't like the idea of any of her colleagues running into the main guy.

"Are you heading out now?" Matt asked as he hung the tea towel over the oven door handle.

"Yeah. Will you come back tonight?" She clenched her hand to stop biting her fingers.

"Didn't we agree I would?"

"It's not fair for you to keep driving back and forth."

"One of us will always have to if we're going to make this work." He kissed her. "I don't mind."

She smiled. "All right. You'll need to get a bigger bed if I'm staying out at the Ridge with you."

"Then I'll see you for dinner," he said.

Georgie locked her apartment and then drove the short distance to the fire station. Declan and Penelope were already there. She wandered over to them. "You won't get many fires out on the ocean," she said to Penelope.

"When there's a fire, it's all hands on deck," Declan said.

"It will be an interesting experience." Penelope smiled politely. Her red hair was in a tight braid again and her clothes were ironed.

Georgie hadn't had a chance to get to know her, but she seemed very efficient. "How are you settling in?"

"I've unpacked all the boxes," she said. "I know my way around town, but I'm still not used to the quiet."

Georgie smiled. "City girl?"

"All my life. It's so dark and quiet at night. And so many stars."

"You'll get used to it," Georgie said. "When I moved to Perth for uni, it didn't take long for the noise and light to become normal."

Declan went over to greet some of the other staff.

Penelope hesitated and then said, "I need a new hobby. What's there to do around here?"

She didn't sound thrilled about finding a hobby, which was kind of odd. "My brother's fiancée runs an adult riding class on Saturdays, and there's always scuba diving and snorkelling."

Penelope smiled. "I've never ridden a horse."

Georgie shook her head. "Never? You'll have to come out to the Ridge. I'll take you for a trail ride."

"What's the Ridge?"

"My family's sheep station. It's about an hour from town."

"I'd like that. Thanks." Her smile was more genuine this time.

It was the least Georgie could do. She remembered

how hard it had been moving to the city and not knowing anyone. "How are you finding the job?"

"I met all the tour boat operators last week," Penelope said. "Jimmy said to say hello."

Georgie smiled. "He's great. You won't have any issues with him. He takes a lot of pride in his business."

"Good to know. I understand someone just bought Rob's business."

Georgie nodded. "Brandon's best friend, Sam. He's moving up in about a month."

"He knows he has to reapply for a licence to do the whale shark tours, doesn't he?"

"I don't know." Hopefully Faith's father had covered it during the sale. "It shouldn't be a problem, should it?"

"Not if he meets all the criteria. What's his experience?" Penelope screwed her nose up at the instant coffee from the drinks station and made herself a cup of tea.

Georgie thoroughly agreed with the sentiment. "He's been in the army since high school. Joined when my brother, Brandon did." She got her phone out of her pocket and showed Penelope Sam's photo.

Penelope sipped her drink as she glanced over. She choked, eyes wide and coughed, gasping for breath. "Wrong hole." She took a moment to get it under control and then said, "Wow."

Georgie grinned. It was nice to see some genuine emotion. The photo was the best one she had of Sam, taken at Brandon's wedding when he was lounging against one of the posts on the verandah wearing suit pants and shirt. She'd called it his model pose. "He's fit too, and deadly. Could probably kill a person with his bare hands."

"When did you say he was moving up?" Penelope said, fanning herself.

"Within the month." Georgie grinned. "I take it

you're single?"

The smile faded and she nodded.

There was a story there. Georgie kept her tone light. "He's going to be beating the single women off." Most had already gone through their options of local single men. Maybe she should warn Sam. Though it would be fun to see how he fared on his own. She grinned. "He's bought a town house near the harbour."

"Nice. I go jogging in that area."

Declan clapped his hands together. "Let's get started."

The chief of the volunteer fire brigade distributed personal protective equipment and then took them through their paces. About an hour in Georgie's phone rang. She winced and dragged it out of her pocket. "Sorry, I should have set it to silent."

She hesitated when she saw it was Darcy. He wouldn't call her unless it was urgent. She turned away and answered. "What's wrong?"

"Is Matt with you?"

Dread dropped over her and she moved away from the group. "No. He should be at the Ridge by now." Had he had an accident? Was he lying upside-down in his car like her parents had, waiting to be rescued? Her heart raced and she gasped for breath.

"OK. Don't worry. He's probably fine. I'll call Dot and check the roads." Darcy's voice trembled. He'd be having flashbacks of finding their parents.

No way was she letting him deal with this by himself. "I'll drive from this end. We can meet in the middle."

"No, stay where you are. You're safer there. This could be a Stonefish ruse."

"I'm not sitting here twiddling my thumbs." Her phone beeped to notify her of an incoming call. Matt. Her heart leapt. "It's Matt. I'll call you back." She hung up on her brother and answered. "Matt, where are you?"

# Chapter 20

Matt drove out of town after following Georgie to the fire station to make sure she arrived safely. He'd have to thank Nhiari for arranging things with Declan so Georgie wasn't alone today. The police were still looking for the gunman but he could be anywhere by now. They'd all sleep better when he was found.

He turned down the road which led to the Ridge and slowed as he spotted a four-wheel drive with the bonnet popped. The tall male driver stepped out from behind the car and frantically waved him down. He was lean and wore a polo shirt and shorts with boater shoes. Maybe a corporate type who jogged regularly. Two kids' bicycles were on the back and Matt could just see their car seats peeking over the back seat; one definitely had a child in it.

He couldn't leave anyone stranded out here. It might be hours before someone else came past. Matt pulled to a stop behind the car and got out. "You got a problem?"

"I think it overheated," the guy said.

His voice gave Matt goosebumps. Matt stopped, glanced in the back passenger window. One child seat had a blow-up doll in it. What the—?

Something hard pressed into Matt's back. "You're going to do exactly what I say."

Fuck. Matt's skin grew clammy. He never should have stopped. The man's reflection in the window was the same height and build as the gunman. "Are you going to shoot me?"

"Not yet. I need you for something. Get in the front."

He was so screwed. This man would kill him without hesitation. Somehow, he needed to call his sister. No, he needed to delay. He'd called Darcy before leaving town to check whether they needed anything. When he didn't show in an hour, Darcy would raise the alarm.

Assuming he noticed the time and realised Matt hadn't radioed in.

But overpowering the guy wasn't an option. No way he'd avoid a gunshot directed to his kidneys. He moved around the front of the car and climbed in, the gunman right next to him.

"Call your girlfriend."

"No." No way was he involving Georgie. She was safe in town.

"Call her or I'll shoot you."

"You're going to shoot me anyway."

The man scowled, his dark eyes like daggers. "I'm going to enjoy killing you." He pulled out a cable tie and tied Matt's hands together. "Give me your phone."

"It's in my pocket." And almost impossible to get out while sitting and wearing jeans.

The man swore and he fumbled with Matt's pocket, the gun still pressed against Matt's side. Any move and Matt was dead. Chills went through him, too scared to be impressed by the man's dexterity. No chance to overpower him.

The man used facial recognition to unlock the phone and then scrolled through it. "Her name's Georgie, isn't it?"

"She won't come. She's smarter than that."

"Then she'll have to live with knowing she caused your death."

Nausea swirled in his stomach. Georgie already had guilt over Charlie's and her parents' deaths. She would do whatever the guy said. Matt lunged for the phone, but the gunman was too quick. He stepped back and slammed the door in Matt's face, locking it so he couldn't get out. Then he shut the bonnet and got into the driver's seat, placing Matt's phone in the hands-free cradle. So responsible.

He did a U-turn and headed back towards town, one hand on the wheel, the other still holding the gun.

The doors were locked so no way Matt could jump out. Not that it was a viable option at the speed they were going. But perhaps he could convince the man not to shoot him. "Why are you doing this?"

The man didn't answer.

"We haven't done anything to you."

Again silence.

"The police will be watching Georgie."

"The police will be too busy to notice she's gone."

What had Stonefish organised? Concern for his sister added to his other concerns. Was she all right?

As they reached the area where phone reception kicked in the gunman pressed dial on Matt's phone. Georgie's voice came over. "Matt, where are you?"

His heart squeezed, but before he could speak, the gunman pressed the gun against his head. Matt froze.

The gunman chuckled before saying, "Matt's currently tied up in my car."

***

The unfamiliar chuckle made Georgie want to throw up. "You're the gunman." She said the words quietly, but Penelope and Declan shot her looks of concern. Georgie

222

gestured them over and turned the volume up so they could both hear the caller without putting it on speaker.

"I might be," the man answered. "You're going to leave the fire station quietly and meet me at the base of the ranges close to where you discovered Lance."

"I want proof Matt is alive."

Penelope's eyes widened and she mouthed, *What's going on?* She got out her phone.

"Say something," the gunman ordered. In the background it sounded as if they were driving, but there weren't many places along the road to town where there was reception.

Georgie mouthed, *Call Dot* to Declan. He had to know something about what had happened.

He nodded and stepped away to make the call.

"He refuses to speak. I'll show you." The man switched to video, being careful not to show his own face. The image was jerky as the car bumped over the road, but Matt sat in the passenger seat, his hands tied together.

"Don't come, Georgie," Matt shouted. "Stonefish set up a diversion for the police."

Rage swept over her. She would not lose another person she loved. The video switched off and the gunman spoke. "You have an hour."

"I need more time," Georgie said. "I don't have a four-wheel drive." And they were definitely on the dirt by the way the car had been jerking about.

"Parks and Wildlife does. You have one hour or he dies. If I see anyone else, he dies." The man hung up.

Georgie's pulse raced. Penelope grabbed her. "What's going on?"

Georgie shook her off. "I don't have time."

"Dot wants to speak with you." Declan shoved his phone at Georgie, but Georgie refused to take it.

"I can't. If he sees the police, he'll kill Matt."

Declan opened his mouth in protest.

"I've got to go." She ran out of the fire station. She still wore her fire suit and it was a little bulky to get into her car, but she managed it. With everyone at training today, there'd be cars at the office.

She sped over to the building as her phone rang. Nhiari. Shit. She couldn't ignore Matt's sister. She'd be frantic too.

"I'm going alone."

"You can't," Nhiari said. "He wants the both of you so he can kill you. The only reason he didn't kill Matt immediately was to lure you there." She sounded so calm. How could she be so calm?

"I can't let him die. He said he'll kill Matt if he sees anyone else."

"He's going to the base of the ranges, isn't he?"

How did she… Penelope must have told her. "Yeah."

"OK. There's a track across the top, somewhere we can watch from above."

"He'll spot you. He must have people in town watching me. He knew I was at the fire station." She braked hard in front of the PAWS building. "Matt said Stonefish had set up a diversion for the police."

"Yeah, Colin's staying behind to deal with it."

Georgie dashed inside, stripping off her fire-proof jacket as she did so. The receptionist looked up, eyes wide.

"Georgie, what are you doing here?"

"I need the four-wheel drive keys." She strode past her to the room out the back which had the gun safe. Quickly she unlocked it and drew out the rifle, taking the box of bullets with her.

Karen gaped at Georgie. "What are you doing?"

"I'm helping the police." She hadn't done the required training to be allowed access to the gun, but she didn't care. She wasn't going in unarmed.

Nhiari shouted something that was probably denial as Georgie grabbed the keys from the hook and raced outside again.

If the gunman shot Matt, all bets were off.

On the phone in the background were urgent shouts. "Shit," Nhiari said. "I've got to go. We'll be there as soon as we can."

Georgie hung up. That suited her. If the police were busy, she could deal with the gunman on her own.

Was Matt even still alive? There was no phone reception out there, so no way she could call and check before she arrived.

Her chest tightened and her fingers gripped the steering wheel so hard they hurt. She wouldn't consider any option except Matt being alive.

Her phone rang as she hit the town limits. Darcy. He deserved to know what was happening. "The gunman has Matt," Georgie said.

Darcy swore. "Where?

"I can't tell you. He wants me to meet him."

"Don't be stupid, Georgie. He'll kill you both."

"He'll kill Matt if I don't."

"Then we'll back you up."

She shook her head. "I can't risk it. If he sees anyone else, he'll shoot Matt."

"You're not going alone. We need to call the police."

"They know. Declan called them." Maybe he'd think they were backing her up.

"Do they have a plan?"

"Yeah," she lied. "I'm about to go out of range. Stay at the Ridge." She waited a second and then hung up. She exhaled.

Time to get her head into the game. She'd spent time in the area. The gunman could hide at any spot along the track and shoot her while she was driving in. If he'd already killed Matt, he could wait somewhere up the slope of the ranges and get a shot at long range.

Her throat closed over. This was madness. She didn't have the skills to take on a killer. There were too many variables, and this guy hadn't hesitated to kill three others.

Georgie gasped for breath as she turned off the bitumen and had to slow on the track. In front of her the red ranges soared into the air, the only thing to see for kilometres.

She glanced between the track and the ranges, trying to spot anything out of place; a glint off glass or a colour that didn't fit in.

As she neared the rendezvous point she slowed and wound down her window, listening for anything out of the ordinary, fearing to hear a gunshot.

Every muscle in her body was tight. She reached over and pulled the rifle closer so it was within her reach.

Not far now.

This could be the last thing she ever did.

***

Matt jolted as they went over a particularly nasty bump and winced as the plastic cut into his wrists. The skin was raw where he'd been trying to break the ties. He was surprised the gunman hadn't thrown him out of the car and shot him when he'd hung up from Georgie, but maybe he didn't want to risk Georgie spotting the body.

They were close to where the animal traps had been which meant he had very little time to free himself. Nothing in the front seat he could use as a weapon. His best chance was attacking the guy when he got out of the car.

The car bumped over the track and rounded a corner where it widened. Standing in the middle of the area was Lee.

Matt's mouth dropped open. What was he doing

here?

"Good," the gunman muttered.

Great, Lee was in on this. Georgie should have reported him to the police when she'd first seen him. This was going to give Georgie another level of guilt she didn't need.

"I thought you'd like to be reunited with a friend," the gunman said as he turned off the engine.

Matt had no idea where Lee or this guy sat in the Stonefish hierarchy. Was there any point attempting to overpower the gunman when Lee could simply shoot him?

He had to try.

The gunman got out, came around the side to unlock the passenger door and pointed his gun right at Matt's face. "Move."

His blue eyes were like ice, containing no emotion. Chills ran down Matt's spine. Still no way to escape, not without risking a bullet in his brain.

Matt slid carefully out, keeping his eyes on the gunman, waiting for a moment when his attention lapsed, but he stared at Matt the whole time, ignoring Lee behind him.

Lee glanced at Matt impassively as if they hadn't shared a beer around the campfire before, and then turned his attention to the gunman. "This is why you brought me here?"

"There have been questions about your loyalty," the gunman said.

"Only from you." Lee sounded bored. "What do you want me to do, shoot him?"

"Yeah, and the bitch who's coming for him."

Lee turned to Matt. "You've got a girlfriend?"

Matt ground his teeth. "It's Georgie. He wants you to murder Georgie."

Georgie had taken Lee horse-riding and arranged for

him to go on the whale shark cruise. If he could seriously shoot Georgie after spending so much time with her, then he was irredeemable.

Lee took his gun from the back of his jeans. "Do you want me to shoot him now, or when Georgie arrives?"

Matt wanted to be sick. His legs went weak, and he swayed before he managed to strengthen them again. "You'd really kill her?" He had to keep her alive.

"You don't seem to care you're about to die," the gunman said.

Matt met Lee's gaze when he answered. "I care more about a woman who brings joy to everyone she meets."

Lee said nothing, his face a statue. Not a guy to play poker with.

"She deserves to be in this world."

"Let's wait until the girl arrives," the gunman said. "I'd like to see them suffer after all they've put us through."

"I warned the boss the Stokes wouldn't give in easily." Lee shifted slightly closer to Matt. "They're stubborn."

"Are you suggesting my father made a mistake?" The gunman stiffened, the first sign of real emotion Matt had seen.

"Never," Lee said. "He's run the organisation successfully for over two decades. He gets results."

This was Matt's chance to get information. If he somehow made it out alive, he wanted a lead. "He seems rather fixated on the Ridge to me."

"It contains something that is rightfully mine," the gunman said.

Was he talking about the treasure? Matt frowned. "It's Bayungu land."

The gunman waved the comment away. "Your people have no idea of its value."

How dare he! Matt growled and stepped towards the man.

The gunman raised his gun. "Don't."

It was that kind of attitude they'd been fighting against their whole lives. Matt exhaled, but before he could speak a vehicle rumbled in the distance, the sound growing louder. Georgie. He had to get away before she arrived. The gunman looked away for a moment. Matt's muscles bunched, ready to pounce at the gunman.

"Don't," Lee barked.

The gunman focused on Matt, steadying his aim.

Damn it. Matt relaxed, glaring at Lee. He'd get another moment.

"What car is she driving?" Lee asked.

"I told her to take a PAWS vehicle."

Lee swore. "They have rifles to shoot injured animals."

Matt's mouth dropped open, and a fly immediately tried to take up residence. He spat and said, "She wouldn't be so stupid." Sure, she knew how to shoot, but she couldn't shoot anyone. She wouldn't be fast enough against these two. Though she didn't know about Lee.

Lee glanced at him. "If it meant saving you?"

Fuck. He glanced towards the track entrance. If Georgie came in guns blazing, the gunman would shoot without hesitating, not bothering to wait for Lee to shoot her.

When he returned his gaze to the clearing, Lee was gone. Shit.

The gunman smirked at him. "She won't know what hit her. Lee's the best we have."

No. Matt scanned the bushes and caught a glimpse of Lee. He was out of view of the gunman. Lee met Matt's gaze, pressed a finger to his lips and mouthed, *Please*.

What? Was Matt not supposed to warn Georgie?

Both Georgie and Ed had sworn they didn't think Lee would hurt them, but Lee could have been lulling them, trying to get them to trust him.

Lee disappeared into the bush and indecision plagued Matt.

The gunman had spoken about Lee needing to prove his loyalty, so perhaps Stonefish had had doubts.

Maybe Georgie and Ed were right.

But if he chose wrong, Georgie would be dead.

# Chapter 21

Georgie stopped the car just before the end of the track. No need to make it easy for the gunman to shoot her between the eyes. She grabbed the rifle from the seat, loaded it, and slipped out of the car, not shutting the door behind her. Her heart pounded as she stepped into the bush. The only sound she heard was the ticking of the engine.

Was Matt already dead?

She crept closer to the clearing but scanned the ranges to see if she could spot anyone up there.

"Georgie! Lee's out there." Relief hit Georgie at Matt's voice, but then his words sunk in. She spun to check her surroundings only for the rifle to be snatched from her hands before she even registered Lee was there. She fell to the ground and scrambled back as he pointed the rifle at her.

"Lee, please don't." Her voice hitched as terror filled her. His shirt and jeans were clean, though still wrinkled, and he no longer looked as if he'd been living rough.

"Get to your feet," he said, his stare hard.

Shit. Nhiari was right. She shouldn't have brought the gun.

"Please don't kill us, Lee," she scrambled to her feet. "I didn't report you." Surely he owed her for that. Her whole body prickled with sweat as she waited for his reaction.

"I told you to stay out of this, Georgie." He gestured for her to walk towards the clearing.

Anger filled her. "I tried," she retorted. "It's not my fault Stonefish is so damned incompetent." She strode into the clearing. "I mean they left cairns pointing right to their location."

"What?" the gunman shouted, fury on his face.

She barely registered him. Matt stood there, alive, uninjured, his hands cuffed together. Relief made her dizzy as she ran to him and hugged him. "You're alive."

"You shouldn't have come." Matt yanked his hands down, breaking the ties, then spun her around, pushing her behind him and backed them both away from Lee and the gunman.

Damn him trying to protect her. "I wasn't leaving you to be killed alone."

A sound which might have been a strangled laugh came from Matt. "I'd rather be killed alone if it meant you lived."

"Shut up, both of you," the gunman yelled. "And stop moving."

Georgie grabbed Matt's hand and stepped next to him. "We face them together," she murmured.

"Georgie." His frustration was clear.

Lee stood on one side of the clearing holding the rifle, and the gunman was on the opposite side with his handgun. She and Matt made up the third point of the triangle.

"What's this about cairns?" the gunman demanded.

"They were to show the men to the rendezvous point," Lee said. "The Stokes shouldn't have noticed them."

Well that made sense, though Lara would be disappointed they didn't point to treasure.

"You should be more careful," the gunman said to Lee. "You've made too many mistakes. Now's the time to prove yourself. Kill them both."

"You realise this will intensify the police investigation into our operations?" Lee said.

"I don't care. They ruined our smuggling ring."

"We've got more people out there, more arms of the business."

"The smuggling was mine," the gunman's tone held a hint of petulance.

Georgie tugged on Matt's hand and stepped backwards. Maybe they could escape while the two were arguing. Matt moved with her and they reached the edge of the clearing before the gunman noticed. He pointed his gun at them. "Stop right there."

Georgie glanced behind them and froze. A huge Golden Orb spider web spanned their escape path and right in the centre was the resident spider, its bulbous abdomen catching her eye before she took in the eight legs. Her throat closed over.

"Georgie? We'll get out of this," Matt murmured.

She couldn't answer him, but squeezed his hand tightly.

"Relax," he whispered. "When they start talking again, we'll run."

"No!" she gasped.

"Move towards us," the gunman said.

"Don't worry, they won't go that way." Lee held the rifle nonchalantly, always lifted, but not pointing it directly at them. "Georgie's terrified of spiders and there's a web right behind her."

Matt swore and tugged her forward away from the web. "It's all right," he soothed.

This could not be happening. She was about to be

shot and she was too scared of a stupid spider to run for her life. "You have to pull me through," she whispered. She could do it if Matt was by her side.

"I've had enough. Just shoot them already," the gunman ordered.

"Run!" Matt pushed her towards the spider web. She took two steps, almost at the web when the gunshot cracked.

"No!" She spun and Matt grabbed her, hauling her close. Behind him the gunman sprawled on the ground.

What?

It took a moment for her to take in the whole situation. The gunman dead, Lee still on the other side of the clearing, rifle pointed at the gunman, and Matt alive and uninjured, but shaking as he held her.

"We're all right." She squeezed him and said to Lee, "You killed him."

Matt let go and turned, putting himself between her and Lee.

Lee strode over, skirting Matt. "Are the police coming?" He handed Georgie the rifle and she took it automatically, still trying to process what was happening.

"I don't know. They might be up there." She pointed towards the ranges.

Lee swore. "Hopefully Stonefish's diversion slowed them enough. I need you to do something for me." He pulled her towards where he'd been standing.

Matt jerked him away. "Don't touch her."

Lee glared at him. "I just saved both of your lives."

"By killing one of your own."

Lee shook his head. "I'm trying to stop them."

"Then why tell me not to warn Georgie?" Matt demanded.

"Because I didn't want her to shoot me accidentally."

"Are you undercover?" Georgie asked.

"If they find out I shot Clark, then I'm dead. I can't

stop them if I'm dead, and I'm getting closer."

"You want to stop them?" Matt asked.

"I have to," Lee answered. He shook Matt loose and continued. "Georgie, you have to say you killed him."

She gaped at Lee and pinched herself as Matt said, "No way. She's not going to gaol for this."

"She won't have to. I just need a little more time and then I'll come clean."

Lee had saved Tess and now Matt. It was a no-brainer. "What do you need me to do?"

"Georgie!" Matt protested.

"He's our best chance of stopping Stonefish," she said. "And he saved us."

Lee nodded. "Here's what happened. You arrived before we expected you. You gave me the slip and while I was searching for you, you doubled back and tried to rescue Matt. You shot Clark when he was about to shoot you—self-defence. I cut my losses and ran."

"The police won't believe it," Matt said.

"They might," Georgie said. "Nhiari knew I would save Matt any way I could."

"Wait. What about Stonefish? If Clark's the boss's son, won't that make Georgie a target for revenge?"

Lee shook his head. "The boss is pragmatic. You make a mistake, you deserve the consequences. He won't appreciate Clark kidnapping you."

That was a relief. She glanced at the ranges. "Were you up there when I caught Lance?"

Lee nodded. "How did you know?"

"I saw the sun reflecting off glass."

"Clark was with me. He wanted to shoot you, but his handgun didn't have the range. I convinced him he'd get caught if he moved closer."

She shivered. So Lee had saved her twice. "You should go. Do you want to set up some kind of code in case you need help?"

Lee smiled for the first time. "No. I've got this. You just need to stay away from the shipwreck."

Matt studied him. "We will. You need anything, you let us know."

The sound of a car came from the distance, somewhere above them. Georgie looked towards the ranges. "That must be the police. You should go—"

Lee was already gone.

***

Matt swore when he noticed Lee had disappeared. "He's good." He took the rifle from Georgie and then wrapped his arms around her, inhaling the sweet scent of her shampoo. She was alive. He was alive. They were safe.

He trembled.

"Hey, we're all right." Georgie stroked his back.

He could barely believe it. Lee had saved them. He would never doubt the man's word again. Whatever he was doing, he had Matt's full support.

He kissed Georgie's forehead as he got his emotions under control. "Come on, we need to report in and then we need to get our story straight." Somehow, he'd convince her to let him take the blame for Clark's death.

He avoided looking at the dead man as she led him to the car and while he placed the rifle on the back seat, she radioed the office.

"Georgie! Are you all right? What's going on?" Karen demanded.

"Can you get the police to radio me?" she asked.

A minute later Nhiari came through. "What's happened?"

"Matt and I are safe. You need to get here."

"Is it like yesterday?"

It took a second for Matt to understand, but Georgie answered. "Not as many."

Of course, if Stonefish was monitoring the radios they

didn't want to give away too much information.

"We'll be right there."

"Can you let Darcy know?"

"Will do."

Matt wasn't willing to lock away the rifle yet. Stonefish might have people other than Lee monitoring the situation, particularly if they thought Lee was no longer loyal. After Georgie hung up the radio, he pulled her around the car, out of sight of the ranges, then held her. "I almost lost you. You shouldn't have come."

She snorted against his chest. "Of course I was coming. You wouldn't have left me if the situation had been reversed."

"That's different." She'd put her life in danger for him. His life was already hers.

"No, it's not." She kissed him. "I love you. I wasn't letting Stonefish kill someone else I love."

How had he ever deserved her? How had he kept himself in denial for so many years? "I love you, but don't you ever put your life in danger for me again."

She laughed. "Then don't be in danger ever again. I'll always come to your rescue."

She had that stubborn look he knew so well. He sighed. "I'll try."

"How did it happen?"

Matt scowled. He'd been stupid, lulled by the thought of children in need. "He was on the side of the road with the bonnet popped and waved me down. The car had kids' bikes on the back, but the head I saw in the backseat as I pulled up was a dummy."

"So you stopped to help someone in need. That's very heroic."

"Except that it led to this."

He wanted time to process everything, particularly what Lee had said, but right now he just wanted to be as close as possible to Georgie. "We'll say I shot Clark."

Georgie pushed him away. "No, we won't. It makes far more sense that I did."

"Georgie, I can't let you be arrested for this."

She rolled her eyes. "Then how did you get the gun from me?"

He bit his lip trying to figure it out.

"See, it doesn't make sense. Plus you know indigenous people get harsher sentences. I won't risk that."

His gut clenched. He still didn't like it. "We could say you sneaked around behind me and gave me the gun."

"Neither Dot nor Nhiari would believe it, particularly if they notice the spider's web."

"We could tell the truth."

Georgie sighed. "I've thought about that, but Dot and Nhiari would have to put in a report, and we know Stonefish has people in the police. Lee saved Tess's life and ours. He's in the best place to take down Stonefish."

Unless it was a long con. Matt shook away the thought. No, he owed the man his life. "All right, but if it looks as if you're going to gaol, we tell the truth. I won't lose you."

She smiled and slipped her arms around him. "Not going to happen. Now I know how you feel, you're stuck with me."

"I can deal with that." He wished he could be as optimistic as her.


It took over an hour for Dot and Nhiari to arrive on the scene, but Matt was content to sit in the shade with Georgie and wait. As long as she was by his side he could wait forever. After they got their story straight, they didn't speak much but Matt spent a lot of time thinking.

Now the immediate danger was over, he didn't need to stay with her, but he'd wanted to move in anyway.

They'd make the difference in distance work

somehow.

Georgie had a few more months on her lease and hopefully by then, with Lee working to stop them, Stonefish would be history. With Stonefish no longer causing problems, the Ridge might finally be able to get on top of their finances.

Then he and Georgie could look at building their own house at the Ridge.

When he heard a car engine, he pulled Georgie to her feet. "Radio to make sure it's them."

Georgie did so and a few minutes later, the police car pulled up. Nhiari was first out of the car and she strode towards him and pulled him into her arms. "I told you not to go anywhere by yourself."

She squeezed the life out of him, but her arms trembled. "I'm all right, *gunyjan*."

She turned to Georgie. "And you! Karen said you'd taken the gun. Why? He could have overpowered you."

"He already had a gun," Georgie pointed out after she'd been similarly squeezed.

"He's dead?" Dot asked.

Georgie swallowed and nodded, pointing further down the track.

Dot smiled and both officers went to look, returning shortly afterwards. Nhiari radioed the station and Dot asked, "What happened?"

Matt told them about the kidnapping.

"Why didn't he shoot you as soon as he knew Georgie was on her way?" Nhiari asked.

"Because Lee had to prove his loyalty to Stonefish."

"Lee was here?" Dot asked.

Matt nodded. "Lee was supposed to shoot both of us, but I warned Georgie he was out there, and she managed to avoid him."

Nhiari studied him the way she had when they were kids and she was trying to figure out whether he was lying. He forced himself not to squirm. "So Lee slunk away after Georgie shot the gunman?"

Matt nodded. "It all happened so fast. Georgie appeared with the rifle and the gunman turned his gun on her, but she shot first."

Georgie shuddered and stepped closer to him.

"What else can you tell us?" Dot asked.

"The gunman was pretty angry about us ruining his smuggling operation. From the sounds of it, he was in charge of that aspect of the business."

Georgie nodded. "He said his father would be furious."

Dot glanced at her. "His father is in charge?"

"Yeah."

"And he told you this before you shot him?"

Matt cut in. "He told me, and I mentioned it to Georgie." Crap, they were really bad at lying.

"We need to ID this guy."

"His name is Clark," Matt said.

"He told you that?" Nhiari asked.

"That's what Lee called him." He shifted, wanting the questioning to be over. "Could we get back to the homestead? Darcy will be keen to see us."

Dot's smile was a little predatory. "A few more questions."

Matt stiffened. She wasn't buying their lies.

The few questions lasted for half an hour as the two police officers double-checked their answers. He seriously wished neither of them was good at their job.

Finally Dot sighed. "Go, but don't leave town. We'll be in touch."

Matt nodded and ushered Georgie back to the car.

As Georgie drove them away, she said, "That was harder than I expected."

"They knew we were lying," Matt said.

"So what now?"

"We can't ask them to lie on their reports."

"Can they charge us for making a misleading statement?" Georgie asked.

"Probably." But they had limited choices. "We owe Lee to buy him as much time as we can."

When they reached the bitumen Georgie turned towards town. "I need to return the car and explain why the police have taken the rifle into evidence. I really hope they don't fire me."

"Why would they?"

"Because I ran out of a training session, took the car and gun without permission and lost the gun."

"Declan will understand." He was a decent bloke, and Dot would smooth things when she got back to town.

"I hope so."

Her concern made him pay more attention. They hadn't discussed her job much. "Are you enjoying it?"

"Yeah, I am."

"What about the ocean stuff?" It had been her dream for such a long time.

"There's still potential opportunity with PAWS and I don't want to live anywhere else. I'll look at roles which involve studying animals up here, or that will only take me away temporarily." She smiled. "It turns out I'm a homebody at heart."

"We'd all support you if you wanted to move elsewhere," Matt said. His life had always been about this land. Could he leave it to help her follow her dream? He thought so, but Georgie had thought moving to Perth would be epic and she hadn't enjoyed the experience.

He had to consider it for the future—their future together.

At the PAWS office, Georgie handed Matt her car keys. "I hopefully won't be too long."

"Do you want me to come in with you?"

She shook her head. "Declan's probably still at the

fire station. We'll stop there next."

She kissed him and then strode into the office as if she owned it, not even twirling her hair.

He was so proud of her.

# Chapter 22

Georgie's hand shook as she clutched the keys of the four-wheel drive in her hand. For all her bravado she was scared this would be the end of her career.

Karen jumped up from behind the desk. "You're all right! What the hell happened?"

Georgie handed her the keys. "It's a long story, but Matt's safe. Is Declan still at the fire station?"

The woman nodded. "Everyone is."

"Thanks." Georgie walked out before Karen could ask any further questions and got into the driver's seat.

"Everything OK?"

"We need to make one more stop." Her heart thumped as she parked outside the fire station. Her colleagues were doing hose drills out the back with Penelope on the hose. Georgie grabbed her fire jacket from the back seat, skirted the building and approached Declan.

He glanced behind her to her car. "You're both alive."

She nodded. "I'm sorry for running off like that."

"Are you going to tell me what happened?"

"I don't know how much I can say. Dot will fill you in."

"Did she catch who did it?"

She bit her lip. "The danger Dot told you about isn't an issue anymore."

His eyes widened. "Arrested?"

Word would get out eventually. "Dead." She took a breath. "The police have taken the PAWS rifle into custody."

He shifted slightly away from her. Not much, but enough. "Are you under arrest?"

"No." Not yet. She hadn't considered how her taking the blame for Clark's death would make others treat her.

"Can you tell me anything else?"

She shook her head. "Can I skip the rest of the day? I'll organise to attend some of the volunteer fire fighter sessions to catch up on what I missed."

He nodded. "Take a couple of days if you need it. I'll call Dot later."

"Thank you." Her muscles relaxed.

Penelope strode over. "You're OK. Where's Matt?"

"In the car."

"What happened?"

"I can't say." Georgie hugged her. "Thanks for your help today."

Penelope stiffened and then relaxed, hugging her back. "I didn't do anything. Did they catch the guy?"

Declan winced.

This would be her future when word got out. People being uncomfortable around her. Georgie nodded, her throat growing tight as she saw Clark's dead body on the ground. "I've got to go. I'll talk to you later."

She hurried to the car and slid behind the wheel.

"Everything all right?" Matt asked.

She shook her head as she backed out. She wanted to get away from here, away from everyone except her family.

"He fired you?"

"No." Georgie took a breath to get her emotions under control. "I told Declan the kidnapper was dead. He thinks I killed him, and it changed his whole demeanour. People are going to treat me differently."

"Then we tell the truth."

She shook her head. She couldn't. Lee had asked this one thing of her. She could deal with the side-glances for a few months if it gave him time to put a stop to Stonefish. It wasn't as if he wanted her to take the fall. He was already wanted for one death. "I have to trust him."

"He's lied to us the whole time we've known him."

No. She had a gut feeling about this. Maybe she was being played, but she would do what she could to help him. "I need to do this," she said. "I need to believe Stonefish can be stopped and life can go back to normal."

Matt squeezed her knee. "I'll support whatever you decide, Georgie, but I don't like it."

"I know." She smiled at him and let out a breath. "Let's go home."

This time when Georgie pulled up behind the farmhouse her whole family rushed out. The only ones not there were Faith and Lara who were at work and school. Matt parked next to her as they'd stopped so he could get his car on the way.

Darcy practically yanked her out of the car. "I'm so glad you're all right." He smothered her until Brandon said, "Give the rest of us a turn."

Georgie chuckled, glad to feel safe again as Brandon replaced Darcy, and Darcy turned to Matt. "I thought I was going to lose another brother."

She didn't hear Matt's reply because Darcy had smothered him as well.

"My turn," Amy said, bumping her husband aside.

"I'm glad you're both OK. Come in, I've got lunch prepared and whisky on the table."

Perfect.

Amy and Darcy fussed around them getting drinks and food while Brandon stared as if trying to get the story from them mentally. They had discussed telling the family the truth but decided the fewer people who knew the better. Her brothers were likely to tell Dot the real story in order to protect Georgie.

Georgie inhaled deeply. The scent of freshly baked scones, coffee and home. She squeezed Matt's hand. They were truly safe.

Matt told his side of the story first.

"Wait, Lee was there?" Amy said. "He was going to kill you both?"

Georgie hated not telling her. Amy and Lee had been friends. Instead, she nodded. "Matt warned me, and I managed to avoid Lee to get to Matt." When she got to the bit about shooting the gunman Brandon studied her. "You killed him?"

She nodded, taking a sip of her whisky-infused coffee and not looking at him.

"That's awful," Amy said. "How do you feel?"

Shit. She probably should be a mess if she'd really killed him. She swallowed. "It was shoot him or Matt would die. It wasn't a choice."

Matt squeezed her hand.

"We can talk later," Brandon said. "The first person you kill is always hard."

Georgie jolted. She hadn't considered Brandon might have killed people while he'd been in the army. Foolish for sure, but he didn't talk about that part of his life.

"Let's skip telling Lara all the details," Darcy said. "We can tell her the police caught the guy. She doesn't need to know about the kidnapping. She's been through enough and I'm worried she's going to start having nightmares."

"She still needs to be careful," Georgie said. "Stonefish are still out there." She yawned, exhaustion settling over her.

"You two should have a nap before Lara gets home," Darcy said.

It sounded like bliss. "We could push the two beds in the spare room together," she said to Matt. She didn't feel like being squashed in a single bed.

"I really need to get a double," Matt said.

"Except it won't fit in your room." Georgie stood and led Matt towards the spare room. She smiled at the new photo from Brandon and Amy's wedding. It wouldn't be too long before there would be newborn photos as well. They had to get rid of Stonefish for good so her family could grow and be safe.

Matt shifted the small bedside table which sat between the two single beds and then they pushed the beds together. Georgie shut the door and stripped off her clothes. Perhaps she should shower, but she really couldn't be bothered. Her bed called to her.

Matt climbed in next to her and pulled her close, his hold tight.

"How are you coping?" Georgie asked him, stroking his back.

"I've never been so scared in my life."

"It must have been terrifying when he pulled a gun on you."

Matt shifted back. "No, I was more scared of losing you. I didn't want you to come. I wanted you to stay safe."

She shook her head. "That fear you felt for me, is what I felt for you. No way was I leaving you there without trying to rescue you."

He sighed. "I love you."

She smiled and snuggled closer. "Right back at you."

He stroked her back. "You know, I've been thinking."

Her eyes were heavy as his hands soothed her. "Hmm. What about?"

"About us moving in together."

Georgie blinked, more alert now. "Have you changed your mind?"

"No. I can have my whole room packed in under an hour, if you can make space for my stuff."

"Done."

Matt grinned. "That easy."

"That easy," she agreed.

"So, what if I asked you to marry me?"

Georgie lost her breath. Her mouth moved, but her brain couldn't decide what to respond. As Matt smirked at her, the perfect response came out. "How about you ask and find out?"

His smile grew wider. "Georgie, will you marry me?"

Elation gave her such a high her head spun. "Yes."

He kissed her and for a moment she forgot about everything except him.

"You really are something special, Georgiana."

"I've been trying to convince you that for years."

He laughed. "You always said I was a bit slow."

"Not anymore," she replied. He was moving at just the right speed.

# Thank you for reading!

When I wrote this book I found myself wanting to know exactly what was in Lilian's journal. I wanted the details of how she fell in love with John and just how horrid the journey from England was. So in the end I wrote the whole journal.

If you want too want all the details, the journal is available exclusively to my reader group.

Sign up at

https://www.claireboston.com/reader-group/

# Acknowledgements

I received a grant from the Department of Local Government, Sport and Cultural Industries to help fund a research trip to Exmouth which is the town Retribution Bay is based on. That enabled me to chat to a number of people including Joe Morgan from Parks and Wildlife who was so generous with his time. I might have taken a few minor liberties with the truth for the story, but most of what Georgie does as a Park Ranger is accurate.

I also spoke with Toni Roe, a Yinggarda woman, and Hazel Walgar, a Bayungu elder, who answered many questions to help me write Matt's story. At the time of writing, Hazel was setting up cultural tours in the area. If you're ever up near Coral Bay, make sure you check out Baiyungu Dreaming.

Some of you will notice the different spelling of Baiyungu/Bayungu. This is due to the written translation of the name. I went with the spelling I found on the Bayungu Dictionary published by the Wangka Maya Pilbara Aboriginal Language Centre. I also got the Bayungu words used in the book from the dictionary.

Thank you to Sergeant Craig Carter who answered my questions about the police while I was in Exmouth as well.

Finally I must thank my team, Ann Harth, Teena Raffa-Mulligan and Mayhem Cover Creations for their editing and cover design.

# Beached in Retribution Bay

Aussie Heroes: Retribution Bay 5

Keep an eye out for Sam's story coming in 2022.